THE DARK ROAD

Marissa Farrar

THE DARK ROAD
By Marissa Farrar

Paperback Edition
ISBN 978-0-9571524-0-3

Warwick House Press

For my best friend, Sam, who was with me on this journey.

Acknowledgements

I would like to thank my editor on this book, Shontrell Wade of Wade-Staten Services. Even though this book had been previously published, I knew to get the book up to a high standard would take a lot of work. I was right. Several months later, and with a lot of patience and a keen eye, my editor has helped me bring this novel up to what I hope is the highest quality. Having a great editor is a bit like having a literary best-friend; they'll always tell you when you're about to leave the house with toilet paper stuck to your shoe.

I would also like to thank my cover artist, Rebecca Treadway, for both producing a totally original cover and also giving great advice when it was needed.

Author's Note:

Many years ago, as a young twenty-something, I took the same trip as the characters in *The Dark Road* make. While much of this book is fiction, some of it is based on my real-life experiences. From the cold behavior of the Cambodian officials at the border, to the lack of decent roads, to the old tin-can of a bus we were made to ride in hour after hour—all of these things were true. I experienced the same terrifying lightning storm my characters witness, the sensation of total isolation, and even the driver and his young assistant stopping at regular intervals to check beneath the bus (for what, to this day I have no clue!). But the idea for *The Dark Road* hit me, when, as the lightning storm continued around us, I was sure I saw something running alongside the bus. As for the rest of the story, well you, the reader, will have to decide which is fact and which is fiction.

CONTENTS

CHAPTER ONE
THE PHONE CALL

When the phone rang, Sasha Mills was tucked on the sofa, a half-empty glass of wine sitting on the side table, and Merlin, her Siamese cat, curled up beside her. She'd been expecting the call, but all her muscles still tightened in anticipation as she reached across and picked up the receiver.

"Hi, baby." Nick's voice was starting to become more familiar than his face.

"Hi, you," she said, squashing the phone between her ear and shoulder, settling back into the comforting arms of the sofa. "When are you coming home?"

Sasha asked every time he called. The question was usually just her teasing him, but this time she was serious.

For the past twelve months, Nick had been teaching English to children in Cambodia. In a week, he was due to fly home to the flat they shared in London—the flat they *used* to share. For the last year, Sasha had been living alone.

They'd been happy together for almost two years before he left, but Nick had become disillusioned with the rat race and decided he wanted to do something to make a difference in people's lives. Having gone straight from university into work, Sasha thought him spending a few months discovering the world outside of London was a great idea. She supported his decision and suggested Cambodia. She'd spent a number of months traveling the country in her early twenties and the experience left her with a lasting impression of the innocence and strength of the children.

It hadn't taken long for Nick to arrange some volunteer work teaching English to Cambodian children in a remote village. Within weeks of making the decision, his bags were packed.

Now, only silence met her question and a sickening sensation churned with the wine she'd drunk. Her right hand flicked unconsciously to her left and she twisted the diamond solitaire binding her third finger.

"Nick?"

He sighed down the phone."Look Sash, I've been thinking. Why don't you come out and join me for a bit? You could work out here. They're always looking for more teachers..."

Acid rose from her stomach and burned the back of her throat. They'd had this conversation before. The first time had been six months ago when he'd been first due to come home. He was only supposed to have been gone a few months. Sasha could have gone with him. Nick wanted her to, but she'd already finished that chapter of her life and didn't want to retrace old steps. Naturally, she was upset when he left, but she'd believed the experience would be good for him, good for *them*. He would return more fulfilled. Sasha never contemplated the idea that he wouldn't want to come back.

"Please don't do this to me, Nick. You know I can't."

"Of course you can, Sash. We can short-let the flat and your mum would look after Merlin. She dotes on that cat."

Sasha sighed. "It's not about practicalities. My life is here and I don't want to go away again. It would be like putting my life on hold."

"You don't have much of a life, Sash. You go to work, watch television and go out drinking in bars. No one is going to notice if you're gone."

Sasha bristled and spoke through gritted teeth. "I may not be out changing the world, but I happen to love my life."

"More than me you mean." Bitterness tainted his voice.

"Don't forget, you're the one who left me, Nick!"

"I wanted to make a difference."

"How noble..."

They fell silent, hurt and anger buzzing through the phone line.

Eventually, Sasha asked, "So what are you really saying, Nick? That you don't want to come home?"

"I want you here with me."

"Just be fucking straight with me will you," Sasha yelled. "Are you coming home or not?"

"I can't leave here, Sash. These people mean too much to me."

"And I don't mean shit!" She swallowed hard, trying to dislodge the burning lump choking her.

"Don't be ridiculous."

"I am *not* ridiculous!" She trembled with anger. "It is not ridiculous to want my fiancé home, or to not want to traipse off to some foreign country at the drop of a hat."

Nick spoke again, his voice distant and even. "I'm sorry but I'm not coming back, not yet at least. I've changed my flight back to London. I'm going to Bali for a couple of week's holiday instead. I want you to come, but if you're not here by the time I leave, I'll assume you don't love me enough to make the effort."

He hung up.

Heat rushed to Sasha's cheeks and her mouth dropped open.

The sheer nerve! He could at least have come home for a couple of weeks, spent some time with her. Now, not only was he not coming home, but he also expected her to give up *her* life to fly out to him and go to freaking Bali!

Sasha yelled in frustration and flung the phone across the room. The handset landed with a crash and Merlin, who had been sleeping soundly, oblivious to the drama unfolding around him, shot out of his seat.

"Oh, I'm sorry, Merlin! I'm sorry, baby. I didn't mean to scare you."

Sasha got up and tried to coax the shivering Siamese cat from under the television stand. He let out a pitiful yowl. She reached under and pulled him out by the scruff of his neck. Clutching him in her arms, she buried her face in his soft fur and let the tears come.

Despite not seeing each other for a year, Sasha believed Nick to be her future. She'd thought it from the moment they met, but now that future seemed to be disintegrating. What he'd said about her life hurt and she was bitterly disappointed about not having him back in London.

Was she being selfish for not going? Was Nick right in thinking her simple, normal life was not enough? Or was he the one being selfish by asking her to give up everything to be with him?

Sasha didn't know what to think.

She had less than eight days to decide what to do. In eight days, she'd either be sitting at home crying while he boarded a plane to fly away from her, or she'd be on a plane herself, going to meet him.

Her boss would go mad.

Was she seriously contemplating this?

Yes, she thought. *Why not?*

She could fly to Cambodia, on to Bali, spend a couple of weeks with Nick, remind him what he was missing and then come home again. After all, it didn't have to be forever. Just long enough to save their relationship. Perhaps the trip wouldn't be such hardship; she imagined loads of women would love to be in her place.

Sasha's tears subsided and she wiped her face in her cat's already-damp fur.

The next morning, Sasha jumped on the tube for the short ride to her office near Angel Station. She'd been working as a recruitment consultant for almost three years now. There shouldn't be any reason why she wouldn't be able to take some time off, but she couldn't ignore the nerves tugging at her insides. Sasha caught herself chewing at her nails, a habit she'd dropped years ago. Disgusted, she pulled her hand away.

Her boss, Alison Killery, though only a few years older than Sasha, was one of those focused, career-minded women who always made Sasha feel slightly inferior and intimidated.

Sasha got into work, went to her own desk and sat down. She waited for Alison to drink her first cup of coffee and trawl through her emails before she got up the courage to approach.

Alison glanced up before Sasha reached her desk.

"Hey, Sasha," Alison said, smiling. "Everything all right?"

Sasha smiled back. Her heart thumped audibly and sweat slicked the palms of her hands.

"Actually," she said, "I have a huge favor to ask."

"Sounds ominous," Alison said, raising her eyebrows.

Sasha took a deep breath. "I need the next three weeks off." She hurried on before Alison cut her off. "I've not had a holiday since last year. I've got days I need to use up and Nick is still in Cambodia..."

"Nick is still in Cambodia?" Alison frowned. "Isn't he supposed to be coming back next week?"

"Yeah, but he's sick." The lie slipped out and Sasha's cheeks flushed with shame.

"Oh, no." Alison's genuine dismay made Sasha feel even worse. "The poor thing. It's nothing serious, I hope."

Sasha shook her head. "They don't know yet." Her mind ran through numerous potential illnesses. "I think they're testing for malaria."

"When do you need to go?"

"As soon as possible," Sasha said.

Alison leaned forward and tapped some keys on her computer. She frowned at the screen.

"Tony is supposed to be taking a long weekend next week. No one else is off, so I guess we can survive without you."

Sasha stopped herself hopping up and down, and clapping with excitement. Instead, she tried to put on a concerned, yet relieved face of a worried fiancée.

"Thanks Alison, I really appreciate it."

She turned away from the desk and walked back to her own, keeping her smile tightly locked behind her lips. The small lie meant she couldn't start raving about her trip to her colleagues. And she would need to tell everyone Nick hadn't contracted malaria when she got back.

At least she was able to go.

Sasha spent the rest of the day trawling the Internet, trying to find a flight. She secured a flight from London to Bangkok, but had a three day wait before flying to Siem Reap

During her travels years ago, she'd flown from Bangkok to Siem Reap, in Cambodia, but traveling by road hadn't been as safe back then. Plenty of people caught buses between the two countries now. Perhaps that would be a better way to go? She'd leave the day after she flew into Bangkok and gain a whole extra day.

Sasha typed an email to Nick letting him know of her plans. The village Nick taught and lived in was miles away from any technology and he went into one of the larger communities once a week to use the phone or computer. He normally picked up his emails and made phone calls on a Sunday, and as today was Monday, he would only get the email the day before, or even on the day she arrived in Cambodia. The timings weren't ideal, but she had no other way of contacting him. Maybe he would have enough sense to check his emails sooner considering the circumstances. If he really did want her to come, and missed her like he said he did, surely he would make the effort to check every day hoping to hear from her?

That evening, Sasha picked up the phone to call her mother. After three rings, her mum answered.

"Hello?"

"Hi Mum, it's me."

"Hello, Sasha-love. How are you?"

"I've got a favor to ask," she said for the second time that day.

"Oh yes?"

"Nick has asked me to go away with him for three weeks and I wondered if you would like to flat-sit?"

"What do you mean, 'Nick has asked you to go away'? Isn't he supposed to be coming home?"

Sasha inwardly cringed. She didn't want to explain things to her mother. Her mum wouldn't hesitate to point out Nick's flaws and right now Sasha didn't want to hear them.

"Yes, but there's been a change of plan. He wants us to take a holiday together before he comes home."

She tried to tell herself she wasn't telling another lie; technically the trip would be a holiday and Nick was still going to come home at some point.

Her mother's pause told her more than words could, disapproval radiating through the phone.

"Please Mum. Merlin would hate to be here by himself for three weeks and getting someone to pop in and feed him isn't the same. You know how he hates to be left by himself."

Her mother huffed air out of her nose, snorting into the phone. "Well I suppose I could do with some time away from your father." She lowered her voice. "He's caught a cold and he's had the damn football on all day. All he seems to do these days is sit in front of the television and complain."

Sasha smiled. She knew her parents loved each other, but they'd been married over thirty years and sometimes even they needed time apart.

"So, is that a yes?"

"When are you leaving?"

"In two days."

"Wow, Sasha!" Her mother didn't even try to hide her surprise. "That's short notice."

"It's been a bit of last-minute thing. You won't need to get here until the day after I leave. You've still got your keys haven't you?"

"Yes, of course."

"So will you do it?"

"I suppose so."

"Thanks, Mum," Sasha said in relief. "I love you, and tell Dad I hope he gets better soon."

She didn't wait for her mum to say anything else. She didn't want to push her luck. Instead, she simply said her goodbyes and then sat back, wondering what the hell she was getting herself into.

Chapter Two
Leaving Home

The following two days passed in a blur. By the time Sasha washed and packed the clothes she needed to take, unpacked and repacked about four times, and tidied up any loose ends at work, the days flew by. Before she registered what was happening, she found herself stood at the airport, her oversized rucksack adorning her back like the shell of a giant turtle.

Years of long trips to the States, Australia and New Zealand had quickly grown her immunity to boredom and she enjoyed the flight, relaxing with a paperback after the past few days of frantic activity. She put the uncomfortable niggle in the pit of her belly down to nerves over seeing Nick again for the first time in a year.

The flight landed and Sasha made her way through arrivals before jumping on a bus that would take her to the Khao San Road. Though her finances were significantly better than in her backpacking days, she found herself heading back to the guesthouse where she'd stayed years before.

With delight, she discovered little had changed.

Though the guesthouse was located off the main drag, people still filled the street. Backpackers loitered everywhere, standing in small groups talking or buying things from the stalls lining the street. Vendors sold everything from clothing and food, to burned CDs and DVDs. Music blasted from small stereo systems in most of the stalls and the different songs jostled over one another. The faint aroma of stale beer and urine underlay the chaos; an unpleasant reminder of the party that had not only happened the night before, but took place every night.

Ahead of Sasha was the guesthouse. The ground floor of the building opened onto the street, tables and chairs spilling into the gutter. Inside, scruffy travelers lazed on cushions chatting to each other, reading or staring at the movie showing on a couple of televisions attached to the walls. A wall of large windows partitioned off a room filled with computers where people sat typing their stories to those they'd left at home.

On the opposite side of the street, food carts filled the air with their exotic spices and hissing steam. Noodles mixed with tiny, fiery chilies. Fried rice thrown into searing skillets. Indeterminable meats stuffed into rolls. All were made and sold from the carts. Pancake mix was cooked in front of the passers-by; chocolate and bananas were bound within crepe casings and served on thin paper plates. An elderly Thai woman nursed a cart stuffed full of fresh oranges, ice and bottles of fresh juice.

"Orange juice ten baht..." she cried over and over again, her English words blending together causing people to frown in their efforts to decipher her—'On-jue ten bah'. She must have said the words a million times a day, always with a huge, toothy smile, earnestly beckoning people over.

Despite the simplicity of their food preparation, Sasha noticed how clean everything was—how clean every*one* was—unlike some of the countries she had been to.

Sasha's stomach grumbled.

I'll get some Pad Thai noodles as soon as I've checked in, she promised herself.

Sasha made her way through the maze of travelers and up to the reception desk situated on the back wall of the guesthouse. A young Thai girl manned the desk. She glanced up as Sasha approached.

"Hello," the girl greeted her with a smile. "Welcome to Sun-Hi Guesthouse."

"Hello," Sasha said, putting her passport and three hundred baht on the counter. "I need a room for the night."

"You want room only one night?" the girl said in surprise.

"I've been here before," Sasha said. "And I have to get to Cambodia tomorrow."

"You have visa?" she asked, picking up Sasha's passport and the money. She turned to where the room keys hung from a wooden board and selected one. Sasha stared at the girl's back, and then raised her hand to her forehead in dismay.

Shit, shit, shit.

She hadn't even thought about needing a visa.

"How long does it normally take?" Sasha hoped her desperation didn't show in her voice. She couldn't remember getting a visa the last time she'd visited. But many years had passed and things changed.

The girl placed the room key on the counter and shrugged. "Two, maybe three days."

"No!" A lump clogged her throat and her eyes unexpectedly filled with tears. "I have to get there before then. It's really important."

"Maybe you pay extra money and you get quicker...?"

"Yes, yes," she said, wanting to reach across the counter and hug the girl. "I'll pay anything."

A smile tugged at the girl's mouth and her delicate eyebrows rose at Sasha's outburst. She pointed to a man sitting behind a desk in the corner of the room.

"You talk to Dang. He will help you."

"Thank you so much. You've been really helpful." Sasha picked up the key and dragged her bags across the room.

The man behind the desk appeared to be a boy from a distance, but as she got closer, she realized him to be closer to middle-aged. She marveled at how people aged here; they either looked young or ancient, there didn't seem to be any in-between.

Dang glanced up from his newspaper. "Please, sit."

"Thank you." Sasha sank onto a red plastic chair opposite. "I need a visa for Cambodia and I need it today. I have to travel tomorrow." She leaned forward, gripping the edge of the desk.

"Visa no problem," Dang said, folding up his newspaper. "I can get visa, but tomorrow not good day to travel. Can get you to border, but not Siem Reap."

Sasha sat back, surprised.

"But you have notices everywhere advertising trips to Siem Reap." She glanced up at one hanging directly above his head. "The notice says the buses run every day of the week."

"Yes, yes, but not tomorrow."

"Well..." she was at a loss for words. "Why not tomorrow?"

"Tomorrow not good day to travel."

Sasha felt like she was going round in circles. She tried again.

"Is there a particular reason why I cannot travel to Siem Reap tomorrow?"

Dang shifted in his seat and fiddled with a pen on his desk, staring at the object. Sasha bent her head and peered up at him, trying to catch his eye. She wondered if he didn't know the English words to explain.

"Is it a public holiday?" she suggested.

Dang lifted his face to hers. He nodded, a smile lighting his face.

"Yes, tomorrow is public holiday. No travel tomorrow."

"But I have to," Sasha said, starting to feel desperate. If she didn't travel tomorrow, she would almost certainly miss Nick. The journey was a long one. If she couldn't leave tomorrow, her chances of catching him would disappear by the hour.

Her eyes burned with hot tears. She was going to lose him.

"What about extra money?" she asked, thinking about the visa. "If I pay extra money, can I go tomorrow?"

Dang picked the pen back up and turned his attention back to his fiddling. Sasha reached across the desk and grabbed his hand, forcing him to look up.

"Please," she begged. "Please help me. It's a matter of life or death. I have to leave tomorrow."

Dang gave her a tight smile and picked up the phone.

"I must make calls. Come back in one hour."

"Thank you. Thank you so much."

She shook his hand furiously. Dang took his hand back and raised it as though to dismiss her.

Sasha pushed her chair back. She stood, heaving her backpack onto her back and picked up her room key.

"Thank you," she said again, but Dang was already talking rapid Thai on the phone. He didn't even acknowledge her, so she turned and walked back through the guesthouse.

Behind the reception desk was the flight of stairs leading to the rooms. Attached to the wall at the bottom of the stairs was a notice listing room numbers and their coordinating floors. Sasha glanced at the large wooden tag attached to her room key. The number seventy-four was carved into it.

She correlated the room number to the right floor and groaned. Eight flights of stairs with her backpack; she would never make it. Sasha glanced around hoping they'd installed a lift since her last stay. She wasn't surprised to see they hadn't. The girl behind reception caught her eye and gestured up the stairs. Sasha smiled weakly and nodded.

"Okay," she said to herself. "Come on feet."

Sasha reached her floor, the thirty kilos on her back taking its toll. The humidity, combined with exertion, caused beads of sweat to drip from her face into her cleavage. She wiped her forehead with the back of her hand; the salt stinging her eyes.

Her chest heaved as her lungs labored over the effort of breathing through the thick and cloying heat. She paused at the top of the stairs, hanging on to the railing to stop her legs from collapsing beneath her.

The long flight and lack of sleep were also taking a toll. Sasha glanced up to see another, smaller notice pointing her toward her room number. She forced her legs to move and headed down the narrow hallway. The cheap linoleum floor squeaked beneath her flip-flops as she walked down the corridor and located her room.

The room was nothing more than a square box with a window looking out onto another corridor. The only item of furniture was the bed. The narrow, hard bunk looked as though it should belong in a prison cell, but Sasha had never seen anything so inviting. She flicked the switch for the overhead fan and flung herself down.

Almost asleep with her eyes open, Sasha stared at the fan washing tepid air over her. The rapid spinning of the fan blades caused the whole contraption to swing ominously and Sasha imagined the ensuing carnage if it broke loose.

The imagery woke her up.

Her stomach grumbled loudly. She remembered her promise of noodles after she had checked in, but her skin was covered in a film of dirt from traveling. She unpacked her toiletries and towel and made her way back down the hall to the showers. The doors she passed on the way were identical. Muted music blared from one behind one of them.

Sasha smiled a hello at a young couple who held hands as they walked toward her. They nodded back before brushing past. The sight of the couple evoked a pang of loneliness and she suddenly missed Nick. She didn't want to be here alone.

Three basic, clean showers were lined up, the toilets and sinks in separate cubicles next door. Each door held a warning about peeping Toms.

Sasha rolled her eyes. Nothing changed.

The cold water was a relief from the heat. The grime and sleep washed away, and she left the shower both refreshed and famished.

Food first, she thought and then she would find out about her visa and ride for tomorrow.

Sasha dressed quickly and trotted down the stairs faster than she'd made it up. She stepped out in the hazy Bangkok sunshine and smiled to herself. Glancing around, she allowed memories of her time here to wash over her like the heat rising from the street. She could barely believe she was back.

During the day, the streets of Bangkok bustled with life, filled with an eclectic mix of tourists, businessmen and locals; but at night, the city showed its true colors. In the evening, the city became an adult's fairground. Elephants walked the street begging for the peanuts their owners sold to tourists. Old VW vans, their roofs removed, were transformed into street bars selling cheap shots and cocktails, while the lady-boys danced in them as if they were on floats in a carnival. Carts trundled around the street selling fried crickets, cockroaches and even scorpions for people to snack on.

The recollections made Sasha's smile blossom and she looked forward to the evening ahead. Any doubts she'd had about seeing Nick again were pushed to the farthest corner of her heart.

Chapter Three
A Chance Meeting

"**Hey, mister! You still want** to go tomorrow?"

Startled, Josh Thomas looked up from his paperback. A young Thai girl stood above him, smiling. He recognized her as the daughter of Mr. Kim, the man who ran the guesthouse where he was staying.

"I'm sorry?" he said. "What did you say?"

"My father say bus leave tomorrow now. You can go if want."

"Really?" Josh said, surprised.

Neither he nor his fellow travelers had been able to work out why no buses were available on Saturday.

"But I've already bought a ticket for the day after," he said.

"No problem. Just change ticket, no more money."

"Great!" Josh smiled at her. "Do I need to tell your father?"

"No, no," she answered. "I will tell him. Bus leave six o'clock tomorrow morning."

"Okay. Thanks."

She gave him a little bow and ran off.

Josh settled back in his seat. He picked his book up, but didn't read any more. Instead, he stared at the words.

To leave tomorrow suited Josh. He was on a bit of a whirlwind trip of Southeast Asia. A year ago he'd bought an 'around-the-world' ticket. The ticket allowed him a certain number of flights within a year. Unfortunately, he only backpacked through South America before moving on to New Zealand, where he met a local girl called Kyla.

Josh moved into Kyla's flat within a matter of weeks, but things didn't pan out as he'd hoped. It soon became clear they weren't as compatible as he first thought.

Josh cringed at the memory.

He pushed a hand through his scruffy dark hair and shifted in his seat, trying to get more comfortable. With his left hand, he rubbed at the swirls and lines of the half-sleeve of tattoos etched into the skin of his opposite arm. His book remained open, but unread.

He'd been stupid. Hoping he'd found his home, the place he finally belonged, he'd jumped into the relationship feet first.

They'd barely known each other when they moved in together. The things Josh found exciting about Kyla—the partying, the reckless sense of humor and unpredictability—quickly wore thin. He longed to be settled, but that seemed to be the last thing Kyla wanted.

One night she went out without him and didn't come home until late the next morning, reeking of booze, stoned out of her head and stinking of sex. When he asked her where she'd been, she laughed at him and told him to mind his own fucking business.

What happened next was the worst thing Josh had ever done. The memory clutched at his throat, leaving him breathless. It stirred something dark inside him and he cringed.

Josh pushed the memory away, not wanting to relive the experience.

After that, he left. There was no other choice. The confrontation revealed a part of him he never knew existed and it scared him. He didn't want to become that person and he needed to get away as quickly as possible.

Doing what he always did when he lost himself—when he didn't know where life should be taking him—he went back on the road.

Josh's funds were now running low and he only had three flights left on his ticket. He decided to use one to fly from New Zealand to Bangkok. From Bangkok he would travel overland through Thailand, Cambodia, and Vietnam. This plan allowed him to see as much of the continent as his lack of time and money permitted. He could then fly from Vietnam back to Bangkok and finally back to London.

Because of his tight schedule, gaining this day made all the difference. It meant an extra day exploring the Cambodian temples of Angkor. A day that would otherwise have been wasted hanging out in the numerous Thai bars lining the Khao San Road.

The guesthouse owner's sudden change of mind still puzzled Josh. Mr. Kim had been insistent, aggressive almost, when Josh asked him for a ticket to Siem Reap for Saturday. Arguing had not gotten Josh anywhere and he'd thought a flicker of fear had gone through Mr. Kim's eyes.

Well, whatever the problem, it must have been sorted now. He would need to watch what he drank tonight if he had a six a.m. start.

How strange to think he would be back in London in a few weeks. This year away felt like a lifetime. His life back in London seemed unreal, disjointed from him somehow. His past life was almost a dream and his only real life, the one he spent traveling.

He wondered if he'd settle back into a 'normal' routine back in London or if he would get itchy feet. Josh liked the idea of having a base again, an actual home rather than a temporary pit stop. He missed having his own things around him, having the comfort of routine and being able to sleep in his own bed. He carried all his possessions in his backpack, most of them battered and worn.

The idea of a job—a nine-to-five in an office—didn't fill Josh with enthusiasm. He'd worked in New Zealand, but only part-time jobs in the bars Kyla's family owned. The money just about kept his head above water. He wouldn't be in such a good position back in London. Friends had agreed to let him stay in their spare room for a few weeks, or at least until he got himself sorted. His background was in IT and there was still plenty of need for someone with his skills so Josh didn't think he would find too much difficulty in finding work. He found the idea suffocating, but he needed to get on with his life; he couldn't wander the earth forever.

Later that evening, Josh found himself sitting in a restaurant nursing an ice-cold beer, despite his earlier good intentions, and pushing rice around his plate with his fork. Like most of the restaurants on the Khao San Road, it opened out onto the street. So many chairs, tables and people littered the area, he struggled to tell where the road ended and the restaurant started.

Loud music filled the restaurant and even the people sitting at the roadside tables had to raise their voices to be heard by friends and family, sitting only feet away. Josh thought the music to be up-to-date chart songs from back home, until he realized they were actually Thai covers.

He smiled to himself as two girls, both in their early twenties, jumped up and started to dance around their table. Both of the girls were pretty, but had masked their appearances with nose and lip rings; one even had bright pink hair. Before long, a group of young men leapt to their feet to join them.

Other diners started to clap in time with the music. The girls twirled, wriggled and raised their hands in the air; responding to the attention of their fellow dinners.

Josh's smile turned to laughter. He looked around at the happy faces of the different nationalities present, trying to imprint the scene upon his memory like a photograph.

Someone caught his attention and, for a moment, the noise and laughter of the restaurant faded into the background.

A young woman sat alone in the middle of the madness and seemed oblivious to it. Her long, dark hair hung down one side of her face. The fingers of her left hand absently twirled and twisted it. Her other hand held her fork, but she stared down at her plate of rice without lifting any of the food to her mouth.

Josh watched as the girl gave her head a slight shake and then looked up, as though remembering where she was. Her face broke into a smile and she started to clap, joining in with the rest of the restaurant.

The song ended and the pierced pair took a bow to their audience before sitting back down. They laughed at each other and hid their faces in their hands in sudden mock shyness. Josh glanced back over at the girl who had caught his attention, wanting to go over and speak to her. With the entertainment over, she'd picked up a book and had her face hidden in its pages. It was impossible for Josh to make eye contact with her.

What was he thinking anyway? The last thing he needed right now was to be distracted from the rest of his trip by another woman.

Before Josh could give the idea any more thought, someone dragged back the chair opposite. A large figure of a man sat down, completely blocking his view.

A hugely overweight man sat across the table. Flesh fell in folds over the neck of his t-shirt and his belly strained against the thin material. Small dark eyes that looked as though they'd been squashed into his face as an afterthought peered at Josh.

"All right, mate!" the man said, almost shouting over the music. "Thought you looked like you could use this."

The stranger pushed a fresh glass of beer across the table. He saw Josh hesitate and nodded encouragingly before giving the glass another little shove as if proximity to the drink would entice Josh to accept it.

"Thanks," said Josh. "But I'm trying to avoid too much booze tonight. I've got an early start tomorrow and I've spent the last three days either drunk or hung-over."

The man laughed. "I know the feeling! Where are you headed?"

Josh realized this was going to turn into the typical travelers talk: where are you from, where are you going, where have you been...?

"Cambodia," Josh responded. "Siem Reap to be precise. I'm getting a bus at six tomorrow morning and

I've managed to miss enough forms of transport on this trip because of beer. I don't intend to add this one to the collection."

The man flung his head back and bellowed with laughter. He straightened up, wiped tears of mirth from his eyes and held out a chubby hand.

"My name's Graham," he said, "but you can call me Goose. Most of my friends do. You know, Goose?"

Josh didn't know if this was supposed to be a rhetorical question and just stared at him.

"Goose! From the film, *Top Gun*."

Josh smiled weakly.

"People like to have me by their side; be their wing man." Goose continued, apparently oblivious to Josh's lack of enthusiasm. "I'm a good man keep close."

He winked, causing Josh to cringe.

"And you are...? Goose asked, hand still out held.

"Josh." Reluctant, he put his own hand into the one offered. It felt exactly as Josh had anticipated—hot and clammy. He resisted the urge to wipe his hand on the napkin in front of him.

"So, Cambodia huh?" said Goose. "I hear they put weed on the pizzas. I'm heading out that way myself. Wanted to go now, but there's some sort of problem with the buses." A frown transformed his forehead into a row of sausages. "Hey, how come you managed to get a ride?"

Josh shrugged. "Just luck. The guy in my guesthouse sorted a ride for me."

"Oh, wow! Really?" Goose leaned forward. "Which guesthouse are you in."

"Sawatdee House," Josh told him, hoping he didn't know it. Unfortunately, he did.

"Cool. I'm right next door." The idea lit up on the other man's face as if someone had flicked a switch in his brain. "Why don't I come back with you and find out if they've got a spare seat? Then we could travel together and I really could be your wing man."

Goose raised his beer toward Josh. He had no other choice than to clink his own glass in salute. Josh knew it looked as though he'd agreed to Goose's plan and did his best to backpedal.

"The thing is, Goose, I kind of prefer to travel alone."

Goose went unperturbed. "Don't be dumb. No one travels alone. You might start out alone, but no one actually *travels* alone."

Josh smiled through a clenched jaw. He couldn't argue with Goose's point. Everyone took similar routes so he often ended up traveling with other people.

Goose took his silence as a sign of agreement and clapped him on the shoulder with a meaty hand. Josh almost felt the sweat print sinking through to his skin.

"Come on then, buddy. Drink up and we'll go and make sure I can get a seat."

Reluctantly, Josh drained his glass. Though he had been trying to avoid beer, he suddenly needed it. He slipped a folded bill under the empty mug, more than enough to cover what he'd eaten. He pushed his chair back and stood, clearing his view of where the dark-haired girl had been sitting. A blond man had taken her seat; she was nowhere in sight.

Fate had determined he wouldn't meet a beautiful, melancholy woman, but was destined to spend his time with this moron instead. He'd obviously pissed someone off.

Josh stepped out into the busy, balmy night.

Within moments, a tiny Thai woman approached. No bigger than a ten-year-old child, she appeared to be wearing a bulky dress made of hundreds of strips of fabric. Each strip was a different color and pattern: reds, greens, blacks, triangles, stripes and spots. On many, tiny shells and beads had been sewn on. Only when she got closer did Josh realize the bulkiness was actually hundreds of fabric belts and scarves wound about her body.

She held part of her clothing out to them. Josh smiled and bowed his head gently, while his newfound 'friend' snatched up the large camera that hung around his neck and blinded her with its flash. The woman didn't react. She simply held her hand out toward them.

Goose stared at her and Josh nudged him.

"If you take her picture you should buy a belt."

"But I don't want a bloody belt," Goose said, blinking in surprise, his voice edged with irritation.

"It's only a couple of baht and it's a matter of respect."

Goose glared at Josh, forgetting his buddy-buddy attitude for a moment. Clocking the expression on Josh's face, his shoulders deflated.

"Well, I suppose they're all right," he grumbled. He took a belt from the woman and dropped sixty baht into her open palm. She smiled and nodded her thanks before moving on to the next tourist.

Josh and Goose continued their walk down The Khao San Road. They got closer to the guesthouse and Josh found himself crossing his fingers, hoping the travel desk would be closed.

As they passed one of the VW vans, the lady-boys who adorned it whistled and cooed at the men. Josh smiled, ignoring their advances, but Goose flipped them the bird. The lady-boys showed no signs of being offended and increased their catcalls.

"They must be kidding," Goose said. "Who the hell do they think they are? Do I look like a gay-boy?"

Josh cringed at Goose's choice of language. He wondered why Goose even bothered to leave London if he wasn't going to accept other people's cultures.

Goose was soon distracted by a group of attractive girls wandering past.

"All right ladies?" he called out as they walked by.

The girls ignored him. Goose turned, walking backward to leer and whistle. Goose seemed oblivious to the fact he was mimicking the calls of the lady-boys he so despised.

Josh stared at the ground, embarrassed. People would sum him up and lump him in the same category as this uncouth creature.

The pair finally reached the guesthouse. The travel desk was still open and manned by the young Thai girl who had told him of the ticket change earlier. She was talking to a blonde couple, pointing out routes on a large map covering the whole of the desktop. She must have heard them come in as she lifted her head. She caught Josh's eye and smiled.

Damn.

Goose noticed the eye contact and bustled over to the girl. Josh sank onto one of the plastic chairs lined up against the wall.

"My mate over there reckons you can get me on a bus to Siem Reap tomorrow," Goose said, talking loudly over the conversation she was already having.

The young couple glanced up in surprise and the Thai girl looked back over at Josh. Josh hid his face in one hand, marveling at what incredible bad luck had brought this awful person into his life.

"I am sorry sir," said the girl. "I am busy at moment, please come back in ten minutes."

"But it won't take a second."

"I am sorry sir," she repeated, slow and loud, as though speaking to a small child. "You must to wait." She turned back to her couple and continued where she left off.

Goose stared at her until he realized she was going to continue to ignore him. He turned away and skulked back to Josh, his demeanor that of a schoolboy who had just been dismissed. Her rebuke delighted Josh, even more so when she lifted her eyes to his and gave him a tiny, secret smile. Goose said nothing as he dropped into a chair beside Josh. He stared at the girl—his face red, lips pressed together—until the couple stood and walked away.

"Come on then," Goose said, leaping to his feet. "Let's make sure I can get on that bus tomorrow."

Josh rolled his eyes at Goose's retreating back, but didn't follow him to the desk. Goose didn't even notice. He had already sat down and started talking to the girl about his trip. He spoke in a fast, loud voice, gesturing with his hands. Josh realized she was nodding in return and tried to send her desperate looks. He hoped the fear in his eyes would make her understand what he was trying to say.

Goose shifted in his seat, the flimsy plastic bending under his weight as he took his wallet from his back pocket. He opened it and handed the girl a huge wad of notes; easily twice what Josh paid. The girl gave Josh another smile.

Goose had been ripped off, but he was getting the bus.

Josh put his face in his hands, exhausted. He felt Goose's presence back beside him, and lowered his hands.

Goose waved his ticket in the air, creating a slight breeze in the humid night.

"Time for a beer I think!" Goose declared.

Josh put his head back in his hands. Goose thumped him on the shoulder and Josh wearily lifted his head.

"Come on, mate. You can sleep when you're dead. Let's party!"

"Goose," he said, shaking his head. "I need some sleep. It's going to be a long day tomorrow."

Even longer now thanks to you, he thought.

"Spoil-sport." Goose switched back to sulky boy behavior.

Josh got to his feet. "I'll see you in the morning," he said, hoping with all his heart that he wouldn't.

Chapter Four
The Beginning

Sasha's alarm startled her from sleep. The small clock played an annoying rendition of 'You Are My Sunshine' in a high-pitched tone. Over the years, Sasha found this was the only alarm she couldn't ignore.

Sleep had come easily, but she'd woken throughout the night. The strange bed, hollow slamming of doors and unaccustomed heat made sleeping undisturbed difficult. She also had the seven-hour time difference to compete with and her body was telling her that *now* was the time to go to sleep, not get up.

Only steely determination got her legs swinging off the narrow bed and her weary head off the rock-hard pillow.

After stumbling down the corridor to the bathroom, Sasha blasted herself with an ice cold shower, hoping to wash away the desire to crawl back into bed. Her shoulders and neck felt stiff from carrying her pack around, her muscles unused to the exercise.

Her bag seemed to have doubled in both size and weight during the night. Sasha briefly debated the possibility of someone sneaking into her room and replacing her pack with one stuffed full of bricks.

She braced herself and heaved the bag onto her sore shoulders. Every muscle groaned in pain as she prepared herself for the hike down the seven flights of stairs.

Thank God, she could just sit on a bus for the whole of the next day. She intended to do nothing other than stare out of the window, doze and daydream about seeing Nick again.

Thinking about Nick, her heart gave a nervous jolt and her breath caught in her chest. She had checked her email again last night but he'd not sent a reply. Sasha prayed he knew about her coming and was waiting for her. The idea that she would get there, only to find him already gone, didn't bear thinking about.

She wished for the thousandth time that he had gone somewhere a little less remote, somewhere that at least had mobile reception.

"Positive attitude," Sasha said, under her breath. "Don't want to tempt fate."

'What about preparing yourself for the worst?' an annoying voice, sounding suspiciously like her mother, chirped in her head.

"Oh, shut up," she answered out loud, ignoring the strange look she received from the young Thai girl she passed on the stairs. "He'll be waiting with tickets to Bali in his outstretched hand..."Sasha allowed herself to slip into this daydream as she continued to plod down the stairs, her knees and thighs trembling under the weight of her pack.

As she entered the main reception area, she was surprised to be blinking against bright sunshine. Her room and the stairwell had been windowless. Because of the early hour, she'd been expecting it to still be dark.

The locals all appeared to have been up for hours. Plates and dishes clattered and banged, people shouted to each other. The warm scent of pancakes and toast tempted her, but she didn't have time to stop for breakfast. The receptionist nodded as she dropped her key on the desk and made her way through the guesthouse and out to the road.

Years of London living had made her forget the pleasure in having beautiful weather first thing in the morning. As she stepped out on the street, the heat from the new day warmed her skin and a jolt of excitement speared through her.

Sasha squinted against the bright light and looked around for the bus. The street was empty apart from locals setting up their stalls. She struggled again, this time to get out of her backpack. She dumped the bag on the ground and, with a sigh, sat on top and rubbed her already aching thighs. She hadn't realized she was so unfit. Her sporadic gym trips hadn't made much of an impact.

Sasha fished her paperback novel out of her daypack, but had barely opened the book before a minibus came bumbling around the corner.

She stood and waited for the vehicle to stop. A young Thai boy, only in his early teens, jumped out of the passenger seat.

"You have ticket to Cambodia?" he asked.

"Oh, yes, I do," Sasha answered, thinking, *where the hell did I put it?* Frantic, she searched her pockets. She located the piece of paper and handed the ticket over to the boy, who in turn handed it to the driver. He took the ticket without bothering to look at Sasha.

"This your bag?" the boy asked, as though a crowd of people waited to embark.

Sasha nodded. He lifted her bag easily onto his back and threw it on the roof, before climbing up to secure her pack to the rest of the luggage.

"Thanks," she said, wondering if she should tip him.

At the door to the minibus, Sasha ducked her head and pulled herself up into the vehicle. The bus was old and rusted, and she tasted diesel on the back of her tongue. When she lifted her head, she was surprised to see the number of people already seated.

At the back of the vehicle sat a young family; a blonde mother and father, and an even blonder boy of about six. They all sat with their eyes closed. The boy lay across his parents' legs, his head in his mother's lap. The aisle ran down the center of six benches, three on either side. In the last one on the right side, sat two girls with piercings and colorful hair. Sasha thought she recognized them from the restaurant she'd eaten at the night before. A couple with dark hair and tanned skin sat on the other side of the aisle.

In front of the pierced girls sat two men, opposite in looks. One was large and meaty with sandy-colored hair, the other dark haired and broad-shouldered. Sasha couldn't see the sandy guy's face as he'd twisted around in his seat to talk to the girls behind. In doing so, he'd squashed his companion against the window. The squashed man glared in annoyance at the large man and, at first, didn't seem to notice her joining the group. When he looked up, Sasha was sure she'd seen something like surprise register in his green eyes.

Across the aisle from the two men, a blonde girl sat alone. In front of the two men, and to Sasha's left, was a dread-locked man, also on his own.

Sasha realized all eyes had now turned to her, and she smiled and waved, feeling like she was on a game show.

"Hi. I'm Sasha," she said, resisting the urge to add 'and I'm an alcoholic'.

The green-eyed man seemed to recover. He pried himself out of his seat and leaned past the man in front, hand offered.

"I'm Josh," he said with a smile. He opened his mouth to say something else when his companion got in first.

"Goose is the name," the big guy said. "Wear it out if you want."

"Hi Goose," said Sasha, trying not to raise her eyebrows at him. "I'm Sasha."

"Good to have you along for the ride, Sasha."

"Thanks. It was almost a ride I didn't get."

"Well, if you're ever in need of a different ride, you know where to come."

Sasha watched, horrified, as he winked lewdly at her. Slowly she turned away Maybe she'd been mistaken and had taken his comment the wrong way?

She hoped the rest of the backpackers would be more personable.

The only free seat on the bus was just behind the driver, so she sat down and then twisted back around.

The two girls, sitting behind Goose and Josh, spoke next.

"I'm Steph," said the one with pink hair. Sasha thought she recognized an American or, more probably, Canadian accent. "This here is Vicki. You'll have to excuse us if we're not too chatty right now. We only got in about two hours ago."

Sasha grinned, recognizing herself several years ago.

"No problem," she said, glad to have some interesting people on board. "Talk when you've recovered."

The two girls grinned before plugging into their iPods, shutting themselves off from the rest of the world.

She moved to get her own iPod from her bag when she realized she was being stared at. From across the aisle, she caught the eye of the lone man. In his late twenties, his chin length, dirty blond hair had been twisted into scruffy dreadlocks. Ice-blue eyes fixed hers with a look somewhere between amusement and hostility. His head tilted to one side in a way that reminded Sasha of an animal listening for its prey. He smiled with his mouth only and Sasha saw he had one canine out of line with the rest of his teeth, like a fang.

Although only a fraction of a moment passed, it was long enough to make Sasha uncomfortable and she shifted, moving her gaze to the girl in the seat directly behind.

She too was blonde, but in a completely different way. She swung hair as fluid as water behind one shoulder as she leaned forward, holding out a manicured hand.

"Hi, I'm Dawn," she said with an English accent. "It's good to have another single woman along. I've only just got here and it's all a bit scary."

Dawn's eyes flickered to the dreadlocked man, but she quickly recovered and flashed Sasha a bright smile.

Sasha didn't want to make conversation with another London girl. It reminded her too much of what she'd left behind, of what she'd not wanted to leave.

"Good to meet you," Sasha said and turned back around, continuing to rummage in her bag for her music.

Everyone else on the bus had lost interest in her, the early start taking its toll and they were all now either staring out of the window or asleep.

The boy who had hoisted her bag onto the roof finished securing it and swung open the passenger door, before jumping in beside the driver. The boy turned back to them, a wide smile revealing perfect, small white teeth.

"Okay, all ready?"

Most of the passengers managed an obligatory 'yeah'. The boy was about to turn back when Josh leaned forward.

"Are we picking up anyone else?"

"No, no. The lady was last."

Relief softened Josh's even features as he must have realized he wasn't going to spend the next fourteen hours squashed up against Goose on a tiny bus with no air-conditioning. Sasha watched as he pulled his body out of the small gap between Goose's large frame and the hard metal of the bus and slid down the aisle to sit next to the scruffy-looking stranger.

Josh knew he was being inexcusably rude to Goose and sensed the annoyance of the stranger at suddenly having to share his seat, but he didn't care. With relief, he settled into the spare seat.

Sasha had watched his antics with obvious amusement and Josh realized he'd not exactly been subtle.

Josh still couldn't believe she'd found her way onto his bus. It never failed to surprise him how often he ran into the same people time and time again. Most backpackers did travel similar routes, but they covered huge distances and there were plenty of other variables that would prevent people from bumping into one another.

Not that he was complaining. This 'small world syndrome' might have brought Goose into his life, but it had also brought the dark-haired girl to compensate.

Josh frowned and forced himself to look away. The last thing he needed right now was another woman. He was no good for anyone and, though he knew nothing about the woman on the other side of the bus, she deserved better than him.

Despite his best intentions, he glanced back over at Sasha. She sat with her eyes closed, her head rested against the window.

Josh sighed and turned to look out of his own window.

The bus rattled and shook over the fairly smooth roads and Josh wondered what it would be like in Cambodia. Several other travelers had told him the country had no real roads, but he found this hard to believe. People tended to exaggerate their stories for impact.

Because of the early hour, the busy streets of Bangkok were still not up to full capacity. Each passing minute brought more and more vehicles onto the roads.

At each set of traffic lights tuk-tuks, bicycles, cars and motorbikes jostled for position. The minibus weaved and swerved between the traffic, threatening at any moment to hit or be hit. Horns blared, not at anything in particular, but simply to be heard. Smog rose from engines, creating a layer of gray above the city, dampening the sunshine.

Josh reached in his daypack and pulled out a squashed roll, stuffed with some unidentifiable meat, he'd bought the day before. He didn't know when they would be stopping next and had learned to be prepared from previous experiences. Taking a bite of stale bread, he chewed slowly and contemplated the journey ahead.

CHAPTER FIVE
A STOP

A small hand pulled at Sasha's.

The awkward position she'd been sitting in had left her neck stiff and she lifted her hand to touch an imprint on her cheek where the material from the seat had pressed into her skin.

Sasha realized she'd slept.

Bleary-eyed, she squinted out of the window, somehow expecting to be able to identify her location. The road gave no clues and the surrounding landscape could have been anywhere in Asia. Small houses, no more than shacks, dotted the countryside. Dirty-looking sheep and cows, with their bones poking painfully through their skin, grazed the sparse ground. The Bangkok traffic had disappeared and Sasha felt like they were the only people on the road.

The small hand tugged again.

Surprised, having forgotten what woke her, Sasha turned to discover the bright blue eyes of the blond child staring at her.

"Hello," Sasha said. "What's up?"

Delighted she was awake, the boy scrambled up on the seat beside her.

"Mum and Dad are still sleeping. They get mad if I wake them."

Sasha smiled, noticing he didn't have any problems waking total strangers.

"And why would you want to wake them?"

The boy stuck a thumb into his mouth, suddenly shy, and mumbled something. Sasha gently pried the thumb back out.

"Say that again."

"Need to go toilet."

"Ah, I see."

She leaned forward and got the attention of the Thai boy in front.

"When are we stopping? This little boy needs to go to the toilet."

The Thai boy said something to the driver and he abruptly pulled to the side of the road. Everyone on board started to move, roused by the sudden swerve and then stop of the vehicle.

Sasha glanced back to see the child's mother wake. Immediately, she looked around.

"He's up here," Sasha called out. "He needed to go to the toilet."

His mother jumped to her feet and moved to the front of the bus.

"I'm so sorry," she said. Her blue eyes were wide and the exact same color as her son's. "Was he bothering you?"

46

"No, not at all," Sasha said, lying. "I don't think he wanted to disturb you."

"Hmm." The boy's mother looked down at him disapprovingly, but was unable to hide her smile. She ruffled his baby-fine white hair. "That doesn't sound like him at all."

The boy grinned around his thumb and his mum took his other hand. The Thai boy pulled open the door and the two of them climbed off.

Recognizing a chance to stretch their legs, everyone else began to scramble to the front of the bus. One by one, they followed the boy and his mother out on the road.

The heat hit Sasha as soon as she stepped out the door. Though she'd thought the bus didn't have air-conditioning, she was clearly wrong.

Without the smog acting as a filter, the sun in the countryside was more intense than in the city. The beams beat down on the top of her head. Sweat ran down her back, making her thin cotton top cling to her skin.

"You look like you could use some of this."

Sasha turned to see the dark-haired guy, Josh, holding out a bottle of water. The sight made her notice her dry throat and she took the bottle thankfully.

"I guess I forgot to pack some myself," she said. "I didn't think."

Josh shrugged. "No problem. Keep it. I've got another one in the bus."

The water was on the warmer side of cold, but Sasha took several long gulps. She'd gone without breakfast and was amazed she could still function without her morning coffee.

As if reading her thoughts, Josh said, "I don't think it's far to the border. We'll need to stop before to get our visas checked and fill in some forms for the Cambodian officials, so we should be able to get something to eat soon."

Sasha hoped her visa was real. Her passport had been left at the desk and she'd been called over to pick it up late last night. She had no idea what the visa was supposed to look like, as she had nothing to compare it to. She prayed she hadn't been ripped off. She might end up left floundering on the border like a refugee.

"I am a bit on the hungry side," she admitted. "But my stomach still thinks it's the middle of the night."

"You've only just arrived then?"

"Yeah, I got in from London yesterday, so I'm still a bit jet lagged."

"I'm not surprised," said Josh. "You didn't stay long in Bangkok?"

"I've been to Bangkok a couple of times and I'm in a rush to meet someone."

"Sounds mysterious," he said with a grin. "Do I hear a story in there somewhere?"

"It's going to be a long trip," said Sasha, trying not to sound rude. She couldn't put her finger on the reason, but she didn't feel like discussing her situation. "Plenty of time for stories."

She paused and held up the bottle. "Thanks for the water."

"No worries."

Sasha turned and got back on the bus, happy to escape the direct sunlight and heat. The Thai boy was rounding the others up, hustling them like sheep.

Josh had been right about being close to the border and within half an hour, they pulled up at what looked like someone's house. The wooden building was isolated.

Scrawny chickens ran around the outskirts of the property, scratching in the dust.

As the troop piled in, a friendly Thai woman rushed over.

"Come, come," she said, racing around pulling out wooden benches from the tables. The inside was clean and spacious. Fans in each of the corners of the room kept the hot air moving.

"Please, sit," she said.

Her enthusiasm was infectious. The woman probably only got a couple of busloads of people a week.

Sasha stood, awkward. Everyone had already formed little groups and she was unsure of where to sit. She felt as if she were back in school and had walked into the canteen at lunch, only to find there was no one she knew and no free tables. She didn't want to sit with Josh. Though he seemed like a decent guy—and the green eyes, dark curls and tattoos had caught her eye—she didn't want him to get the wrong idea.

The mother of the blond boy sat down at one of the tables and caught Sasha's eye. The woman smiled and gave a slight nod of her head, beckoning Sasha. Relieved at not having to spend any more time hovering, Sasha went over and sat down opposite.

"Are you sure you don't mind me joining you?" Sasha asked. "I hate to impose just because I'm friendless!"

The woman laughed. "No imposition, I promise. It's nice to have someone else to talk to. As much as I love my family, you can hear the same stories once too often."

"Hey!" her husband exclaimed, sitting down beside her. "I heard that. Are you telling me you don't like my stories?"

"The first time they're funny," she said, patting him on the back of his hand. "It's just by the tenth time I find myself zoning out a little."

Her husband shrugged his broad shoulders and grinned. His teeth were white and straight in his tanned face.

"Ah, well. What can you do?"

"I'm Laura, by the way," the woman said with her slightly nasal Australian twang. "This is Greg, and that little terror over there is Ben."

Sasha smiled. "Sasha."

The Thai woman walked back around the tables putting simple plastic menus listing chicken, shrimp, or beef with either noodles or rice in front of everyone.

Within a few minutes, everyone had ordered and shortly after, a cold Coke was placed on the table in front of Sasha. She gulped the drink down, needing the fluid, sugar and caffeine.

"I am so impressed you're out here with your son," Sasha said. "Everyone I know takes their kids on package holidays to Majorca."

"We wanted to raise Ben with as much of our own education as possible," said Laura. "There's only so much a kid can learn stuck in a classroom, so we try to expose him to real life and the real world as much as we can."

"Isn't it difficult traveling with a child?" Sasha asked. "I have enough trouble getting myself from A to B; I can't imagine trying to keep a small child entertained."

"Ben is great." She smiled at her son who was now crouching in the dirt, trying to poke at the chickens with a stick. "He keeps himself entertained and he is so outgoing, he makes friends pretty quickly."

Sasha thought back to the incident on the bus and grinned. "Yeah, I noticed that."

"The Asian people love children too," she continued. "They're twice as helpful when they see we have a child with us. If there are other kids around, he'll play with them. The language barrier doesn't seem to be a problem when you're six. A ball is a ball and kids will play with it, whatever country they're from."

Sasha couldn't agree more. She hoped that when she had children she would have the insight and ability to be able to show them the world and teach them about accepting other ways of life and cultures.

The food they'd ordered was put in front of them and Laura called Ben back to the table. He sat down and devoured his chicken and rice, talking between mouthfuls about the places they'd been and all the friends he had made.

Sasha still had a western stomach and, after noting they were a fair distance from the sea and having seen the state of the cows, she too opted for the chicken, but with noodles. Her stomach rumbled and she could barely eat fast enough. Good, simple food tasted amazing when she was hungry.

Glancing around, everyone else seemed to be enjoying his or her meals as well.

Josh, Goose, Dawn and the two pierced girls sat at a table together. The young, dark couple sat together at another table. At another table, separate from everyone else, was the dreadlocked man. Sasha couldn't help hoping that he stayed away from the group for the rest of the trip. He gave her the creeps.

The driver and the boy ate with the woman who ran the restaurant. They all spoke loud and fast, and all at once.

After the group finished eating, forms were handed around. Each of the travelers filled in reasons for their visits to Cambodia, along with their passport and visa numbers. As Sasha copied from her passport, Josh spoke over her shoulder.

"It's probably a good idea to buy some bits and pieces for the rest of the trip." He pointed over to a chest fridge, which contained bottles of water, old cans of soft drinks and cans of beer. Wire baskets held packets of crisps and small loaves of bread. "We don't know what the border will be like or how long we will have to wait there."

His words surprised her. "Wait there? What do we have to wait for?"

"For our bus." He nodded over at the driver. "Those guys won't be coming into Cambodia with us. They'll want to get home to their families. It'll be Cambodian people who drive us to Siem Reap."

"Of course," she said, feeling a little stupid.

"I wouldn't have known either if someone hadn't told me."

He smiled down at her. She was struck by the green of his eyes and the way the corners creased. His dark, curly hair spiraled out of control, falling over his forehead.

Wow, he's cute, she thought, her heart suddenly tripping a beat. Immediately her cheeks flushed and she glanced away.

Josh must have seen her reaction for he looked away, as though embarrassed for her. Sasha stared down at the table, lost for words. Goose interrupted them with a shout and, with relief, she turned her attention.

"Hey guys!" he said, standing by the fridge, a can of beer in each hand. "I've found a way of making the trip more interesting!"

He went to throw a beer each to the two girls, but they both shook their heads and grimaced.

"I'll pass. I'm struggling enough," said Vicki.

"If I ever touch alcohol again it will be too soon," Steph added.

Dawn screwed up her tiny nose. "I can't stand beer. I'm purely a vodka or white wine kind of girl."

Goose, disappointed, turned to Josh and Sasha. "You two will join me though?"

"Goose," said Josh, unable to hide the weariness in his voice. "It's barely even lunch time and we've got the border crossing to deal with."

"Well, I'm going to have one," he said, cracking open a can. "And I'll take the rest with me for later."

Goose called the owner over, pointed to the beer, and pushed a wad of cash in her hand. Her eyes widened in delight, a smile splitting her face, and she started to help Goose transfer the cans into his daypack.

Sasha turned her attention back to Josh. "Is he a friend of yours?"

"God no! I met him in a restaurant last night and made the mistake of letting him know I was traveling to Cambodia today." Josh pulled a face. "There weren't supposed to be any buses running today, but a stroke of luck got me on this one."

"I offered them a ridiculous amount of money so I could travel today."

"Really? I paid the same price because I already had a ticket to leave the day after. The people who ran the guesthouse told me I could go today instead if I wanted to."

Sasha laughed. "I guess the amount of money I paid was enough in itself to get the locals to give up their bank holiday."

Josh frowned. "Bank holiday? Was that the reason they gave you why they weren't running the buses?"

"Yes. Why, what did they tell you?"

"Nothing really," he said, shaking his head. "They were very mysterious about the whole thing, they even seemed worried. That's why I was so surprised when they said I could travel today after all."

"Oh well." She shrugged. "I guess the main thing is we're here."

"Very true." Josh glanced back over his shoulder. "I think we had better help ourselves to some supplies before Goose empties the fridge."

Sasha got up and together they went to the fridge. They both selected a couple of drinks, crisps and a loaf of bread. The bread was softer and fresher than Sasha expected, but the idea of eating dry bread didn't appeal. It was easy to be picky when she had a stomach full of good food.

She paid for her selections and put them in her bag. Whatever happened in the next few hours, at least she wouldn't go hungry.

With full stomachs and paperwork clutched in their hands, the backpackers piled back on the bus.

Chapter Six
The Border

It turned out they were still over an hour away from the border. As they approached, large, concrete multi-story buildings loomed from the Cambodian side. They stood like a strange oasis in the landscape; a surprising statement of wealth among the wooden shacks, dirt and poverty. Even the banner stretching between two huge stone pillars welcoming them to Cambodia did not have the glamour of these buildings.

Curious, Sasha pointed them out to Josh.

"They're casinos built for rich Thai businessmen," he told her.

"Why can't they go to casinos in their own country?"

"It's illegal to gamble in Thailand, so they build the casinos here for easy access. Unfortunately, the locals don't benefit because they're all Thai owned and run."

"That's awful," she said. "It must be horrible for them to have so much wealth on their doorstep when they've got nothing."

"They don't know any different," said Josh with a sad smile. "And their government doesn't do much to help."

The bus pulled over about five hundred yards from the border and Sasha joined everyone else in climbing from the vehicle. One by one, they collected their bags from the roof. Sasha took hers, almost staggering under the weight, and hoisted it back onto her shoulders. Each of the backpackers thanked the boy and the driver, who simply pointed to the border as if to tell them to go.

Sasha clutched her passport in her hand, her stomach churning. What would she do if they turned her away? Nothing had been said back at the restaurant, but these were government officials who would be much more likely to spot a fraud. She started to regret her decision to push her visa through so quickly. Trying to dispel the worry, she conjured up an image of falling into Nick's arms, him ecstatic to see her, but even that didn't help. The image prompted worries of its own.

Josh must have seen the color draining from her skin for he turned his attention back to her.

"Are you okay?" he asked. "You're pale."

Sasha pushed her passport in his hand. The piece of paper that made up her visa had been stapled in its pages.

"Does this look right to you? I had it all rushed through yesterday and I'm a bit worried the visa might be forged."

Josh flicked her passport open to where the slip of green paper was attached to one of the inside pages. He opened his own passport to an identical page and studied it, a small frown creating lines between his eyes.

"What do you think?"

Josh lifted his eyes to hers. "Well, I'm no expert, but they look exactly the same to me. I'm sure you'll be fine— you're not the typical illegal immigrant."

He smiled and a weight lifted from her heart. "I hope you're right."

"Stick with me. If they refuse you, I'll smuggle you inside my bag."

"You'd never lift me."

"Want a bet?"

Taking Sasha by surprise, Josh picked her up and flung her over his shoulder. She let out a shriek and hit him on his back in protest. He set her back down, grinning.

"See? No problem. You're only a little heavier than my pack."

Sasha glanced down at Josh's huge, eighty-liter bag.

"Charming," she said, but couldn't help grinning back. She smoothed down her hair and wished her face would go back to its normal color.

"Maybe for the time being you should just walk," Josh said. "Come on."

The rest of the group had already reached the border, so they trailed after. Sasha felt better, but she couldn't shake the apprehension. She wondered how much of it had to do with seeing Nick again.

She glanced guiltily out of the corner of her eye, catching the sun-freckled skin and strong profile of the man walking beside her. She didn't have time to analyze the little jolt the sight gave her. Before she knew what was happening, she was handing in her passport.

The small, dark-eyed man behind the counter stared at her. Sasha trembled under his scrutiny and her cheeks burned. If only she had more control over her body's blood flow, life would be much easier. She tried to smile to relax the atmosphere, but the man made no move to smile back. He grunted as he returned her passport.

Relieved, Sasha grabbed the document back. Josh had waited behind her so if she had any problems, she wouldn't be left alone on the wrong side of the border. The small act of kindness touched Sasha and when she set foot on Cambodian soil, a sense of belonging and purpose strengthened her.

A local man ushered the backpackers toward a couple of large tuk-tuks and the group shared a nervous glance.

Steph was the first to voice their doubts. "We're not going the rest of the way in *that*?"

Josh frowned. "I've heard horror stories about people being stuck in pick-up trucks for most of the journey, but this is ridiculous."

"It would take forever," Steph said as she climbed on board, Sasha and Josh following close behind. Steph leaned over to the driver. "Hey? We go to Siem Reap in tuk-tuk?"

The driver stared at her before processing what she had said. He burst out laughing, leaving Steph red-faced.

"No, no. Tuk-tuk only to bus station."

The group heaved a collective sigh of relief.

The sigh, however, was premature.

As they were whisked through the streets, the tires churned up the dry dirt road. Dust caught in the back of Sasha's throat and bit at her eyes. She clung to the bars of the tuk-tuk, terrified they would tip over if they went around a corner too fast.

Ten scare-inducing minutes later, they were deposited at the bus station.

The feeling of disbelief returned. The bus stop consisted of nothing more than bare, redbrick walls and a corrugated iron roof. Only more dirt and dust made up the floor and a couple of battered plastic chairs were the only furniture.

"I hope the bus isn't going to take too long to arrive," said the female part of the dark-haired couple.

Sasha realized this was the first time either of them had interacted with the group and she was surprise to hear a soft Irish accent. She'd assumed from their lack of communication that they were foreign.

"I'm sure it won't," said her partner, touching the back of her neck. He looked around at the rest of the group. "What do you guys think?"

Everyone glanced at the uncomfortable surroundings, unable to give him an answer.

"Well, I don't intend to stay in this dump for any length of time!" Dawn said. "Certainly not when there are perfectly decent hotels around the corner. Why don't we go to them and wait at one of the bars?"

"Sounds good to me!" said Goose, lifting a half-drunk can of beer up in a salute.

Dawn raised her eyebrows and chose to ignore him.

"How about you, Josh?" she asked, flashing him a smile.

Josh frowned. "I'm sure we won't be here for too long. And you can't wander off. We'd never find you again. In the meantime, just use your pack to sit on. At least we've got shade."

Dawn rolled her eyes. "Fine, but we'd better not be here for long."

Sasha glanced up at Josh as everyone found themselves their own seats and corners to settle in. Sasha watched him put his pack where he stood and she dropped her bag down beside it. They both sat on top of their packs and wriggled down to create small dents and pockets of comfort in the overstuffed bags. Though they were in the shade, the corrugated tin roof seemed to store heat, turning the little shelter into an oven.

"I hope you're right," Sasha said.

Josh raised an eyebrow and grinned at her. "So do I."

They sat in silence for a moment, taking in their sparse surroundings.

"Go on then," said Josh, "Tell me a story."

Sasha widened her eyes in surprise. "Like *The Three Little Pigs* or something?"

"No," he laughed. *"Your* story."

Sasha stared at the ground. "I haven't got one. My life is pretty normal. I work as a recruitment consultant; I live in London; I have a cat. No story to tell."

Josh laughed and lifted both hands, palms up. "What about all of this? If your life is so dull, what are you doing sitting in a shack on the Cambodian border?"

"I told you already. I am visiting someone."

"A someone in particular?"

Sasha realized he wasn't going to give up without getting something out of her.

"Ten days ago my boyfriend, who works in Siem Reap, called me to tell me how much he missed me and that he'd bought me a ticket to come out and visit. So I got on the plane and here I am."

Josh raised his eyebrows and gave a low whistle. "Wow, that's commitment. You flew all the way out here on a whim? So is that why you needed to get to Siem Reap today, because you missed him too?"

"Yes, of course," she said, her face reddening at both the white lie and the fact she'd admitted to being spoken for. She realized she was embarrassed she'd been emotionally blackmailed into flying out. She would never admit to anyone that Nick would rather be sunning himself on a beach in Bali then seeing his fiancé for the first time in a year. As she ran the situation over in her head, the first thread of doubt wound its way into her heart. She tried to push the sensation away, but it clung like a poisonous tentacle.

"So how long has he worked out here?" Josh asked.

"It's been a year now," said Sasha, her shoulders sagging.

"And you don't mind?"

"I encouraged him to come," Sasha said.

"But he must fly back and visit you?"

"Well, he was supposed to be on a plane about now, but he decided it would be better for me to come out here. We might end up flying on to Bali"

"Sounds like fun"

Sasha's mind wandered but she wasn't allowed to dwell on her relationship for too long. Goose, who had been hanging out by himself outside, poked his chubby face into the shelter. Red-faced and sweating heavily; the heat and sun had taken its toll. The alcohol probably wasn't helping. He took another long swig from the can in his hand before yelling out to them.

"Hey! You guys. Come and look at this."

Josh grimaced at the sound of Goose's voice. Sasha thought he was going to ignore him, but then he answered, "What is it, Goose?"

"Come and see. You'll like it, I promise."

Josh took a deep breath and gritted his jaw. "We're fine here, Goose. You come and show us."

"I can't," Goose whined. "You have to come here."

Josh looked at Sasha. "He's not going to shut up until I go, is he?"

Sasha smiled and shook her head. Josh pushed himself to his feet and she stood to follow him.

"You don't have to come," Josh said. "He's my curse; I have to live with him."

"Don't be silly. Whatever it is will be more entertaining than sitting by myself," Sasha replied, inadvertently dismissing the nine other people sitting around her.

Together they walked out into the bright sunshine.

Sasha realized what Goose had been getting excited about right away and her heart melted a little for him.

A group of children, aged anywhere from three to ten, surrounded Goose in a semi-circle. Threadbare t-shirts and ragged shorts hung from their bodies and their feet were dirty and bare. Dust coated their lustrous, black hair and large dark eyes of the smaller ones peeked inquisitively from behind fingers and older children's legs. They spoke to each other, gabbling in Cambodian. One of them said something loudly and they all giggled, hands held over their mouths.

Sasha's broke into a smile. Josh hunkered down beside her so he was on the same level as the children. He reached into his daypack and pulled out the bread and crisps he'd bought earlier. The children left Goose and crowded around Josh. A girl, one of the little ones, shyly tapped him on the arm, pointed to the bread and then to her mouth.

Breaking off enough so all the children would get some, Josh tore the bread into pieces. Delighted, each child snatched a portion before running off with brothers, sisters or friends to a safe distance to compare and consume their prizes.

Sasha nipped back to the shelter and took her own bread from her bag, along with the crisps and fizzy drinks.

Josh saw her and called out, "You might want to save a little of that. We still don't know how long we are going to be here for."

Sasha shrugged dismissively, but rethought. She didn't want to appear selfish, but she didn't want to get stuck in this kind of heat with no fluid. A bottle of water, a can of lemonade and a small piece of the bread went back in her bag and she took the rest out to the children.

Seeing her return with an armful of food, the children rushed back, smiles lighting their faces. Sasha pulled open the bags of crisps and taught the first child to cup his hands. The others copied and she shook the slivers of fried potato into their hands, trying to be as fair as possible. Josh cracked open a can of lemonade and the children held the can in both hands, drinking solemnly, before passing the can on to their neighbor.

Sasha knew this would be an image that would stay with her forever. She thought briefly about getting her camera, but it seemed wrong to want to take holiday snapshots of hungry children.

She and Josh sat huddled on the ground, content to take in the sight of the children. The heat and sense of contentment lulled Sasha into a kind of trance. Josh broke the serenity with a yell.

"Goose! What the hell do you think you're doing?"

His sudden shout made Sasha jump. She looked over at where Goose was standing and jumped up, astounded at the idiocy of the man.

"What?" protested Goose. "They like it—see?"

The children around Goose weren't holding a can of soft drink; but a can of beer.

Josh strode over and crouched down next to the child holding the can. Gently he took the can from the child's fingers.

"Sasha, have you got any more soft drinks?"

Sasha ran back to the shelter and took the last can of lemonade out of her bag. She raced back out and handed the can to Josh. He cracked open the drink, took a tiny sip and made yummy noises. Then he took a sip of beer and screwed up his face as though the can contained diesel.

Immediately, the child reached for the lemonade and Josh gave it to him before standing up. Goose stood a little way off, watching the scene with a sulky expression on his face. Josh walked back up to him. He pushed the beer can back into his hands, crushing it and spilling beer down Goose's front at the same time.

Goose lifted his hands. "Hey! Watch it buddy!"

Josh's face got closer to Goose than would have been physically comfortable for either of them. He spoke in a low, controlled voice.

"If I see you pulling a stunt like that again, I will personally make sure you *never* get to Siem Reap. Do you understand?"

Goose stared back at Josh for a moment, then, realizing he was serious, shifted his gaze to the floor and pushed his foot around in the dust.

"Do you understand?" Josh said again.

Goose grunted a 'yes' and Josh turned away and walked back to Sasha. The children had lost interest in them by now and had wandered away with their treats. Josh was shaking with anger and Sasha instinctively put a hand on his arm to calm him.

"I hate how there is always one person who spoils things for everyone else," he said.

"At least you stopped him."

"The problem is, there are people like him all over the world and quite often no one tells them what they're doing wrong. It's stupidity and ignorance more than anything else."

Josh was right. Goose wasn't a bad person; just thoughtless and spoilt. He was someone who had never lived with the consequence of his actions, so he didn't notice the effect simple ill-mannered gestures had on the people he interacted with. He now sat with Steph and Vicki who chatted to him, having perked up after their naps on the bus.

Sasha thought no one else had witnessed the scene outside at first, but then she saw the dreadlocked man sitting alone at the front of the bus shelter. He smiled his strange, fanged smile. Sasha couldn't tell if he was trying to be friendly or weird. She didn't want to judge a book by its cover; he couldn't help the way he looked. She gave a tentative smile, but he shifted his gaze back down at the ground, concentrating on the cigarette he was rolling.

No one else appeared to pick up on the frosty air surrounding Josh as they went back into the shelter.

"I'm almost tempted to pick up my bag and move it away from Goose," said Josh.

Sasha gave him a smile of sympathy. "That's not going to do much good, I'm afraid. We're all going to be stuck in the very confined space of the bus for the next ten hours."

"If it ever shows up."

As if his words conjured up the vehicle, a dirty, white minibus pulled up outside the shelter. No one spoke for a moment, a silent pact not to jinx the possibility of this being their ride, but then a young Cambodian boy jumped down from the passenger seat and hailed them from the entrance.

"Hello people! Come, come! You want to sit in dirt all day?"

The group shuffled to their feet like old women. Sasha joined them, lifting her bag once again. Though she was pleased to see the bus; the size, rust and apparent lack of air conditioning didn't make it look like the most comfortable ride.

"At least it's not a pick-up truck," Josh commented.

Sasha raised her eyebrows. "It might as well be."

Once again, packs were strapped to the roof and they all piled on the bus. The seats were smaller and harder than the previous ones, but the group copied the seating pattern of earlier. The one exception was Josh. He slid across the aisle and into the seat next to Sasha.

He gave her an apologetic smile.

"I know I'm playing musical chairs." Under his breath he added, "I just don't think I can stand ten more hours next to that guy. I fear we both wouldn't make it out alive."

Sasha laughed. "In that case you should definitely sit here. I don't want to be responsible for you getting into another fight."

"Thanks, I'll try not to bore you too much."

Sasha smiled, but didn't answer. So far, he'd been the most entertaining part of the journey.

CHAPTER SEVEN
APPROACHING DUSK

Before long, the group realized the tales of Cambodian roads were true.

Shortly after leaving the border, the dusty roads deteriorated to dirt tracks. Every bump and rut felt ten times the size they really were. A four-by-four would have struggled over the track and this twenty-year-old bus with no suspension made for an uncomfortable ride.

The travelers held on to their seats and the backs of those in front. Despite their efforts, every time the bus hit another rut, someone bounced, hitting their head on the hard metal roof. The groans and half-laughter of the injured parties filled the bus.

The metal exterior of the vehicle absorbed the heat of the day and all the windows were opened wide, trying to coax any small amount of breeze inside the vehicle. The lack of tarmac held other problems. The wheels churned up the dry dirt so a red dust rode on the breeze, coating them all in a rusty mist.

They'd been traveling for a long time without a break and Sasha's muscles ached from being in the same position for too long. The bus trundled through a rural area where even the small villages they passed through seemed to be deserted. She spotted the occasional person outside their small, wooden houses, but as soon as the local caught sight of the bus, they disappeared inside. Sasha couldn't remember the last time they passed another vehicle, although that could be a blessing as the road was so narrow in places, she struggled to imagine how they would pass without going off the road and into the submerged grasslands on either side.

Sasha leaned forward and tapped the boy, whose name she learned to be Chay, on the shoulder.

"Are we going to stop anywhere soon?" she asked. "We've been driving for hours."

The boy shifted around in his seat so he faced her.

"Most travelers' stops closed today or we stop earlier," he explained. "We find somewhere soon."

"Are they closed because of the bank holiday?"

Chay's smooth, young forehead crumpled in confusion. Then he seemed to recover and laughed. "Yes! Today is 'no travelers' holiday."

His attitude left Sasha puzzled. She wanted to ask him about it further, but he'd turned back. Chay began to speak in Cambodian to the driver. The driver glanced back at her and laughed.

Sasha shifted uncomfortably in her seat and glanced at Josh. Had he heard? Josh sat back in his seat, eyes closed, listening to his iPod. She was without an ally.

Finally, they stopped at a restaurant for food.

The group piled off the bus, groaning and stretching cramped muscles. Though late afternoon, the sun's strength hadn't waned and the air remained thick with dusty heat. Even so, Sasha was relieved to be able to stretch out. After a while, the confines of the bus started to feel claustrophobic.

Once again, a wooden shack made up the restaurant, but it served cold drinks and the standard fare of rice, noodles and bread. The group found seats as the family who ran the restaurant watched them with narrow-eyed suspicion from behind a counter at the back. It was hard not to feel uncomfortable under this sort of scrutiny and the travelers glanced at each other, not wanting to say anything.

The reception was a sharp contrast to the warmth and enthusiasm of the Thais.

The family placed food in front of them without any kind of smile or conversation; even Chay and the driver were treated with aversion. The tension bled to the group causing their own conversation to be muted and stiff.

Despite the cold atmosphere, the food tasted good; hot and spicy. Whatever they'd done to upset the locals, at least they hadn't taken it out on the cooking.

Wanting to escape the tension of the room, Sasha bent down and picked up her daypack. She stood from the table and walked over to the glass-fronted fridge that contained a selection of drinks. She chose a two-liter bottle of water and handed over an American dollar to pay. From the lack of a smile and the way the man took the money without looking at her, she didn't expect to get change back.

Sasha slipped out the door and headed around the side of the restaurant. Apart from a couple of chickens scratching around, the small yard was deserted.

Sasha cracked open the bottle and poured the water over her face, arms and chest. The velvet coolness quenched her skin. She stripped off her vest. Panic gripped her that someone would catch her standing in her bra. Working quickly, she used the wet vest to wipe herself down, before pulling on a clean top from her pack. The water had run pink and red dirt streaked the old top she'd been wearing, but she felt cleaner and more refreshed than she had in ages.

As she stuffed her old shirt in her bag, she sensed eyes on her. She spun around to see the dreadlocked guy standing at the corner of the building. He leaned against the wooden wall, his arms folded across his chest. He gave her a cool smile, before he turned and went back inside.

Sasha's cheeks flushed. How long had he been there? Had he watched her change? She couldn't say anything; after all, she shouldn't have stripped out in the open. It wasn't as though he'd spied on her in the bathroom. Even so, his presence made her uncomfortable and she hung outside for a moment, hoping when she went inside, he would already be on the bus.

By the time she went back in the restaurant, the others were getting up to leave. Sasha added another couple of dollars to the small pile on the table to pay for her food, and headed back outside. She shouldn't want to be back on the uncomfortable bus, but given the awkward silence and stares from the Cambodian family, it was a welcome relief.

As she climbed back on, she couldn't help but glance in the direction of Dreadlocks. He faced the window, paying her no attention, and she told herself to relax. The incident had probably been an accident. Perhaps he came outside for a cigarette and hadn't been watching her for as long as she assumed.

A sense of unease hung over the group as they headed deeper into the country, the wheels of the old bus slowly eating the miles. The empty streets and lack of people was painfully noticeable, but nobody mentioned the lack of life; as though putting voice to the strangeness would make it more real.

Sasha had been to Cambodia before, but she couldn't remember ever feeling uncomfortable or threatened. She was certain the people had been more than welcoming. Of course, she'd visited several years before; attitudes had obviously changed.

Several hours later they stopped for dinner only to be welcomed with the same awkward atmosphere. The family running the restaurant took orders in a hushed silence, and retreated to a back room.

Two Cambodian children, a boy and a girl, about five and seven respectively, played a game with a wooden hoop outside. Ben saw them and his eyes lit up. He loosened his grip on his mother's hand and ran over.

The children smiled, shy and uncertain, at each other. The girl reached out, offering the hoop to Ben.

Ben didn't get the chance to take the toy. From out of nowhere, the children's mother appeared. She grabbed both children by the arm, one in each hand. Their feet scuffed in the dirt as she dragged them toward the back of the restaurant and to the room out back.

Ben stood alone, blinking in the fading sunlight. His lips pressed together in his effort not to cry in front of people.

Laura had watched what had happened with the same stunned disbelief that was now on her son's face. Anger tightened her features but, obviously not wanting her son to realize how upset she was, she fixed a smile on her face and went up to Ben.

"Hey honey," she said. "Are you going to come in for some food?"

Ben blinked again, but managed a nod.

Laura crouched in front of him and reached out, rubbing his arm in comfort.

"I expect they were just out past their bedtime," she said. "That's why their mum came to get them. She was annoyed with *them*, sweetie; it had nothing to do with you."

Ben continued to stare at the ground, his mouth in a tight line.

Laura pulled him towards her and gave him a fierce hug.

"Mum!" he protested, the embarrassment of his mother's public affection snapping him out of his upset. He untangled himself from her arms.

She grinned at him. "I can't help it," she said, reaching out to ruffle his blond hair. "You're too cute."

"Mum..." he said again, still embarrassed.

Laura got to her feet. "Come on. Let's eat."

They sat back down on the long wooden bench table running down the middle of the room. The driver and the boy sat on one end, away from the rest of the group, and Dreadlocks sat at the other end, still refusing to interact. Small holders of salt, pepper and dried chili flakes ran down the center of the table; plastic utensils wrapped in stiff paper napkins protruded from separate pots.

Sasha shot Laura a look of sympathy, but the older woman pressed her lips together and gave a slight shake of her head.

What's the matter with them? her look said.

Sasha gave her a brief smile and shrugged. She didn't have the answer. The rest of them weren't going to leave it at that.

"Why do I feel like something isn't quite right?" said Josh.

The two girls sat opposite.

"Maybe they're pissed off they've had to open for us," said Steph. "I've heard the Cambodians like the American dollar too much and they're always trying to sell things to backpackers and can be a bit pushy, but when I've spoken to other travelers about the Cambodian people, everyone said they're friendly enough.

Vicki spoke in a low voice. "But they seem almost scared of us." She shivered despite the heat. "They're giving me the creeps."

Steph noticed the shiver and laughed. "You're way too sensitive, Vicki. They probably just don't like foreigners."

"They're sure in a funny business if they don't like foreigners," she grumbled.

"They're country folk and they are probably just a bit wary of strangers," said Josh. "I'm sure as soon as we get into the towns the people will be more accepting of us."

Dawn raised her eyebrows. "I should hope so. We're giving these people our business. The least they could do is crack a smile." She ran a hand through her hair and grimaced. "I wish someone had warned me how gross this place was going to be."

"I'm sure you can survive a few weeks without getting your hair done," said Steph. "And I'm sure these people have more important things to worry about. Haven't you seen all the people with lost limbs and deformities because of the land mines?"

Dawn shrugged. "It's not my problem?"

Steph shook her head in disbelief and turned away.

The restaurant was situated in a small hamlet. The countryside around was completely flat, stretching to the horizon. An occasional, awkward stunted tree broke up the vast expanse of land. Though the day remained hot and dry, and the road little more than dust, most of the land surrounding them was flooded. During the drive, they'd passed solitary wooden shacks built high on stilts to keep them elevated above the water. Children played in the dirt and the family's buffalo waded in the water beneath the house, grazing on submerged plants.

They were now on marginally higher ground, which allowed for sturdier ground-level buildings, but the poverty was still obvious. Despite the icy service they received, the entire group left obscenely large tips.

As they piled back on the bus, Sasha caught sight of a group of locals silently watching them from across the street. Instead of playing, the children stood with their small hands clasped in the hands of the adults, their faces solemn, as if at a funeral.

A cold finger traced down Sasha's spine and she shivered.

She sat down next to Josh and nudged him gently. "What were you saying about something not being right?"

Josh turned in the direction she nodded and frowned.

"Wow. What's up with them?"

"I don't know, but I don't like it." Sasha leaned over to Chay. "Why are the locals staring at us like that?"

The boy looked over at the statuesque group and shrugged dismissively. "Today is not good day for travelers."

"Just because of the holiday?" she tried again, probing for more information.

Chay shrugged. "They don't like people traveling on the holiday."

Sasha couldn't be sure, but she thought Chay was avoiding her eye.

"It is tradition," he said and turned away.

"I guess everyone has their customs," said Josh. "Who are we to judge?"

"I guess so."

Sasha settled back in her seat. She couldn't help but watch the stony faces grow smaller as they drove out of the village and back into the unrelenting expanse of water and land. The terrain stretched continuous on either side, making the road like a never-ending bridge

With full stomachs, the group settled into silence, some dozing, most watching the strange scenery go by. Only Goose continued to talk, oblivious that no one either listened or responded to him. The several cans of lager he'd consumed had thickened his already alligator-like skin, and he continued to tell tales of drunken exploits from his travels. When the sound of his voice bored even himself, he plugged into his iPod and started to wave his arms about and 'dance' to the music. Though he sat alone, the size of the bus wasn't ideal for a six-foot, overweight dancer, and Josh turned around to glare at him.

Immediately, Goose exaggerated his dancing, but then must have realized he was about to exile himself from the rest of the passengers and calmed down.

"Idiot," said Josh under his breath.

Sasha smiled to herself and continued to admire the unique landscape from the window. In a short space of time, the bright light reflected off the water changed its hue, deepening and softening. Birds finished their day's feeding and took to the darkening sky, searching for places to roost. The occasional family they'd seen darting into their homesteads as the bus passed began to thin out. With no electricity feeding their homes, the rural Cambodians rose with the light and slept at dusk. The place took on an eerie, quiet calm; the only sound being that of the bus and the tinny music from their personal stereos.

It's as if the vehicle separates us from our surroundings, Sasha thought. *As though I'm looking through a portal and witnessing a different world, a different reality.*

The idea made her uncomfortable and she quickly looked away from the window.

"What's wrong?" Josh asked, a concerned frown marring his forehead.

"Nothing, nothing," she said, trying to shake the sensation. .

"You've gone white."

"You're only saying that because I'm lacking the traveler's tan," she said, trying to lighten the sudden heavy atmosphere pressing on her shoulders.

"You won't be pale for much longer, especially if you go to Bali."

Surprised, Sasha realized she hadn't thought about Bali for hours. In fact, she hadn't thought about the reason for her trip since the border. As the distance between her and Nick lessened, Sasha became more certain that she shouldn't have come. She couldn't imagine the meeting; the two of them reunited after a year apart. They would be like strangers again. She wanted to imagine a romantic reunion, but all she could think of were questions that made her stomach churn and doubt their future together.

She didn't want to think about it.

Sasha turned her head to look back out of the window. Darkness had swallowed the land; the inside of the bus was all she had.

A bolt of blinding lightning cut through the sky, lighting the bus so brightly it was as if someone had flashed a floodlight into the vehicle's interior. Sasha heard herself and several others, both male and female, let out a scream of surprise. Another flash followed and she watched the extraordinary landscape transformed for a split second into the backdrop of a science fiction movie. A fork of lightning joined the water to the sky, the petrified trees standing silhouetted and alone.

Another bolt struck again, then another and another, like a strobe.

A nervous murmur went around the group. Thunder—loud enough to make the glass shake in the bus's windows—cracked and rolled above them.

At the back of the bus, Ben started to cry. He buried his head into his mother's chest and Greg wrapped his arms around his family as if to protect them from the storm.

Josh glanced back at the crying child and smiled nervously at Sasha. "I think I know how he feels."

Sasha's own heart raced and her stomach churned with a mixture of fear and excitement. She wasn't usually scared of storms, she even enjoyed them; but normally she was able to watch them from the safety of her flat.

"I don't like the idea of quite so much lightning on a very flat plain when we're the only metallic object for miles," said Josh.

Sasha scowled. "I was trying to ignore that fact!"

"I don't think we'd be injured because the tires would ground us, but it would be an experience to be hit."

"It's an experience I can live without."

She looked back out of the window, marveling at what was occurring around them. Their isolation—no city or hospital for hours—was worrying and a little frightening. She told herself storms like this were probably common for the rainy season and surely she would have heard if busloads of backpackers were killed in storms whilst trying to cross Cambodia. During all her years of travel, she'd never seen anything like this lightning.

Another roll of thunder crashed above and Sasha cringed.

"Do you think it will last long?" Vicki yelled over the noise.

Goose pulled out his headphones. "Who wants it to stop? This is the most exciting thing that's happened for ages."

"I'm sure it will pass," said Laura, a stern undercurrent in her voice as she glanced deliberately at her crying child.

"What do you want to bring a kid along for anyway?" Goose replied.

"I agree," said Dreadlocks, finally speaking up. "This is no place for kids. Why ruin the trip for the rest of us?"

Greg glared at both men and Dreadlocks returned the stare with a snide smile. Sasha didn't think it was possible, but the atmosphere in the bus had suddenly got worse.

Chapter Eight
Missing

Goose faced the front again and shrank down in his seat. He reached in his bag and pulled out another can of warm beer. If everyone else was going to be miserable, at least *he* intended on having a good time.

The thunder clapped again. He jumped at the sound and then scowled in annoyance. He was stuck on this bus with a bunch of boring wimps and couldn't let his guard down for a minute. The slightest little thing, like giving that kid some beer, seemed to antagonize them. What gave Josh the right to threaten him anyway? The guy wouldn't know fun if it jumped up and bit him on the ass.

The strain on Goose's bladder wasn't helping his mood. They hadn't been going for long since their last stop, but the amount of fluid he'd consumed had built up. He shifted in his seat, trying to relieve the pressure. He knew he couldn't ask them to stop now; he'd never hear the end of it. If he waited awhile, the kid or someone else would want to go.

The lightning continued, lulling Goose into a rare moment of appreciation for the almost supernatural beauty. The rhythmical flashes cleared his mind of all thought and when another clap of thunder made the rest of the group laugh nervously, he didn't even hear them. Instead, he heard someone calling his name:

"Graham..." A soft and feminine voice.

Laughter bubbled beneath the surface. Something about the sound caught his heart; tears pricked behind his eyes and a lump formed in his throat.

"Graham..."

He tore his gaze from the window and turned to the girls behind. Deep in conversation with each other, they didn't pay him any attention.

He interrupted them anyway. "Did you want me?"

Vicki raised an eyebrow. "No Goose, we don't want you."

He scanned the rest of the bus, but the other members of the group seemed to be deliberately ignoring him. The young couple had barely spoken to anyone during the whole journey and the Australian family was too wrapped up in their precious child to bother about anyone else. The posh girl slept with a U-shaped pillow around her neck and an eye-mask covering half of her face. Goose knew the voice hadn't belonged to the weird guy with dreadlocks who sat in front of him. The only other people were Josh and his new buddy-buddy girlfriend.

Only Josh knew his real name was Graham. He'd shown his visa and passport to the other man that morning, comparing all the stamps they'd collected during their travels. Josh had commented on his real name then.

Goose stared at Josh's head, trying to figure out if the other man was playing a trick on him.

As if he'd felt eyes burning in his back, Josh turned around.

"Something I can do for you, Goose?"

Goose scowled and turned back to the window.

The moment he did so, girlish laughter filtered to his ears, as light and fresh as the tinkling of a stream. He swung his head back around. Everyone ignored him. Another call of his name, this time more urgent, drew his face back to the window.

"Graham!"

Was it possible the voice came from out there? If so, how could he hear it so clearly? No. It didn't make any sense. Who would be calling him? They were in the middle of nowhere and he didn't know anyone in Cambodia.

The gentle laughter came again and fluttered around his ears like butterfly kisses. He pressed his palms and face against the dusty glass. The laughter stirred a strange desire inside him. It suddenly felt as if a thousand bees buzzed in his veins. The continuous flashing blurred his mind, making it difficult for him to string a coherent thought together.

The window beside the girls was the only one that opened fully on their side. Goose twisted around in his seat and clambered up over the back, leaning across the girls to get his head out the window.

"Hey. Watch it," yelled Steph. "What do you think you're doing?"

She thumped Goose on the shoulder, but he didn't even notice.

Josh saw Goose climbing on top of the two girls and rolled his eyes. "This guy is nothing but trouble."

"Is he all right?" Sasha asked, looking at Goose.

Goose's face was pale, his eyes wide and staring. Vicki and Steph leaned away from him with disgusted expressions. Goose hung out the window like a dog in a car.

"He's probably just pissed, the idiot."

"Are you sure that's all?" said Sasha, her eyes wide in alarm. "He looks crazy."

"The guy is a moron," said Dreadlocks, but no one paid him any attention.

"Goose, get off them," Josh shouted above the thunder, making Sasha jump again.

When Goose ignored him, Josh got up and walked in an enforced hunch to where Goose was trying to squeeze his large frame over the back of his seat. As if he were a small puppy that needed punishment, Josh grabbed him by the scruff of his t-shirt and dropped him back in his seat. The moment Josh pulled Goose away from the window he seemed to come to, looking around as though trying to figure out where he was.

"Can't you behave yourself for one minute?" said Josh, angry.

Goose blinked at him. "Huh?"

"What the hell do you think you were trying to do?"

"I'm not sure..."

The dazed glaze returned and his eyes dragged back to the window. Then he seemed to remember something and focused on Josh.

"I just needed to take a leak."

"And you thought you'd climb out of the window of a moving bus?"

Exasperated, Josh ran a hand through his hair. He walked back to the front of the bus, leaned over to Chay and tapped him on the shoulder.

"Can we pull over?" he asked. "A quick toilet stop for the piss-head."

He expected Goose to be riled by the comment, but when he turned back, Goose was staring back out of the window, his head cocked, as though listening to something. The bus pulled to a stop and Josh nudged Goose's shoulder.

"Go on then."

Goose stared blankly for a moment and then dragged himself out of his seat. He pulled open the door and hesitated at the top of the steps. In the seconds between the blinding lightning strikes, the darkness was complete. Goose climbed with unsteady steps down to the road.

Josh went back to Goose's seat and reach under, fishing out his bag. He opened the bag and pulled out the two remaining cans of beer. He cracked one open and tipped the booze out the window. The drink hissed and fizzed as it hit the dusty ground. Josh waited for the yell of protest he expected from Goose. All remained silent and he cracked opened the final beer and repeated the motion.

"Hopefully he'll sleep it off now," said Josh. He turned back to the girls. "You two okay?"

"Yeah, we're tough," said Steph with a grin.

"We've put up with enough drunken idiots in our time," Vicki agreed. "Don't worry about us."

Josh looked at the rest of the gang. Dawn slept, oblivious to the drama happening around her. Dreadlocks watched silently, a smile of wry amusement on his face. The Irish couple sat huddled together, the girl with her head on her boyfriend's shoulder and his head resting on top of hers. They'd had little interaction with the rest of the group, hardly seeming to notice what was happening around them. Laura and Greg were also huddled together with their son. Laura watched her now sleeping son but Greg glanced up and caught Josh's eye. The large man nodded his approval. Josh returned the nod and turned back to the front.

"Goose is taking his time," said Sasha.

Josh sighed. "He's probably doing it on purpose to hold us up even more."

"Do you think we should see if he's all right?"

Josh huffed air out through his nose. "I am starting to feel like the man's babysitter." Still he got up and leaned out the open door.

"Shake it off, mate! Time to go." Josh listened for the sound of hot urine hitting the dirt, the pulling up of a zip or even swearing under breath. There was nothing. The ground emitted the day's heat back into the atmosphere, and the air was still and thick. Josh peered into the darkness, willing his eyes to adjust. More flashes of lightning gave him brief glimpses into the night, but not for long enough to allow him to scan the road completely.

"Come on Goose," he called out, his voice hollow in the empty night. "You're not doing yourself any favors."

Josh strained his ears, listening, but again no reply came. He didn't even hear the sound of movement on the road. The first flicker of nerves spiked through Josh's stomach and he leaned back into the bus.

"Sasha? Could you reach in my bag and grab my torch? I think Goose is hiding or something."

Sasha frowned, her lips pressed together. She fished out Josh's torch and then pulled her own from her daypack. She climbed out of the vehicle and handed Josh his torch. Simultaneously, they switched them on and strong beams of light cut through the darkness. Sasha joined in, calling Goose's name, but answer came. They walked up and down either side of the road, studying the dirt, foliage and water for any sign of disturbance. There was no sign of Goose and they walked back to the bus in silence.

Josh crouched down and peered beneath the bus, but it was empty. Chay jumped out of the passenger seat and joined them.

"What is matter?" he said, standing in their torchlight.

"Goose has disappeared," said Sasha. She turned to Josh."What if he's wandered out there?" she said gesturing to the flooded overgrowth. "He might have passed out or something. He could be drowning as we speak!"

"Damn it," said Josh. "Give me your torch."

With a light held in each hand, he stepped off the road and into the undergrowth. The vegetation was thick and water seeped into his shoes. Tentacles of weeds caught around his calves and he struggled to tear them away and move forward. Another roll of thunder crashed overhead and bolts of lightning speared through the sky, illuminating the land stretched out before him.

Fingers, as hard as steel, grabbed the back of his arm. Josh spun around. Chay's small face peered up at him.

"No Mister! Must stay on path. Still many land mines from war!"

Images of people with lost limbs, or even worse—lost lives—flashed through his head. His legs went weak beneath him as he realized what he'd been about to do. He allowed Chay to lead him back to the road where Sasha waited.

"What are we going to do?" she said, her voice high-pitched and tears trembling in her tone. "We can't just leave him here."

"Well we can't risk other people's lives by wading out to search for him. If a land mine went off, it could kill someone. We can't take the risk."

"I know," said Sasha, starting to pace. "What about trying our mobile phones? We could call for help?"

"No reception here," said Chay. "And still many hours to city."

"We've got to at least check. Someone might have a satellite phone?"

Josh took in the sight of her distressed face and nodded, but the sinking sensation deep in his gut made him suspect this story wouldn't have a happy ending.

Fat droplets of water began to splash on the road, creating miniature craters. Faster and faster, the rain mottled the ground with dark marks. Sasha put her hands out, palm up. The weight of the rain was such that a single drop formed a pool in the center. Another crash of thunder signaled the onset of a torrential downpour and they ran for the shelter of the bus. The couple of seconds it took to reach the doorway was enough to leave them soaked. They climbed back on the vehicle with water running down their faces and their clothes clinging to their bodies like second skins.

Neither Josh nor Sasha could meet the expectant eyes staring at them. Sasha put her head in her hands and Josh stared at the floor. Dawn pulled her eye mask from her face.

"Guys?" said Vicki. "What's going on?"

Josh lifted his head up. "Goose has disappeared. He's wandered off the road or something, and we can't find him."

86

"What do you mean you can't find him?" she said. "We haven't even looked yet. We should all go out and search for him."

"We can't," said Josh, defeated. "We can't wander off of the road because of the possibility of land mines."

"That's crazy," said Steph. "We must be able to do something?"

"You can all check your phones," Sasha said. "If anyone has got reception we can call for help."

For a moment, the bus filled with the sounds of people digging their cell phones out of their bags and beeps as they turned them on.

For the first time, Sasha wished she'd bothered to invest in a decent phone. She'd resisted the whole 'smart phone' revolution and clung to cheap her pay-as-you-go mobile. She didn't think she even had roaming.

As Chay predicted, no one had reception.

"Please, keep checking," Sasha said. "It might change."

An uncomfortable silence settled over the travelers. "Now what?" asked Steph, breaking the quiet.

"We're going to have to search for him," said Josh. "But we can't go off the road."

"The man is a damn idiot," said Greg, breaking his usual silence. His normally gentle face furrowed with anger. "I am not risking the safety of my family to try to find a drunk."

Laura put a hand on her husband's arm and a look passed between them. Greg pressed his lips together, controlling his anger.

"This is Goose's own fault," said Laura. "If he managed to get himself lost, I really don't see what we're supposed to do."

The male half of the Irish couple spoke up. "How long until we reach Siem Reap?"

"In storm, maybe six hours more," said Chay. He turned and spoke to the driver. "Yes, six hours if journey goes well."

"If you don't lose any more passengers, you mean," said Dawn.

Chay shrugged. "Sometimes, if rain is too heavy, bridges..." Chay put his fingertips together and then pulled them apart.

"Collapse?" said the Irish girl, a tremor in her voice.

Chay didn't interpret the worry in her voice and simply appeared pleased at acquiring a new word.

"Yes, yes! Collapse."

"In which case we need to get there as soon as possible," said Laura. "The longer we sit here, the worse the bridges are going to get."

Vicki's voice increased in pitch "So you're saying we should leave him here? Just because he had a few beers, you think he deserves to be abandoned in the middle of nowhere?"

"We haven't abandoned him," said Laura. "He's the one who has abandoned *us*."

"That's crap!" said Steph. "He's probably slipped and knocked himself out. He wouldn't wander right out there, I expect he's by the side of the road somewhere."

Josh shook his head. "We looked right along the roadside and didn't see anything—not even footprints."

"You couldn't have looked hard enough," she said. "You probably didn't even search at all; you wanted to be rid of him."

Sasha stood, her hands held up, trying to quiet the group.

"Hey, people! We're not helping anyone by getting at each other. We need to agree on a plan of action and stick to it. What about the men and myself, as I'm already wet, going back out and having another look? If we still can't find him we'll have no other choice than to go on to Siem Reap and raise the alert."

She scanned the faces of the remaining backpackers, trying to judge everyone's reactions to her suggestions. Vicki and Steph nodded and Greg pulled his large frame out of his seat. He kissed his wife and sleeping son and made his way to the front. The Irish man gave his partner a tight smile and she squeezed his hand. Only the dreadlocked man didn't move, or even acknowledge something was happening. He simply stared out of the window, ignoring them all.

Josh looked at him and frowned. "Excuse me... I'm sorry I didn't catch your name."

He turned around, his ice-blue eyes fixing Josh's. "That's because I didn't give it to you."

Josh didn't say anything, just raised his eyebrows expectantly. The silence between them was tense, each waiting for the other to speak first.

"The name's Seth," he said finally.

"Okay, Seth. Are you planning on giving us a hand?"

"Not really." He shrugged. "I don't see why I should. I couldn't give a damn about the guy."

Josh's jaw tightened, his fists clenched by his side.

"Just leave it," said Sasha, hoping Josh would leave him alone; the guy obviously wasn't a team player and she didn't trust him.

Sasha turned her attention back to the people willing to help. "If we can borrow everyone's torches?" she said.

The search crew marched off the bus and into the driving rain like men in a chain gang. Sasha went to step off with them, but Josh's arm blocked her way.

"There's no point in you coming back out," he yelled, trying to make himself heard above the pounding rain and thunder.

"I don't mind," she shouted back. "I'll feel better if I can help."

"Your choice," he said moving out of her way.

The torches were distributed between the group and those who had waterproofs slung them over their heads. Sasha hadn't thought to pack wet weather gear. Josh handed Sasha his rain jacket. She considered the offer for a moment, thinking the polite thing to do was refuse, but in the short time she'd known him, she suspected he wouldn't let her go without.

"Thanks."

Sasha took the jacket. She threw it over her head and shoulders, holding the hood up with one hand and the torch with the other. The force of the rain almost tore the material from her grip and the hammering sound of rain on plastic was deafening.

The driver had finally joined them, so they divided into two groups of three. One group set off in one direction, with one person walking down the middle of the road and the other two walking on either side. The other group mirrored their actions.

They walked slowly. The intense darkness and rain made it hard to see and everyone wanted to be certain they hadn't missed anything. Sasha set off with Josh and the Irish man. She walked down the center of the road and, with a stab of panic, realized she struggled to distinguish the two men walking on either side of her. Only vague beams of torchlight pinpricked their location. She turned her head to look back. The interior of the bus was now only a vague glow in the distance; the other group was nowhere to be seen.

"This is crazy!" yelled Josh. "I can hardly make out what's in front of me."

"Let's go back," said Irish. "There is no point in risking losing someone else."

The group stopped in silent agreement.

Sasha put her hand over her mouth, suddenly nauseous. "I feel awful."

"This isn't your fault," said Irish. "You've done everything you could."

The three turned around and headed back to the bus. The closer they got, the brighter the torches of the other group appeared. Sasha became aware of the vast expanse of nothingness that lay at her back, and she had to resist the urge to break into a run.

The other group reached the bus first and Greg shook his head at the approaching threesome.

"Nothing?" asked Josh, more a statement than a question.

"Nothing."

CHAPTER NINE
A VISITOR

Wet and subdued, the group continued their journey in silence. The storm hadn't let up. The rain pounded on the metal roof, echoing around their small confined space as though they were in a tin can under a waterfall.

Sasha sat with her forehead pressed against the glass; staring out at the flashing world as they passed. She couldn't help but reflect on the likely loss of life that had just occurred and it sat heavy on her heart.

Goose had been annoying, but he didn't deserve what happened. Nobody set out on a traveling adventure expecting tragedy to befall them. She thought about his family and friends at home, waiting for another exciting email, only to receive news of his disappearance or death. Thoughts of her own family passed through her head. If anything ever happened to her, her mother would be devastated.

Sasha would have given anything to be curled up in front of the television with a cup of tea and her cat purring on her lap. What was wrong with a simple life if it meant comfort and safety?

The heavy rain drove against the window and the continuous thunder cracked and rolled. The night seemed threatening, as though it held a portentous secret; menacing and fateful. The empty seat amplified the tension. The space Goose left was more accusing than the man ever could have been.

Sasha blinked back tears, blurring the already distorted view. The roadside passed more slowly than she would have liked. Each time the white lightning lit up the area, she caught the sight of vegetation protruding from the flooded land and imagined Goose lying tangled in the fronds, dazed, frightened and alone.

Outside the window, the light show dazzled and mesmerized.

Exhausted, Sasha's thoughts wandered. Her eyes burned and each time she blinked, she struggled a little more to open them again. To sleep felt disrespectful to Goose. Part of her still expected him to show up; as though she would turn around and find him back in his seat or he would come running out of the darkness, his arms waving for them to stop.

The brilliance of the lightning continued, compelling her to watch, knowing that even if she did close her eyes, she would continue to see liquid fire raining down from the night sky.

Though aware of her surroundings, her mind drifted to that unseen place occupied in dreams.

Ferocious red eyes glared at her from the darkness.

Sasha reared back from the window, her fingers gripped tightly around Josh's arm, her knuckles and face white.

"Christ, Sasha!" said Josh, his eyes deep with worry. "What's wrong?"

She couldn't speak. She just pointed out of the window.

"What? What is it?"

"I don't know," she said, her voice no more than a whisper. "Something was out there..."

"Whatever you thought you saw, it was just a dream."

"No," she said, shaking her head. "That thing was real."

"What was real?" said Josh, impatience sharpening his tone.

"I... I can't describe it. An animal of some kind was running along the side of the bus and it..." She broke off, a lump in her throat blocking her words. "Was watching me."

"Sasha, you were dreaming. You nodded off. I promise."

Sasha's mind conjured up the thing she had just seen. The lightning had lit the creature like a strobe light, but she'd seen enough to last a lifetime. Though the thing ran on four legs, loping like a wolf tracking its prey, its long black body seemed to wind and contract like a snake's. But its eyes were the worst. Blood red, with pupils as long and elongated as a goats; it had looked at her with a knowledge and intelligence surpassing any animal.

She shivered at the memory. Perhaps Josh was right. Maybe her overwrought mind was playing tricks, but God! The sight of the thing had been awful. The look in those eyes would stay with her forever. Such malevolence emanated from the creature; the shock had been enough to stop her heart in her chest. The idea that her mind could conjure up such evil scared her almost as much as if it had been real.

"Are you okay now?" asked Josh.

Sasha nodded, not trusting herself to speak.

"It's probably things just playing on your mind."

"I know," she said. "Don't worry. I must be suffering from an overactive imagination."

She tried to smile; the expression tight and fake. Josh squeezed her hand and, not for the first time that day, she was absurdly pleased to have him by her side.

Josh felt something pass between them. He was reluctant to let go of Sasha's hand, but this was not the right time. He doubted there would ever be a right time. This was no longer a fun trip, a casual adventure. Someone might be dead and Josh couldn't help but feel responsible in some obscure way. Fate had brought Goose across his path and that chance meeting may have killed him.

Josh hoped he'd done everything he could. He hated to think he would one day find out Goose had been laying only feet away and they hadn't found him. The insane weather conditions had made searching hard enough without the fear of being blown apart by land mines. Josh didn't consider himself to be a particularly brave man, but he didn't think he was a coward either. He'd weighed the risk and the whole group had made the decision to move on. The child and women needed to get to shelter. They were better off making the move to alert the appropriate authorities than sitting impotently on the roadside in a storm.

He hoped this was the truth and he wasn't just making excuses to himself.

Cutting off his thoughts, the bus shuddered to a halt.

The driver spoke to Chay in an urgent voice. They both swung their doors open and jumped out of the bus, not seeming to care about the downpour. The doors slammed shut behind them, making those who had still been sleeping awaken with a jump.

Josh leaned over the front seat, trying to identify the problem. The weak headlights of the bus lit the road ahead, illuminating the figures of Chay and the driver standing in the rain. They had their backs to the bus and appeared to be studying the road. The silhouettes of their bodies blocked Josh's view.

"I hope this isn't what I think," Josh muttered under his breath.

"Why?" Sasha asked, overhearing him. She leaned forward so they were shoulder to shoulder. "What are you thinking?"

He shook his head. "I don't want to jinx things. Let's wait till they get back."

"Whatever the problem, it's not looking good."

The driver turned and pointed to the roof, where their baggage was strapped on with waterproof tarpaulin. Chay stared for a moment and then glanced back at the road and shrugged.

Both men turned and headed back to the bus. The driver climbed into his seat and sat, resolutely ignoring the travelers. Chay also got back on board, resuming his place on his seat, but he turned around so he kneeled, facing the group.

"Hello," he called, making sure no one was left sleeping. "We have a problem. In front of road, there is bridge... "

"Oh Christ!" exclaimed the dark Irish girl. "The bridge is down."

Chay shot her a look of irritation and continued. "Bridge is not down. But, bridge is not good. We must take bags from roof and carry over. Bus is too heavy with people and bags. Okay?"

"You want us to go out in *this*?" said Steph. "Is there no other way of getting across?"

"No," Chay replied. "If bridge breaks, then big problem. Bridge is only small, but bus could get stuck."

Sasha forced a grin. "Well at least most of us are already wet."

"We're not!" Steph protested. "I don't want to go out there."

"Neither do I," said Dawn. "I may only be wearing flip-flops, but they're bloody expensive ones."

"None of us *wants* to go out in the rain," said Sasha. "But if getting wet means the difference between us getting to Siem Reap wet, or being stuck out in this for the rest of the night, I think I'll choose the wet option."

"Okay. Fair enough," said Steph holding up her hands in defense. She nudged Vicki who was staring out of the window. "You ready to get a soaking?"

"Huh?" said Vicki, visibly jumping at the elbow in her ribs. "Did you say something?"

"I asked if you were ready to get wet."

"Why would I want to get wet?"

A frown creased Steph's forehead and she studied her friend, one eyebrow raised.

"Didn't you hear what Chay said? The bridge is no good and we have to carry the bags across to reduce the weight of bus. You must have had your iPod on too loud."

"I'm not listening to music," said Vicki. "I was listening to... "

She broke off, frowning, as though trying to remember.

Steph shook her head. "Listening to what?"

"Nothing, nothing," she said. "It doesn't matter."

Laura piped up from the back. "I don't mean to ask for special treatment, but do you think Ben could stay on the bus while Greg and I carried our bags?" She looked around the group, searching for a reaction.

"That's fine by us," answered the male half of the Irish couple. He opened his mouth to say something else, but his girlfriend shot him a pleading stare that was impossible not to notice, and he closed it again. He put his arm around her shoulders and whispered in her ear. She gave him a tight smile and squeezed his hand.

Josh couldn't help but comment. "Is there a problem?"

"It's nothing," said the Irish girl. "Don't worry."

"It's not nothing," her boyfriend said. "They should know if we're going to get through this safely."

Josh folded his arms across his chest. "If this affects anyone's safety, you'd better tell us."

The couple looked at each other and the girl nodded.

"We need to tell them," she said and turned to the rest of the group. She took a deep breath and began.

"We've been traveling for about two months now, mainly down Southern Thailand and on the islands. When we got back to Bangkok to carry on with our trip," she paused, either to gather her nerves or add drama, "I found out I was pregnant."

A general chorus or 'oh wows!' and 'congratulations!' sounded throughout the group. The girl blushed and her boyfriend's grin cut his face in half.

"What made you decide to continue the trip?" asked Sasha.

"We've only got another a couple of weeks before we fly home. We decided another few weeks wouldn't make any difference."

"Fair enough," said Josh. Then something occurred to him. "I don't think I know your names."

"I'm Paula," said the girl. "This is Alex."

"It's nice to meet you both," said Josh. "Now what do we want to happen? Are you going to be okay walking across, or would you prefer to stay on the bus with Ben."

"I don't want to piss anyone off or anything," said Alex. "But I would much prefer her to stay in the bus."

"I think that's probably best," said Josh. "As long as no one else has a problem and the driver doesn't think it is too much extra weight."

"Hey! I'm not that big just yet," Paula protested, only half-jokingly.

"I don't think anyone will have a problem," said Josh. He looked around the group for their opinion. Most people were nodding their agreement. Dreadlocks shrugged and glanced away, disinterested.

"I don't see why she should be the only one who gets to stay dry," protested Dawn. "She's only pregnant—women do it all the time. Anyway, I'm only a size eight. I don't think I'm going to make any difference to the weight of the stupid bus."

"I don't think that's the point," said Josh, irritation spiking through him. "Being skinny and wearing expensive shoes is not a good enough reason to get preferential treatment."

"But getting knocked up is?" she shot back, claws out.

Josh's face tightened. He gripped his hands into fists as he struggled to control his temper. His short fuse had been the source of all his shame recently and he'd promised himself he wouldn't let it control him anymore. He was stronger than that.

Steph stepped in. "If we've all got to get wet, then you sure as hell have to," she said. "What makes you so special?"

Dawn turned to Steph and cast a snobbish eye over Steph's short pink hair and nose ring. She flipped her sheet of blonde silk back over one shoulder.

"Let's just say some people are more designed for roughing it than others."

"Well you shouldn't even bother doing this type of thing if you can't hack the pace," Steph snarled. "Maybe next time you should stay home with Daddy."

Dawn scowled at Steph and turned her back on her.

"Just leave it Steph," said Josh. "We can't physically drag her off."

"Can't we?" she said, under her breath.

Steph turned to her friend for support. "That girl is such a bitch," she said, not bothering to keep her voice down.

Vicki didn't seem to be taking much interest in what was happening and continued to stare out the window, a strange half-frown, half-smile on her face.

Josh looked at Laura and Greg. "Is it okay with everyone else if a couple of people stay on board?"

"If Paula needs to stay on board, it's fine with us," said Laura. "After all," she said with a smile, "I can empathize."

Josh turned around and explained the situation to Chay.

"That is okay," Chay said. "With child, two woman and driver, not too much weight. But people must carry bags. Okay?"

"Okay," Josh agreed.

Everyone began to rustle around in their bags to find anything they could use to keep them dry. A few organized people had waterproof jackets, but the rest made do with whatever items of clothing they had.

The small bus filled with contorted bodies as people stood and tried to cover themselves best they could in the limited space. Mutter apologies resounded as arms and legs were stuck into places they shouldn't be. Protected against the ensuing soaking, they headed out into the rain.

CHAPTER TEN
TROUBLED WATER

Vicki sat, staring out of the window, making no move to leave the bus. Steph nudged her friend to spur her into action and Vicki turned around, a crease between her eyebrows, her eyes not quite making contact.

"Did you hear that?" she asked.

Steph strained her ears, trying to listen above the noise of the bus and the storm that christened the world.

She shook her head. "I can't hear anything other than the rain."

Vicki grabbed her arm, her fingers digging painfully into Steph's flesh.

"No! Listen," she said, urgently. "I think someone's out there."

"Hey, you're hurting me!" Steph pulled her arm out of Vicki's grasp, rubbing her sore skin. "No one's out there, Vicki. We're miles away from anywhere."

Vicki stared at her, her eyes narrowed, her lips a thin hard line. For a moment, Steph thought her friend was going to hit her and a rush of worry and panic swept over her.

Vicki shook her head as though trying to get water out of her ears and flashed a warm smile. "Come on then. What are we sitting here for? Everyone else is outside already."

Steph looked around at the almost empty vehicle, confirming Vicki's observation. "Are you sure you're all right?"

"Yes, positive. I just thought I heard something."

Steph got up from her seat, stretching her body as much as the confined space would allow. Her limbs felt as though they'd shriveled in the cramped space and she almost groaned with pleasure at the movement. Vicki did the same and the two helped each other get into their jackets.

"I guess it's a good thing we prepared for the rainy season," said Steph.

Vicki stood with her arm half-in, half-out of her jacket, seemingly mesmerized.

Steph jabbed another elbow at her. "It's only water. We'll dry."

Steph walked in a stoop to the front of the bus and began to make her way down the couple of steps. Her feet touched the sodden ground and she realized Vicki wasn't behind her. She turned to see Vicki standing in the same position she'd left her.

Steph reversed up the steps, back into the bus.

"Vicki?" she called over the storm. "What's up with you? It's only a bit of..."

The slow turn of Vicki's head stopped Steph in her tracks.

Vicki's face was deadly white. Her eyes seemed not to focus on Steph, but to peer into a realm no one else could see. Her hand trembled as she reached out and touched the windowpane in front of her.

Her voice was high and strained as she spoke. "I can't."

Steph knew Vicki wasn't speaking to her. A shiver ran down Steph's back, but she shook it off. She ducked her head to keep from banging it on the low ceiling and took the couple of steps to the back of the bus where she grabbed her friend's hand, forcing her to acknowledge her presence.

Vicki looked through her as though she no longer existed.

Josh leaned back in the bus. Everyone else was standing in the rain, waiting for the group to be complete before setting off on this part of their journey.

"Everything all right in here?" he asked, looking expectantly at the two girls and then to Dawn. Paula sat with Ben dozing in her lap.

"Everything is fine," said Steph, trying to keep the irritation out of her voice. "You don't have to keep acting like team leader you know? Vicki's just a bit freaked after what happened to Goose. We're coming now."

"Okay," Josh said, backing off. "Only trying to help."

Steph turned her attention back to Vicki. The color had returned to her face and she seemed more embarrassed than anything.

"Sorry," Vicki said, with a slight shake of her head. "I don't know what happened."

"Don't worry." Cautiously, Steph took Vicki by the elbow. "Let's get out of here before they decide to drag us off."

The pair climbed from the bus and into the relentless rain. Chay sat on the roof of the vehicle, untying the bags. He handed the packs down to Greg, who then passed them onto the girls. Steph took hers, adjusting her stature to take the weight. Finally, Dawn's bag was thrown into the bus with her. There was no point in strapping the tarpaulin back down for the sake of one bag.

Each of the travelers hoisted the bags onto their backs. They made their way to the front of the bus and stood still, assessing the bridge before them, waiting for the next instructions. The darkness and the driving rain blurred Steph's senses. Thunder deafened her, rain blinded. The thick, earthy taste of wet dirt sat in the back of her throat like an accusation.

Moving as a pack, with safety in numbers, the group approached the bridge. The simplicity of the structure was worrying. Two long planks of wood stretched from one side of the crevice to the other, with shorter planks nailed horizontally between them. Black water swirled beneath the bridge and the level appeared to be rising before their eyes.

"Who should go first?" yelled Sasha. "Us or the bus?"

"You go first," said Chay. "People lighter."

"But if we go over and then the bridge breaks, we're stuck on the other side with no shelter."

"If the bus goes first and breaks the bridge, we can't get over anyway," said Josh.

"I still think the bus should first," she argued. "If the bridge starts to give way, we'll be able to stop the bus from going any further and at least we'll have somewhere to shelter until the rain stops and the water goes down."

Josh considered this for a moment and turned to Chay. "I think Sasha is right."

Chay pursed his lips and then shouted something to the driver. The bus grumbled back to life. The group parted down the middle, allowing the bus to move slowly between them. The bridge was just wide enough to take the vehicle and as its wheels mounted the unstable structure, the whole group held their breath. Tension stretched the already charged atmosphere. All eyes fixed on the bus and its precarious position.

Steph saw Sasha glance off to one side and frown. She followed the other woman's gaze see to a lone figure standing still and silent on the edge of the road, silhouetted by the lightning. The color drained from Sasha's face.

"It's okay," said Steph. "It's only Vicki."

Sasha shook her head. "She gave me a fright. What's she doing over there? Is she all right?"

Steph frowned. "I don't know. She's been acting strangely ever since Goose went missing. I guess it has affected her badly."

"The whole situation is scary," offered Sasha. These aren't normal circumstances. I wouldn't blame her for being frightened."

"I'm sure you're right." she said, though she wasn't entirely convinced.

"It's probably best if you go and get her."

Steph nodded and walked back up the road to where Vicki was standing. The rain continued to pound on their head and shoulders, but Vicki didn't seem bothered. Her back was to Steph, her entire body frozen still. The closer Steph got, the more uncomfortable she felt. She couldn't shake the sensation that she was approaching a stranger, not the friend she'd known for almost twelve years. She

106

was within a couple of feet of Vicki, but her friend still hadn't turned around or acknowledged her presence.

"Vicki?" she shouted. Thunder cracked above and she cringed. "What are you doing?"

Her shout elicited no response. Steph reached out a trembling hand and touched her friend's shoulder. It felt cold and hard beneath her palm.

Oh God! She's already dead!

The insane thought leaped into her head.

Suddenly Vicki spun around and Steph let out a shriek of surprise. Her hand clutched her chest, trying to calm her hammering heart. Vicki's face looked perfectly normal and she stared at Steph in confusion.

"Are you all right?" Vicki asked.

"I should be asking you that," said Steph, annoyance creeping into her voice. "What the hell are you doing standing here?"

Vicki shrugged. "I don't know. I just didn't want to get covered in mud. Besides," she said turning her face back to the rugged, black landscape and the light show. "It's beautiful. I bet this is how the world looked before life was created."

"Yeah, whatever," said Steph, not in the mood for a theoretical discussion. "While you've been admiring the scenery, everyone has been waiting for you so we can get over the bridge."

"Oh! Of course, sorry," she said, seeming to remember the others. "I guess I got carried away."

With their head and shoulders ducked low in their rain jackets, they trotted back to the group.

Though the front of the bus had mounted the bridge, the back tires remained embedded in the thick mud. The driver put his foot down and the back wheels spun.

Red mud sprayed from under the wheels, catching everyone in the blast. The heavy splat of mud hitting the plastic of wet weather coats could be heard over the noise of the storm.

Josh's head rocked back as a clod caught him full in the face. He gasped in shock. Rain washed his face clean straight away, but the taste of dirt remained on his tongue. Grit crunched between his teeth. Josh stepped out of the range of the bus and tilted his head back, mouth open. He swilled the rainwater around his mouth and spat on the sodden ground. He could still taste the earth, but that seemed to be the aftertaste of the water.

Sasha saw him and grinned. "Got you in the face, did it?"

He looked down at her mud-spattered jacket, which was his, and then down to her bare legs. The jacket offered enough protection from the rain, but mud still covered her legs. Only tiny patches of skin peeped through the dirt.

"Looks like it got you all over," he said, returning the smile.

The bus wheels continued to spin and Chay shouted to the group.

"We must push," he said, demonstrating with his arms.

The group realized this meant standing in full force of the churning wheels and doubtful glances passed between them. The driver stopped revving the engine, abruptly leaving an eerie quietness.

Suddenly, Josh felt vulnerable. After already losing one of their members, the knowledge that they were in the middle of nowhere, with only the storm for company, was uncomfortable.

The men lined up at the back of the vehicle. Greg, being the largest of the party, stood in the middle, with Josh and Alex on either side. Living up to his loner reputation, Seth stood to one side with his arms folded, making no attempt to help.

Each of the men shoved their shoulders against the metal. On Chay's signal, waving his arms up and down and yelling, the driver put his foot on the accelerator and the men pushed.

The bus edged forward, up out of the mud and onto the wooden planks. Now slick with mud, the wheels spun and skidded dangerously to the right.

"Whoa," yelled Josh, and each of the men grabbed the bumper, making sure the vehicle didn't slide right over the edge. Their feet slipped on the wooden surface, but together they managed to keep the bus on track. The vehicle crept across, until it bumped down over the other side and onto solid ground.

Now that the bus had made it over in one piece, the tension in the group subsided. Though wet and muddy, a huge weight had been lifted from their collective shoulders.

"We need to go two-by-two across the bridge," said Josh.

"You mean like animals onto the ark," Sasha teased.

For once, he ignored her. "Going two at a time will increase the weight, but it'll be safer than going individually. If someone slips, another person will be able to steady them."

Chay and Alex went first—the man and boy testing the way for the women. They trod with care. The water and mud made the wood like ice, and they were careful not to slip. The pair crossed safely and the waiting group clapped and hollered, trying to keep up the camaraderie.

Desperate to be back with their child, Laura and Greg went next. Greg stood on the left and Laura on the right. Greg reached out and took Laura's hand. She smiled at him gratefully and together they took their first cautious step. Laura squealed in fright as the bridge rocked slightly under Greg's weight. He squeezed her hand and they continued their wary walk.

A sudden crack echoed around the empty terrain and Laura collapsed to her hands and knees with a scream. Immediately, her husband was by her side, kneeling down next to her to try to pick her up. She shook her head and put out one of her hands to stop him. Her face was screwed-up in pain.

"Are you guys okay?" yelled Josh. "What's happened?"

"Laura's leg has gone through a piece of wood," Greg called back. "I think she's hurt."

Worry flooded through the group.

Josh walked to the edge of the bridge. "I'm going to come over. We may have to carry her."

Josh realized the outside part of the bridge would be stronger than the middle. If it was able to hold the weight of the bus, it would hold his. Of course, standing right on the edge of the bridge increased his chances of slipping over, but was still safer than falling through.

Crouching to lower his center of gravity, he edged his way out to Greg and Laura. In no time at all, he reached them.

"Do you think you may have broken it?" Josh asked Laura.

"I've definitely broken the bridge," she said with a thin smile. The color had drained out of her face and tears of pain glistened in her eyes. Josh admired her for her attempt at a joke when she was obviously in pain. "I don't think the leg's broken," she continued, "though I think I've cut it on the wood."

"Okay. We are going to have to lift you out and get you across."

Laura nodded. Greg and Josh held her under each arm and gently pulled. The broken piece of wood, still attached to the bridge, poked downward and wedged against Laura's injured leg. As the men pulled, the piece of wood pulled up with her, pushing itself deeper into her leg. Laura bit her lip to stop herself from crying out. Her eyes were squeezed shut, trying to center the pain. Josh felt the resistance and, seeing the expression on Laura's face, he told Greg to stop.

"No, it's okay," she said. "You are just going to have to pull harder."

"Not if it's hurting you!" said Greg. "We must be able to do something else. Make the hole bigger perhaps?"

"If we do that we might end up hurting her even more," Josh said.

"It's okay," Laura repeated. "Just get me out of here. I can handle it."

Greg looked uncertain, but Josh took her at her word and got back in position.

"Come on, mate. Let's get this done."

Greg nodded and took hold of his wife. With more force, the two men pulled. The piece of wood snapped and Laura came free with a jolt. Josh and Greg flew backward, Laura coming with them. Josh's heart lurched into his throat as he hit the fragile, slippery wood. In a horrific flash of premonition, Josh saw the three of them crashing through the rest of the bridge and into the black rushing water below. To his relief, the bridge held.

Josh and Greg carefully got back to their feet and made their way over to where Laura sat, clutching her bleeding leg. The rain had washed the blood away from the wound, revealing a deep gash with large splinters of wood embedded in the flesh.

"That looks nasty," Josh said. "Are you okay for us to move you?"

"I don't fancy sitting here all night," Laura said, trying to smile despite the pain.

"Okay. We'll help you along the edge of the bridge. The edge must be stronger than the middle."

"I'll take her," said Greg. "You go back and tell the others."

Josh looked back to where the rest of the group waited, patient, but concerned. Greg was already lifting his wife. She was as small as he was large so he supported her with ease. Josh prayed Greg wouldn't slip and send them both over the side. He waited until they'd crossed safely, then made his way back to the others and explained what had happened.

Using only the edges of the bridge and with extra care and caution, the rest of the group crossed without incident.

Wet and shaken, they all climbed back on board, the shelter of the bus a welcome relief from the constant tattoo of the rain. They pulled towels and dry clothing from their bags before Chay strapped them back beneath the tarpaulin on the roof. Greg and Laura already sat on the back seat. Greg held a bloodstained t-shirt next to the gash in Laura's leg while he used a pair of tweezers to pull out bits of wood. Paula sat next to them with a white-faced, teary-eyed Ben on her lap. Though she must have been in considerable pain, Laura smiled bravely at her son, trying not to upset him even more than he already was. Ben reached out his small hand and took hold of his mother's, squeezing it tightly. Acutely aware of her pain, the small boy was desperate to comfort her.

Sasha and Josh sat back in their seats at the front. Giving Sasha his jacket meant he was soaked to the skin. Sasha's top half had stayed dry, thanks to Josh, but mud caked her shorts and the material clung to her bottom and thighs. Despite the small confines of the bus, Josh stripped down to his shorts and briskly rubbed himself dry with his towel. Sensing Sasha's awkwardness at their sudden half-naked proximity, Josh climbed over the seat and into Goose's old spot.

How strange to be sitting back in this seat. Goose's disappearance had almost been forgotten in the excitement of getting over the bridge.

A shiver ran down Josh's back. He wasn't normally a superstitious person, but he felt like he was sitting in the place of a ghost. He wished Sasha would hurry up and change so he could sit back next to her. He didn't want to admit it to himself, but he realized he was afraid. All he could do was hope and pray they'd been through the worst.

CHAPTER ELEVEN
LOST

Over an hour had passed since the bridge crossing and the storm still raged with an unrelenting fury. They'd already crossed another two bridges and both times Chay and the driver borrowed torches to check the safety of the crossing. The passengers waited with baited breath, dreading the call for them to disembark once again, to risk being washed away or suffering a worse injury than Laura sustained.

As soon as Sasha had changed, Josh dropped himself back in the seat beside her. She'd smiled at him, so he assumed she didn't mind him sitting back next to her. He didn't think anyone would expect him to stay in Goose's place. It was too creepy.

Laura's leg had been cleaned and bandaged. Soon after boarding it became clear that everyone, with the exception of Sasha, had a medical kit any doctor would be proud of. Though the wound had been attended to, Laura was not well. She lay against Greg, her eyes closed and face ashen. A sticky film of sweat coated her skin and she took hitched and shallow breaths. No one in the group had any medical knowledge and they didn't understand if her reaction was a sudden onset of infection or another illness, which had broken past her defense mechanisms once she'd been injured. Both Greg and Ben watched her with a mixture of love and fear. Neither spoke unless spoken to, all their attention focused on the woman who bound them with the ties of love that made them a family.

The bus moved at a frustratingly slow pace. The darkness, driving rain and poor roads were bad enough; but every time the vehicle seemed to be covering some ground, they had to stop. Josh lost count of the number of the holdups. When the vehicle, once again, came to a grinding halt, he paid particular attention to what the boy and the driver were doing when they picked up the torches and made their way outside.

Josh peered over the top of Sasha's head, watching the movement of the two Cambodians as they walked, heads together like conspirators, around the outside of the bus. Sasha saw Josh's interest.

"What do you think they're looking for?" she said in a low voice, trying not to alarm the rest of the group.

Josh shrugged. "I wondered the same thing myself."

The man and boy crouched down, shining their lights under the chassis.

"Maybe they're checking for damage to the vehicle," suggested Sasha.

"Yeah, that or stowaways!"

Sasha's eyes widened in alarm before realizing he was joking. Josh poked her lightly in her side and nodded his attention back out the window.

"If they're check for damage to the vehicle, what are they looking for now?"

She turned to follow his gaze. The driver and Chay swept their torches away from the bus and across the landscape around them. Another flash of lightning forked the sky and, in the split second of light, Josh saw they were arguing.

The driver, who had remained silent throughout the whole trip, faced Chay, his finger pointed in the boy's face, his own face pushed up close. Chay cowered under the attack, but the driver seemed much calmer. If anything, his self-control was the most intimidating thing about him; that and the malice playing around his eyes.

"Why does that not make me feel good about things?" said Josh, concern clouding his face.

"What do you think they're fighting about?" Sasha whispered, not wanting to draw anyone else's attention to the scene in front of them.

Josh shrugged. "Could be anything. They're probably worried about turning up in Siem Reap one person short. I wouldn't like to have to explain if I were them."

"I hope that's all it is. The driver looks pretty scary to me, I don't think I'd like to... Ouch!"

A well-aimed elbow silenced Sasha mid-sentence just as the man and boy got back in their seat.

"I wish you'd stop doing that," Sasha grumbled.

Josh ignored her and leant over to the seat in front.

"Everything okay?" he asked, deliberately keeping his voice light and bright.

"Yes, yes," answered Chay in exactly the same tone. "Everything okay."

Josh nodded and went to sit back, but a glare of disdain from the driver froze him in his tracks. The driver continued to make his way to his seat but only once his backside was planted on the chair did he turn away. The bus grumbled back to life and relief washed over Josh when the driver's attention focused on the road ahead.

"Wow," said Sasha. "He doesn't think much of you."

"The feeling is quickly becoming mutual, though I've no idea what I've done."

"I expect he doesn't like foreigners. He hasn't exactly been the life and soul of the journey so far."

Josh glanced at his watch. Only half past nine. He'd thought the hour to be so much later. The darkness and storm seemed to have been going on forever. The trip was supposed to take about fifteen hours, but with all the delays and the terrible weather, they would be lucky if they got in before sunrise.

Josh turned, his eyes flicking across the rest of the bus. Everyone slept. His gaze rested on Laura and her injured leg, propped up on a bag in front of her and covered with a sarong. Her skin was pale and beads of sweat decorated her forehead and upper lip. Her head rested on Greg's broad chest, their son curled up beside them. Greg's arms were wrapped protectively around his wife and child.

As Josh watched Greg opened his eyes, assessing the situation, before closing them again and falling back to a sleep.

About to turn back and settle himself down for a sleep, Josh realized someone else *was* awake. Her forehead pressed against the glass of the window and her hand partially covered her face.

Vicki's lips moved in silent words. Occasionally, she paused as she smiled with girlish glee and tilted her head as though listening for a reply.

The sight froze his blood even more than the stare from the driver. He could not explain why, but the look in her eyes edged close to the boundary of madness.

Josh turned to Sasha to say something, but stopped. She too, slept. Her dark lashes rested against her cheek and a piece of hair tickled her nose. Without thinking, Josh leaned over and brushed away the curl. The ease of this motion took him by surprise. How amazing to think he had only met her that morning. He felt like they'd been traveling together forever.

Josh thought back to their earlier conversation. He found it astounding that this gorgeous woman had come all this way on the whim of a guy she hadn't seen for a year. He wondered if he would do the same thing. A year was a long time and people changed, especially when they were in extreme situations and places. Josh couldn't help admiring her trust, but he couldn't imagine sending his partner to live in a different part of the world. Was she trusting or simply naive? If Sasha were his, he wouldn't have left in the first place, never mind stayed away for this long. Josh had heard the hurt in her voice when she talked about her fiancé not coming home to visit.

Josh glanced again at her sleeping face, admiring the smoothness of her skin and the fullness of her lips. He wanted to reach out and touch her cheek, but he resisted the urge, not wanting to freak her out or look like a creep.

Watch yourself buddy, he thought. *You don't want to screw things up again.*

Despite knowing Sasha had come out here to see her fiancé, he couldn't help thinking that they would both be going back to London. In a few hours time they would go their separate ways, but Josh made a promise to himself to convince Sasha to stay in touch. Her fiancé didn't exactly come across as committed and anything could happen.

Then he shook himself. What was he thinking? He didn't trust himself to get involved again, especially so soon. He wouldn't be any good for her. If he cared, he would stay the hell away.

A yell from the back of the bus tore Josh from his thoughts and startled Sasha awake. She looked around with fear in her eyes and Josh unconsciously reached out and covered her hand with his. In unison, they turned to the noise.

Vicki was climbing over the top of Steph. Steph grappled with her friend, trying to hold her in the seat, but Vicki fought to get out of her grasp. One of Vicki's hands pushed in Steph's face, squashing her friend's features into painful angles. Her other hand hooked over the back of Goose's old seat as she pulled herself out of Steph's grip and lurched toward Paula and Alex's seat. Paula, terrified of this sudden insanity, had pushed Alex and herself up against the window, as far away from Vicki as possible.

Vicki's eyes rolled back in her head, the whites, forked with veins of red, eclipsed the socket. Her lips curled in a snarl and spittle foamed at the corners of her mouth. The fingers holding the back of the chair were curled and claw-like; the knuckles white with strain.

Everyone stared, frozen in place by the spectacle. The bus shuddered to a halt, throwing them all forward. A painful gasp from Steph spurred them into action.

Greg caught Vicki from behind, wrapping his large arms around her slight frame to pin her against him. His strength and size left her wriggling and mewling, but unable to fight. Her breath came in deep, heavy snorts through her nose; like a horse galloped to its limit. Her eyes closed and she seemed to relax. Steph was crying from shock and fear for her friend. Red lines scraped down her cheek where Vicki had drawn her nails like claws.

Except for Vicki's breathing and Steph's sobs, silence descended on the bus.

Then Vicki began to wretch, heaves wracking through her whole body, coming from somewhere deep within. Greg loosened his grip on her a little. He turned to the others, nervous with this sudden change.

"What should I do?"

Seth curled the corner of his mouth, his nostrils flaring. "The girl is wasted and she is going to puke at any moment."

"We don't want her throwing up in here!" said Paula, aghast.

Josh nodded. "They're right, let's get her outside."

Josh leaned over and pulled the handle, sliding the door open. Almost doubled over now, the noises coming from Vicki sounded harsh and painful.

Greg still pinned her arms to her side. "There's no way I can keep hold of her and get her out of the bus."

"It should be okay," said Josh. "I think she's too preoccupied to hurt anyone."

Greg let go of Vicki. She bent closer to the floor, her hands resting on her knees, the dry retching sounding even more painful than before.

"We'd better get her outside."

The rain had died down since the last time they ventured out, but it still fell at a steady rate. The lightning continued its remarkable show and thunder grumbled overhead, dark and menacing.

With Josh holding one of Vick's arms, Greg the other, they moved awkwardly in the small confines of the bus. Vicki walked slowly, bent like an old woman crooked with osteoporosis. Josh navigated the steps, his feet making contact with the road. He turned back and helped a still-heaving Vicki from the bus. As she stepped from the last step and onto the road, Greg let go of her arm. The moment he did, Vicki straightened up, the heaving stopped, and she bolted past Josh.

Taken by surprise, he made a grab for her. His fingers closed around her wrist, but the sweat on her skin made her slippery. He held her for only a moment before she slid from his grasp and ran to the side of the road.

Without a pause, Vicki plunged into the swamp-like mass of water and vegetation. Like an absurdly inelegant gazelle, she bounded through the water with incredible speed, leaving the bus full of people watching her, mouths open, muted in surprise and shock.

The darkness swallowed Vicki. When another bolt of lightning lit the plain, she was gone.

CHAPTER TWELVE
ANOTHER SIGHTING

A scream shattered the silence.

"No!"

Steph leapt from her seat and ran from the bus. She ran across the road and plunged off the side. Thick, warm water seeped into her shoes and tendrils wrapped around her ankles, clutching at her. In a moment of hysteria, she imagined the plants winding around her calves, holding her, dragging her down, and she screamed in such a way, sleeping birds startled from their roosts.

Steph fell to her hands and knees, tears coursing down her face. Her fingers sank into thick, squelchy mud and something wriggled and slid from beneath her palm. She barely even noticed. She sat back on her haunches and lifted her face to the sky.

"VICKI!"

Broken-hearted, she screamed her friend's name. With her fists clenched, she tried to stand, but stumbled and fell forward. The slow, steady rain drummed on her head and back. Tears falling from her nose, cheeks and chin joined the swamp-like water that had claimed her friend.

Gentle, warm hands lifted her from her kneeling position, but she fought back at them, knowing they would try to bring her back to the road. She couldn't go back. She couldn't leave this god-forsaken place without first finding her friend.

Like a wildcat, she bucked and thrashed, clawing and biting. She flipped her head backward, trying to butt the person behind, but the hands and arms held strong.

"I'm not letting go this time," said Josh gently.

He continued mutter 'shush' and 'calm down,' until finally she slumped back, sobbing and exhausted. Josh lifted her and carried her back to the road. Her clothes were soaked through and a thin slime of mud and algae coated her arms and legs. Steph didn't care. Sobs coursed through her body, her heart breaking at the thought of losing her best friend.

Josh's stomach tightened and his throat closed at Steph's misery.

He helped her back on the bus and she collapsed onto Goose's old seat, all the energy sucked from her body. Josh climbed on the bus after her and stood looking into the confused and horrified faces.

"Can you pass me some towels?" he said, trying to keep his voice from breaking. Immediately everyone started to rustle around for the towels they had used to dry themselves with earlier and thrust them toward him. He signaled for Sasha to lay one of the towels on Goose's old seat, under Steph, and then he laid one on top of her. Instinctively, she curled up in the fetal position, thumb in her mouth and her finger stroking the top of her nose in comfort. Josh bundled up another towel and put it under her head. Despite the pink hair and numerous piercings, Steph appeared tiny and lost—like a small child. Josh realized she was saying something, but he couldn't understand. He crouched down next to her and gently pulled her thumb from her mouth.

"Please don't leave her."

Her voice was no more than a whisper, but he heard the pain. He didn't know what to say; he just put his head in his hands.

A hand touched the nape of his neck and the contact made him jump. He lifted his head to find Sasha looking down at him, his worry mirrored in her eyes.

"You're all wet," she said, draping his own towel around his shoulders. "Get yourself dry. You'll be no good to anyone if you're sick."

Her hand rested on his shoulder and he reached up and held it tight. Sasha leaned her body in closer to him, for both the warmth and the comfort.

"I can't believe this is happening," he said. "What are we going to do?"

Sasha couldn't answer him.

Alex stood. "I don't know about anyone else, but this whole thing is starting to freak me out." Scared, silent faces stared back. "This is hardly normal. People don't freak out and run off into the night, or if they do, what are the chances of the same thing happening to two people within hours of each other?"

"Goose was different," said Josh. "He didn't freak out. He'd drunk too much and probably passed out on the side of the road somewhere."

The moment the words left his mouth, he found himself thinking back to Goose's behavior before he went missing. In his mind, he saw the dazed, drugged glaze in his eyes and the way he'd clambered over the top of the girls trying to get out of the bus. Had Goose really just been drunk, or was he telling himself and everyone else that to keep everyone sane? If alcohol hadn't caused his behavior and disappearance, what the hell had?

Josh turned his face from Alex's questioning stare. He didn't want him to notice the doubt in his mind or the fear in his heart. Alex wasn't going to let things go so easily.

"Well, what about Vicki?" he said, his voice taking on an almost accusatory tone. "She wasn't drunk. She just went completely nuts."

"The girl must have been on something nasty," Seth said, one side of his mouth raised in a sneer, revealing his strange fang-like tooth. "It's not like she's not the type."

"Shut up," said Steph. "She hadn't taken anything."

"It was awful," said Paula. "Her eyes..."

A shudder ran through her body, the sensation perceived by everyone on board. Something had happened to Vicki, something dark and unexplainable, and everyone knew it whether they were admitting it to themselves or not.

"What about you two?" Alex called out to Chay and the driver. "Have you got any explanations about why we keep losing people off this bus? Is this normal practice? Is your driving so bad, people go crazy and decide to walk?" White-faced and shaking, Alex's voice increased in octaves as he spoke. Paula put her hand on his arm to silence him.

Chay said nothing, but his face didn't hide his confusion. He turned and spoke angrily to the driver, but the man shrugged and continued to stare out of the windshield as if nothing was happening.

125

"What did you say to him?" Alex demanded.

"I say only we must search harder for this one," he answered. "But it is not our fault if tourists run away." Chay did not look at the tourists in question, only stared at the floor, unable to meet Alex's eye.

"She didn't run away," Steph said, sniffling. "Something was wrong with her. She kept asking me if I'd heard things and was off in a world of her own. The way she freaked out, hitting and biting... I've never known her to fight anyone."

Josh lifted his head. "Please don't take offense," he said to Steph. "But *is* there any chance she was on some kind of drugs? Maybe hallucinatory ones, like acid or something?"

Steph thought for a moment, more patient with Josh than she'd been with Seth.

"No," she shook her head. "She would have told me."

"Could she have been drugged?" said Paula.

"Well, yeah, I guess. But when? She's been fine all day and most drugs work fast."

Steph's words caused suspicion to stiffen the air, each person trying not to think the person sitting next to them might be responsible for such violent and irrational behavior. The group hadn't even known each other a day. Imagining one of them got their kicks from meddling with someone else's head wasn't difficult.

The atmosphere throbbed with mistrust and Josh knew he needed to do something. Being at each other's throats was the last thing they needed.

"Let's think this thing through rationally," he said to Steph. "What are the chances of someone being able to slip something to Vicki without her noticing? It would have been in her food or drink, so when was the last time she ate."

"Ages ago at the restaurant," said Steph. "She's been drinking from a bottle of water since then, but I've been drinking from the same one." Horror passed across her face. "What if something's in the water and the same thing happens to me?"

"It won't," said Josh. "Don't think like that. If something was in the water you'd be feeling the effects by now."

Steph wiped at her face with the back of her hand and adjusted her nose ring. Red mud and dust smeared with her tears, giving her the appearance of a tribal warrior. In any other situation, she would have looked funny.

"Perhaps she had a flashback?" Steph said, looking up at Josh in hope. "I mean, I've heard of that happening, people going about their day-to-day business and reliving the trip they did ten years earlier. Couldn't it be something like that?"

Sasha and Josh glanced up at each other, a look passing between them.

'Is that the answer?'

'Possibly. Possibly not.'

'But it's the only answer we've got.'

'And people need answers...'

They both nodded and smiled; making sure the rest of the bus thought the situation was under control. This whole thing was happening to someone else; in years to come, they would be able to say to each other, *'God! Remember when...'*

Even Steph seemed relieved until she realized her best friend was still missing. She burst into tears again. Reaching out, she grabbed Josh's hand.

"We have to find her," she said in desperation. "I can't leave without her. What am I going to tell her family, her boyfriend? I can't desert her out here."

Her voice was high-pitched and breaking, punctuated by tiny, hitching hiccups. Tears continued to stream down her face and her grip on Josh's hand grew tighter.

Josh empathized with her but didn't want to repeat the same process as with Goose—a dangerous search with no result. None of them wanted to abandon Vicki. Guilt in a human heart festered and poisoned. Besides, Goose was different. Goose didn't have someone on board who loved him; Vicki did.

Josh squeezed Steph's hand in return.

She released her grip, but not her gaze. "Please..."

She stared at him with an intensity and anguish he'd never been exposed to before; committing him to a promise he'd not agreed to. An obligation he would not be able to fulfill.

Josh broke the eye contact and looked back up at the group.

"Okay gentlemen," he said. "I guess we've got another search on our hands."

The overwhelming sensation that none of this was real swept over Josh. The feeling gave him a jolt; something deep inside realizing that going down that fantastical route would be unwise. Falling into a false sense of security held its own dangers.

Though he'd agreed the two disappearances might be down to drink and drugs, he couldn't help thinking there was more to it. Josh needed to keep his wits about him.

As the men—except Seth, who once again showed no sign of wanted to help—and Sasha got ready to leave the bus, Steph reached out and touched Sasha's arm

"It should be me who goes," she said through her tears. "She's my friend. I need to look for her."

"I don't think that's a good idea," said Sasha. "You've already been out there and you're soaked to the skin."

"You went out when you were already wet," Steph said defiantly.

"Maybe I did, but you're upset and you might do something stupid."

Steph opened her mouth to complain, but Sasha spoke over her. "And it won't do any of us any good to have you lost as well."

The stubborn expression faded from Steph's face, replaced by a misery that had become part of her. All the fight went out of her and she curled up on the tiny seat, pulling the towel back over her damp body.

When everyone was ready to leave, Josh leaned over and poked Chay between the shoulder blades. "Come on you two. We need your help."

Without turning around, Chay spoke to the driver who replied as though his missing passengers were more an irritation than of any importance. Chay's angry response, however, got the driver moving. He opened his door with a grunt, hoisting his body out of the seat as though he had suddenly doubled in weight.

Sasha spoke to Josh. "I don't know about you, but I would be feeling so much happier about this trip if the person in charge actually gave a shit whether any of us made it or not."

"I know what you mean. Neither of them has been particularly reassuring."

Without talking, the group divided in the same conformity as when they'd searched for Goose. The familiarity and the acceptance of these actions were almost as terrifying as the madness and the disappearances. That they could fall into their parts with such ease increased the weight of despair pressing upon their shoulders.

Mercifully, the rain had grown lighter. Though the thunder still rolled and grumbled overhead, the pounding rain had all but stopped and they were able to hear themselves speak. They called Vicki's name at the top of their voices, listening intently for any replies or cries for help. As the two teams moved further apart, the other group's calls echoed back.

The dust that had been such a problem earlier in the day had turned to mud. Of course, the mud created its own problems as the travelers dragged their feet, trying not to slip as they searched the area.

The foliage seemed bigger here. Plant leaves looked thicker and darker, with veins running through them that were substantial enough to carry blood. The flora seemed to come from an older world.

Beams of torchlight swung across the sodden landscape. The clouds hung low in the sky; a thick blanket insulating the moon from the earth. The darkness was so absolute it seemed to suck in the pathetic beams of light as if feeding on them. Even their voices seemed wrong and unnatural in this world.

Walking down the muddy road, Sasha couldn't shake the feeling they should have been keeping quiet instead of giving away their positions with noises and lights. The sensation might have been irrational and stupid, but she couldn't pretend the cold shivers that clawed their way up her spine didn't exist. She was glad for Josh's proximity and wondered how well she would be coping right now if she hadn't met him.

As if hearing her thoughts, Josh turned and caught her eye. His gentle smile caught her heart and she turned away, flustered and confused.

Sasha opened her mouth to call Vicki's name again. A sudden movement in the beam of her flashlight caused the word to catch in her throat like a lump of meat. She choked on it, her breath trapped inside her lungs, slowly burning. Her airways stopped working, but her heart went on overdrive. Blood coursed through her veins, rushing in her ears. Her body froze in position: left foot forward, arm outstretched, torchlight shaking.

"*Josh!*" she hissed, forcing the name to break the obstruction. Another roll of thunder masked her voice so she tried again, this time loud enough to get the attention of both men.

"JOSH!"

He was at her side in an instant. "What? Did you see her?"

Sasha wasn't capable of answering. "Over there! Look!"

Josh and Alex swung the beams of their torches to join Sasha's. The combined light revealed only empty landscape.

"I saw something," she breathed.

"Yes, we know," said Josh, impatience sharpening his tone.

"It was that thing, the thing from the bus. Its body moved through the light." She paused, trying to steady her shaking voice. "It *wanted* me to see it."

"Are you sure? It was probably just an animal of some kind."

"No. No, it wasn't."

131

"I don't mean to interrupt," said Alex. "But what the hell are you two talking about?"

Sasha glared at Josh, daring him to say something, but he ignored her.

"Sasha had a bad dream earlier and now she thinks it was real." She didn't fail to notice the playful teasing lingering behind his voice. "She thinks it's following us."

That idea hadn't even entered her head, but as he said the words she knew it to be the truth.

"My God," she whispered. "We've traveled miles since I last saw the thing. It *must* have followed us."

"Your imagination is running on overdrive. I'm sure..."

"Help me..." The voice was faint, distant and unmistakably female.

Sasha's sighting forgotten, they called Vicki's name out into the darkness.

Hearing a change in their tone, the other group turned. Greg started to jog toward them, Chay and the driver lurking behind.

"Help me."

The voice came again, a pained, pathetic whimpering that came from all directions at the same time. Though it sounded far away, the voice could also have come from right next to them.

"Vicki?" yelled Josh. "Keeping shouting so we can find you."

Only the sound of leaves bending, heavy with rainfall, to splash their burdens into the water below, echoed back to them.

Four pairs of ears strained to hear a cry. Four pairs of eyes searched the beams of torchlight for the glimpse of a face or a hand.

"I can't tell what direction that came from," said Josh, a hint of desperation marring his normally strong voice.

"We need to be methodical," said Greg. "She can't be too far away for us to have heard her. If we put our torches next to each other and then scan as much land as possible, we'll come across her."

"But what if she's drowning?" said Sasha. "What if she's drowning right now?"

"If everyone would shut up for a minute, we might be able to hear something," snapped Josh.

Everyone fell silent, embarrassed. Then, with no other plan suggested, the small group fell into line, using their combined light to scan the land before them. Intermittently, one of them called out Vicki's name, but the silence was deafening. As the minutes ticked by, the chances of finding Vicki alive diminished.

A thin peal of laughter drifted to the group like a fog, touching each of them individually, causing hairs to stand and skin to crawl.

"That isn't her," said Sasha, tears of fear pricking the backs of her eyes.

Even the men shifted nervously, but they stuck to their self-resolve like drowning men to a life raft.

"The drugs are affecting her," said Josh. "She's out of her head"

"I don't like this," said Alex, fear infecting him. "Something's not right."

"For Christ's sake," snapped Greg. "Someone's life is depending on us and you lot are going to risk it because of a few heebie-jeebies. Get a grip."

"Greg's right," said Josh. "If you don't want to continue with the search, go back to the bus."

Alex flushed pink and began to scan the vegetation with exaggerated care. Sasha wouldn't be told so easily.

"I saw a creature of some sort," she said. "I know I did. I'm not some brainless bimbo. That thing is out there and that is *not* Vicki!"

"Would you shut up?" said Greg, his voice furious. "If you don't want to be thought a bimbo stop acting..."

His words cut off as the beam of light from his torch streaked across a sleek, black body. Scales covered its back, glinting in the light like an oil slick. The thing turned to face Greg, slit eyes red with hatred. Slowly the creature opened its razor-tooth mouth and laughed.

Greg stumbled back in shock. His feet tangled and he fell to the ground and started to pull himself backward, trying to get away from the abomination.

"Oh my God!" said Sasha, staring in fear.

She lifted her torch with a shaky hand and shone it in the direction of the laughter. The light revealed nothing but empty landscape. As she turned to Josh, the laughter floated through the air directly behind them.

Josh bent down and dragged Greg back to his feet. "Let's get the hell out of here."

Though neither Josh nor Alex knew what they ran from, seeing a man like Greg brought to his knees was enough to make them realize they should be afraid. More, they should be terrified. As four pairs of feet pounded across the muddy terrain, they heard the creature's claws dragging through the dirt, its scales scraping the ground. The bus suddenly seemed so far away, farther than they had walked, almost as if someone had picked the vehicle up and moved it while they weren't looking.

Josh couldn't help but try to turn his head to catch a glimpse of the thing chasing them. Sasha noticed him trying to look back and grabbed his arm, pulling his attention back to the direction they were running in.

"Don't be an idiot!" she yelled between heavy gasps of fright and exertion. "Just keep going!"

The bus was now only meters away. Josh pushed Sasha forward, making sure she reached the bus first. The creature's cruel laughter came from close behind—a high-pitched and almost child-like sound that clutched at their hearts like barbed wire. Hearing the inhuman laughter, Sasha knew two things for certain: the thing could catch them if it wanted to and it was enjoying itself.

Sasha reached the bus's door, grabbed hold of the rail that ran up the two steps and swung onto the vehicle. In the few seconds it took her to scramble on board, she squeezed her eyes shut, waiting for the claws she'd heard to tear like razor blades down her spine. Even as her feet left the road and she clambered into the relative safety of the bus, she expected something to grab her legs and pull her, screaming, into the undergrowth. When she realized she was safely on board, she looked around at the set of confused and frightened faces as if waking up from a dream or a nightmare.

The three men collided, jamming up against each other like people trying to escape a burning building. Josh climbed on first, followed by Greg and then Alex.

Blood rushed through Sasha's ears. Her breath left her body in harsh painful gasps. Though the run had been short, the adrenaline surging through her veins sent her body into overdrive. Nobody spoke and she realized they were waiting; waiting for the thing to launch itself onto the bus, to use its wickedly sharp claws to open the vehicle like a tin can.

Seth broke the silence. "You guys want to tell us what the hell you're running from," he said, nervous laughter behind his voice.

The immediate panic over, Josh and Alex stared at the floor, neither one of them having seen anything. Greg sat on the back seat with his family. Laura was awake, but weak. Worry and fear tightened her pale face. Their son sat between them, staring up at them both in turn, his lower lip trembling as he struggled to control his tears.

"It was just an animal," said Greg, trying to reassure his family. "They must have wolves or coyotes or... something." He mumbled the last few words, as if he didn't really believe what he was saying.

Sasha shook her head, her forehead creased in disbelief, eyes narrowed. "Wolves don't laugh..."

"Coyotes do!"

"Like that?" she said bitterly. "Do they laugh like that?"

Greg shrugged and turned his attention back to his family. Sasha couldn't tell if he was being a loving father and husband, or if he was simply using them to hide behind.

"And do you think the animal got Vicki?" asked Steph in the same small voice.

"It's possible," said Greg. "It looked pretty fierce..."

Sasha interrupted him with by a snort of hysterical laughter and he shot her a look of pure venom.

"I'm glad you find this funny," he said coolly.

"I'm sorry, really I am. But that was no wolf or coyote." She held his gaze, trying to make him accept what he had seen. Even before she spoke, she knew she wasn't going to get through to him; his defenses were up—an armored response.

"What you saw wasn't an animal. Remember its eyes, for Christ's sake! Remember the sound it made. An animal does not do that."

"You don't know this country," Greg said. "You don't know anything about the native wildlife here."

"I'm pretty sure someone here will have a Lonely Planet or some other guide book on Cambodia and I'll bet it doesn't have a section on crazed, laughing beasts that stalk buses full of backpackers!"

"Sasha..." Josh said, trying to calm her.

She turned to him, frustrated. "I can't be the only one here who doesn't buy this crap." She looked around at the rest of the group but they avoided her eye.

"Okay," she said, relenting. "Maybe I don't know what I'm talking about. But these guys must know something."

Sasha pointed to the two locals who were so far ignoring the scene playing out behind them. Even when Josh tried to get their attention, they continued to pretend they hadn't heard him. Josh leaned over the seat and tapped Chay on the shoulder.

Reluctantly, the boy turned to face them. As he did so, the driver fired a staccato of sharp words at him. Chay scowled but said nothing in return.

"I think you need to help us out on this one," said Josh. "Is it possible some kind of horrible wolf creature is out there?"

Chay's eyes flicked briefly and nervously to the driver before nodding. "Yes. Big animal..." Then he conveniently forgot most of his English and bared his teeth at the group, raising his hands and curling his fingers into claws. "Very bad," he said. "Maybe they hurt your friends."

"See!" said Greg. "I *told* you it was just an animal."

"Even if it is 'just an animal' we still have to be extra careful," said Josh. "We can't be wandering around out there if these things are prowling around looking for dinner."

"But Josh..." protested Sasha.

He waved a hand to silence her.

"But Josh, what about the laughter?" she persisted. "We heard it, I know we did."

"For Christ's sake, Sasha, can't you just drop it? An animal of some sort is out there, not some weird creature following us."

"Why are you fighting this?" she said. "How the hell do you explain the sounds? We all thought Vicki was calling to us. How could we have mistaken that for an animal?"

"Maybe we heard Vicki at first." His voice was low and curt. "But she obviously didn't make it did she? With the thunder, rain and the strange acoustics of this place; we can't be sure about anything. Now I suggest we drop the subject before you start to freak everyone out."

"But..."

Josh slammed his hand against the back of the seat in front "Enough!"

For the second time in a matter of minutes, tears pricked the backs of Sasha's eyes. She turned away from Josh's stern gaze and angry voice, not wanting him to see her cry. She wasn't just upset about the way he'd spoken to her, she was frustrated and scared. She didn't doubt her own ears and eyes, but no one else wanted to believe her. Josh was the person she thought she could lean on. She had come to think of him as her friend and ally, but suddenly she felt alone and isolated. For the first time since the nightmare began, she found herself wishing she had Nick beside her.

138

Josh put his hand on her thigh. "Sasha..."

Tears threatened to burst like storm clouds. She shifted her weight from him, staring out of the opposite window, willing the tears to stay away. Josh sighed and turned away. One tear escaped her furiously blinking eyes, rolled down her nose and plopped on her lap.

CHAPTER THIRTEEN
A GAME OF CHANCE

Sasha always dreamed the day her future husband proposed would be the most romantic and happiest of her life. In reality, the day had been more traumatic than she ever could have thought. Though the event was filled with romance, knowing that Nick was leaving the next day had tinged the moment with sadness and fear.

Sasha had no idea about the proposal. She'd planned a small leaving party for Nick, an evening in a restaurant with a group of their closest friends. Situated underground, the restaurant had low ceilings and dim atmospheric lighting. She struggled through the meal, relieved only tapas graced the table so she wouldn't be sitting with a large plate of uneaten food in front of her. Each morsel she put in her mouth was the texture of rubber and, even after chewing a thousand times, the food still wedged in her throat when she tried to swallow.

After the tortuous meal, their friends tapped on glasses, banged on the table and demanded a speech. Nick laughed and hid his face behind his hands, his light brown hair flopping into his eye in a way that always made Sasha's heart melt. He stood with hands raised as if surrendering to his friends' demands instead of doing something he had planned and probably rehearsed. As he stood, they clapped and cheered and the rest of the restaurant turned to watch them, admiring the group of young, successful people.

Sasha's heart had swelled with pride and she tried desperately to ignore the gnawing, twisting sensation chewing at her gut. She had to fight to stop herself leaping up and dragging him back down. She wanted to tell him he was making a mistake and she didn't want him to go; she had never expected him to *actually* take her up on her stupid suggestion.

Nick began his speech, thanking everyone for coming and making terrible jokes about Asian 'women' and traveling hippies, but Sasha barely heard him. A strange buzzing sensation filled her ears and her heart thudded in her chest. What would her life be like without him? What if he met someone else? What if this was the one guy she was meant to be with and she had actually encouraged him to go halfway around the world without her?

Nick's hand on her shoulder made her realize he was talking about her.

"The person I really have to thank for this opportunity is my gorgeous Sasha. If not for her, it would never have occurred to me to do something so selfless as go and teach these children. She made me see that I needed something else in my life, something to make me appreciate how lucky I am to have this life and a happy future." He paused and looked around at the expectant faces. "It's because of this future that there is something I need to do before I leave tomorrow."

A collective hush fell across the restaurant and Sasha stared up at him in surprise. Nick pulled her to her feet and she stood, faint and wobbly.

"Sasha, I love you. My life and future will always be with you. To show you how much I mean it, even though it will be a whole six months before we can start our new lives together, I am asking you to be my wife."

Sasha's mouth dropped as her brain tried to process what he'd said. Nick looked at her shocked face, waiting for her to say something. When it became clear she wasn't going to, he gave her a gentle nudge.

"Sash..."

His voice jolted her back to reality and she glanced down at the diamond band gripped between his fingertips. She opened her mouth to speak, but her words stuck in her throat. Her eyes welled with tears, her vision blurring. All she could do was nod and bury her face against him.

"Was that a 'yes'?" he asked, half-laughing and trying to pull her away from his body. She nodded into his chest.

Nick laughed again and held her closer.

"Yes!" he announced. "She said yes!"

The restaurant broke into a cheer and a couple of waiters appeared with champagne. The rest of the night was spent in a whirl of congratulations and excitement.

Later that night, when they were finally home, they lay in bed clinging to each other. Sasha had tried not to fall asleep, not wanting to miss any of the hours they had left together.

She woke late the next morning and Nick was no longer by her side. With a sinking stomach, she convinced herself he'd already left without saying goodbye. When he appeared in the bedroom door with a tray full of breakfast, she burst into tears.

"I don't want you to go," she blurted. "It was a stupid idea and I've changed my mind."

"Oh Sash," he said, sitting on the side of the bed beside her. "We've talked about this. You've already done your traveling thing and you know how unhappy I've been here lately. All I've ever done is work in the city and take two-week package holidays to Spain. Just think, in six months I'll be back and ready to settle down with you."

"As long as it's only traveling you're getting out of your system and not anything else," she said, sniffing through her tears and feeling like a teenager.

He tapped her playfully across the back of her head. "Silly."

"And you'll call me all the time?" she added.

"Of course!"

"And you'll count the days until you get to come home to me again?"

"I'll count the days," he promised.

Sasha woke with a jerk, tears drying on her cheeks, tightening the skin. Thoughts of Nick had followed her into her sleep, so she'd relived their most defining moments in her dreams.

Count the days, my ass, she thought bitterly. *More like string me along. Keep the little woman at home looking after the flat, while he buggers off for as long as he wants.*

"I shouldn't even be here," she said to herself.

"Sasha?"

She turned to find Josh watching her, concerned.

143

"Are you okay?"

Sasha shrugged. "I was thinking about the reason I'm here."

"The boyfriend?"

"The so-called fiancé," she said, holding up her left hand. "I'm not even sure why I'm wearing this stupid ring any more. He's made it pretty obvious he has no intention of coming home anytime soon. So, here I am rushing off to visit him like a complete idiot. I mean, if he wanted to see me, he would have made things at least a little easier for me to get to him. Why make me come all the way out here to try to catch him before he leaves? We could have met in Bangkok or Singapore and flown direct. Instead I'm traipsing across this god-forsaken land to try to catch him." She ran out of steam and put her head in her hands. "He didn't want me to come, did he?"

She lifted her head and fixed her gaze on Josh's green eyes. He gave her a little half-smile of sympathy, but did not respond.

"You must think I'm a real loser, huh? Worrying about my stupid love life when people are probably dead. I'm pathetic."

"Don't be daft," he said gently. "Following your heart isn't pathetic. You're the one who's made the effort; at least you can say you tried. If you ask me, he's the loser for not realizing how lucky he is to have someone like you waiting for him."

Sasha smiled, but her heart was weary. "Thank you. I'm not sure I agree with you, but thank you for being sweet. How long have I been asleep for?"

"Not long, an hour at the most."

The bus bounced and jolted along the mud track, the engine a steady thrum. Sasha rested her head back against the glass, the vibrations of the vehicle buzzing through her skull.

"Have we covered much distance?" she asked.

"Probably not. It's hard to tell in this place, everything looks the same."

"How's everyone else doing?"

"Paula and Alex seem okay; at least they've got each other. Steph cried for the first half hour, but I think she's exhausted herself because she's asleep now.

"What about Laura? How's her leg?"

Josh twisted around. "Hey Greg?" he called softly, so as not to wake Steph. "How's Laura doing?"

Greg looked up with worried eyes. "She's not good," he whispered, his concern more for his sleeping son than Steph. "I think she's got a fever or something, but she doesn't feel warm. She keeps muttering, like she's talking in her sleep, but with her eyes open."

Greg lifted the sarong off Laura's leg. Spots of red seeped through the white of the bandage like ghostly fingerprints.

"Do you think I should change the bandage again?" he asked. "It's been a few hours."

Josh took in the sight of Laura's face. Despite Greg's worries, she was now asleep and peaceful.

"I'd let her sleep," Josh said. "Rest will do her more good. I've got some antibiotics with me—a prescription I got for emergencies—so she can take a couple when she wakes up."

Greg nodded, relieved someone else made the decision. "Thanks, mate. If they both slept the whole way to Siem Reap, I'd be happy."

"I'd like to do the same myself," said Josh with a grim smile. "But try not to worry, the worst is over. The storm's letting up and we seem to be making some distance now."

"I hope you're right. This whole thing feels like a nightmare. I keep thinking 'if only we hadn't bugged the people at our guest house so we could travel today'. What difference would one more day have made? If we had just accepted that we'd have to travel another day, none of this would be happening to us."

"I did exactly the same thing," said Josh. "They told me I couldn't travel today. I insisted and they still said no, even got angry with me when I questioned it. Then later they told me something had come up and I could travel." Josh paused, thinking for a moment. "Makes you wonder, doesn't it? It's almost like they knew or something. Poor Goose, if he hadn't latched onto me he would still be alive today."

"It's not your fault, mate. You didn't know this was going to happen. And anyway, if he was on a different bus in a different country, he would probably still have got himself in trouble."

"It doesn't stop me feeling guilty," said Josh. "I should have told him to get lost when I realized what a jackass he was. I didn't even like the guy."

"That was obvious," said Greg, trying not to grin.

"Does that make me a bad person?"

"If it does, we all must be pretty terrible. I don't think he was the most popular person on this trip."

Josh ran a hand through his hair, trying to tame the curls now drying and springing from his head. "I even feel guilty talking about the guy. I hope there's some way we can tell people what happened to him. I'd hate to think he's got family who won't know what really happened to him."

"The thing is we don't know ourselves. Only that he disappeared off the bus. How are we going to be able to tell his family anything?"

"At least we'll be able to tell them what happened leading up to it, with some omissions of course, and they'll just have to try to figure out the rest for themselves. For all we know, he might have been suffering with some mental illness. I know it's unlikely, but still..."

Laura shifted in Greg's arms and he moved his position to accommodate her.

"You're lucky to have them," said Josh.

Greg looked down at his family and pushed a lock of blond hair away from Ben's closed eyes. Ben's long eyelashes lay against his cheek and he muttered when his father touched him.

"I think our next trip will be a package holiday somewhere like you Brits do. To a three-star hotel with self-catering and nightmare bus transfers!"

"Even this bus trip would be preferable." Josh laughed. "Morning meetings with the travel rep, and Bob and Cindy from Manchester who can't stand foreign food and complain 'it's too hot' the whole time."

"Yeah, well maybe that's not us," he said, grimacing. "Perhaps we should be happy to stay at home. Australia isn't such a bad place."

"I'm not even sure where home is anymore," said Josh, unable to hide the regret in his voice. "At least with a family you always know where your home is."

"You don't have any family of your own?" asked Greg.

He shook his head. "My mum remarried a few years ago and Dad has rediscovered his social life. I don't have any brothers or sisters."

"I'd be lost without these two," said Greg. "Laura and I met when I was twenty-three and she was only nineteen so I can't imagine what life would be like without her."

"How did you guys meet?"

"At a party. Not very original, but it worked for me. Some of my old uni friends threw a Christmas party and Laura knew a friend of a friend."

"So you spotted each other across a crowded room?"

"Something like that. Five years later, we got married and a year after, Ben was born."

"You make it sound so easy," said Josh.

"Well, to be honest, it wasn't all smooth sailing. Laura had to go away for work for a year and we hardly saw each other. That was tough, but we managed to get through it. The year apart made us realize we wanted to be together." He paused, remembering old times. "So you've never been tempted to settle down yourself?"

"Me? No, not yet anyway. I've got too much to do." He paused, considering what he'd said. "At least, I've *had* too much to do. Now I'm not so sure about my life."

"You're traveling, aren't you? Isn't that enough for the moment?"

"To be honest, I've done my traveling. I'm on my way home."

"So you've got nothing lined up?"

Josh shrugged. "Nothing important. I'm kind of hoping things will work themselves out."

Laura moved again and stretched her body. Her leg shifted and nearly fell off the bag it was resting on. Greg somehow managed to use his own leg to stop hers from falling, and he carefully put her leg back into position.

"Greg?" she asked, voice as fragile as snow.

"I'm here honey."

"Is Ben...?"

148

"Ben's fine. He's right here, next to me. He's still sleeping."

Laura smiled weakly and her eyes flickered shut again. She smiled broadly and, with her eyes still shut, said, "Who's singing?"

Greg's head snapped up at Josh. "This is what she was doing earlier." He glanced back down at his wife. "No one is singing honey. It's your imagination."

"It's so lovely," she said, a beatific smile upon her face. "I think Ben's with them; he's singing." She tailed off as she concentrated on the voices only she could hear.

"That's not Ben, baby," Greg said, unable to keep the worry out of his voice. "Ben's next to us." He lifted her hand and guided her palm to Ben's sleeping head. He put her hand on top of her son's head and ran her fingers through his baby-soft curls.

"Do you feel him?" he asked. "This is Ben right here beside you."

Laura snatched her hand away and her eyes shot open. Her nose wrinkled and her lower lip stuck out like a sulky toddler.

"Don't do that!" she said. "That's not Ben. Ben is out there. He's calling me."

Josh's gaze locked with Greg's; his own thoughts mirrored in the big man's worried face. 'Oh no, not again...'

Greg sat with Laura on his left, her head rested on his chest, his arm around her for support. Ben was on his right, his body small enough to lie on the seat, his head in his father's lap. The bus bumped and shook beneath them as the driver navigated the terrible road and conditions.

Until now, Greg had been careful not move or shift his weight, for fear of disturbing his family, but he twisted his body, waking Ben but able to look into his wife's eyes.

What he saw terrified him.

Her eyes were still the same shade of cobalt blue they'd always been, but now something else resided in them; a new, dark quality that seemed to shift beneath the surface like the shadow of a shark in the ocean. He took hold of her shoulders and shook her gently, but she did not seem to see him. If Greg hadn't known better, he would have thought he was staring into the eyes of a blind woman.

The thought stunned him for a moment, but he quickly regained his composure. He shook her again, harder this time, but she didn't even acknowledge his presence. She continued to stare beyond him. The metal shell of the bus didn't seem to exist for her. Instead, she peered into a magical and distant world which held her rapt.

"Laura?" Greg shook her again.

"I know," she said, her voice full of wonder.

"For Christ's sake, stop it!"

"I will, I will," she said in earnest. For a second, Greg allowed himself to believe she was talking to him. Then she said, "I want to be with you."

"Laura!" Greg shouted in her face, loud enough to disturb the rest of the sleepers, but not enough to break her trance.

"Mum?" A tiny voice came from the right of Greg. "What's wrong with Mum?"

Greg turned his attention from his wife to meet the questioning eyes of his son.

"Your mum's fine, buddy," said Greg, trying to give his son a reassuring smile. "She's not feeling too well because of her leg. Don't worry; I'm taking care of her."

"She's going to go missing like those other people," said Ben, his blue eyes welling with tears.

"No she isn't!" said Greg, too sharp. "Don't say that."

This started the tears and his lower lip stuck out in a strange parody of his mother's earlier expression.

Torn between wanting to comfort his son and looking after his wife, Greg looked from one to the other, unsure of what to do.

"Why don't you come and sit up here with us?" Josh called to Ben.

Ben blinked in surprise, his tears forgotten.

"It's fun up here," he encouraged. "You can watch the driver drive the bus."

The tears quickly returned. "But I want to be with my Mum."

Grateful, Greg realized Josh's intentions. He needed to give Laura his full attention.

"Wow!" Greg said. "You lucky boy. Getting to sit with the grown-ups. Only big boys get to sit at the front."

Ben's lips thinned with suspicion. A clever kid, he knew a reason lay behind the sudden desire for him to sit up front. Even so, he was still just a child and couldn't help but be torn between wanting to stay with his parents and the fear of missing out on something more interesting.

Laura had fallen quiet, but she stared into space with a strange half-smile on her face.

Ben's tears began to dry and he wriggled off his seat. After taking another wary glance at his mother's face, he made his way to the front of the bus. Josh helped him up and Ben squeezed himself between Josh and Sasha.

"I can't see," Ben complained, lower lip threatening to wobble.

Josh glanced back at Greg and Laura. Laura's eyes were open again and Greg watched her, his brow furrowed with worry.

"Why don't you kneel on the seat?" said Josh, determined to distract the boy from his mother's disturbing behavior. "You'll be able to see much better then."

Ben did as he was told; maneuvering his small frame into position, sharp knees and elbows jabbing Josh and Sasha as he did so. In his new position, Ben was able to lean on the back of Chay's seat, his arms folded across the top, chin resting in the crook of his arms.

Satisfied Ben was preoccupied, Josh turned back around to Laura and Greg. The rest of the bus was awake now and alarmed by the latest development.

"Oh my God!" said Dawn. "It's happening again, isn't it?" She looked between Josh and Greg, her blue eyes wide with fear. Both men remained silent, too shocked and scared to speak.

"Isn't it?" she demanded, banging both her hands on the back of Sasha and Josh's seat as punctuation. Ben jumped, turned around and promptly burst into tears.

"Well done, Dawn," growled Josh. "We'd just got him settled.

"This isn't her fault," said Paula. "She's only saying what the rest of us are thinking."

"Speak for yourself."

Everyone turned, surprised to hear Seth speak again.

"So it's *not* what you're thinking?" challenged Paula.

He shrugged. "I just don't like people putting words into my mouth."

"What?" she said, incredulous. "Don't you think there are more important issues here than you worrying about your stupid pride?"

"This has nothing to do with my pride," he said, keeping his cool. "It's about people who have no idea what they are talking about speaking in turn for me."

"Whatever," said Paula, holding her palm up to dismiss him.

"You don't know what's going on either," said Dawn, happy to have someone stand up for her and keen to continue the camaraderie.

"And you do?" Despite the panic creeping onto the bus, Seth remained calm.

"Just leave it, the lot of you," said Sasha, trying to comfort a sobbing Ben. "Nothing is going to happen because there is no way in hell we are going to let Laura off this bus."

She looked up at Greg who caught her eye and nodded. He wrapped his large arms around his wife's torso, his huge hands locking together to form a vice-like band around her. His face was grim determination.

As if sensing her husband's resolve, Laura's body became rigid and stiff. Her eyes widened, nostrils flared, head held high like an animal alert for prey. There was no fear in her eyes; nothing about her suggested she was aware of the tension and unease that suffocated the bus. Instead, she seemed eager, unable to restrain the anticipation of going to whatever was calling her.

"I won't be long," she said, her voice husky, almost a whisper. "It's the only place I want to be now, with my family."

Greg shook her, making her head snap back and forth. "For Christ's sake, Laura! We're *here*. Your family is here!"

She shook her head. Her wide eyes pooled with tears and she dropped her chin.

"Not anymore. I need my real family. The ones I am meant to be with."

The sadness in her voice was chilling and Greg's own eyes welled with tears. Josh held Ben back. The little boy cried and called out for his mummy. Josh's face pained with the difficulty he felt at holding a crying child away from his parents.

Greg wished he could hide this horrible scene from his child, but he was too scared to let the boy out of his sight. Though he didn't want to admit it, he didn't want Ben to go outside. There were things out there. Things with thousands of teeth. Things that could bite.

"I just want to be with my family," she said again, tears rolling down her cheeks. "Why are you doing this to me? All I want is to be with them."

"We're here baby," he said, trying to sooth her. "We're both here."

He kissed the top of her head, nuzzling the familiar warmth and scent. His heart hitched with his love for her, but the horrific fear and sudden certainty that he was going to lose her eclipsed his emotions. Her body trembled in his arms, hitching with tiny hiccups as she tried to stifle her tears.

"Please don't do this to me," she said. "Please don't hurt me."

Greg was shocked. "I would never hurt you Laura. Never."

She continued to cry.

Surely it's over now? he thought, feeling wretched. *This isn't like before.*

Not being able to see his wife's face frustrated him. In this position, holding her from behind, he only had a view of the top of her head. If only he could look into her eyes and see Laura there, instead of that black nothingness, then he would know this was over. If he loosened his grip for a moment, just long enough to shift her around so she sat beside him, he would be able to tell.

It will be all right, he told himself. He wanted to believe it, was desperate to believe it. *I'm still here. I'm still stronger and bigger than she is. If she tries to run, I can easily just grab her again.*

"Please Greg, baby," she cajoled. "Please baby, let me go."

Greg made his decision and, as the muscles in his arms lost their tension and his fingers loosened their grip, a foxy expression crept over Laura's face.

"Greg. No!" Alex yelled and flung himself over the back of his seat and against the couple. Instinctively, Greg's arms tightened back around his wife.

"Can't you see what it's doing?" he said, his voice frantic. "It's tricking us. The same thing happened with Vicki."

All heads turned to stare at Alex. Only a split second of silence passed before all hell broke loose.

Laura bucked and thrashed, taking Greg by surprise. He almost lost his grip on her and panicked, crushing her body against his. Her arms were pinned by her side, but her head whipped back and forth, her teeth bared. Her injured leg fell off the bag but madness masked any pain it caused.

"You fucking cunt!" she screamed. "Let go of me, you fucking cunt."

Hearing this language come from his gentle wife's mouth shocked Greg to his core, but made him more determined not to let her win.

"I'll claw your fucking eyes out," she hissed. "Yours and that fucking brat's."

With that, she turned and spat at Ben. The boy cowered and hid his face in Josh's chest.

"Somebody do something," cried Dawn. "I can't handle this."

"Like what?" said Josh.

Laura started to scream, a blood-curdling screech that could have shattered windows.

Both Dawn and Paula clamped their hands over their ears, cringing at the sound.

"Oh my God. Oh my God. Oh my God," Paula repeated over, and over again, as if the mantra would protect her. She squeezed her eyes, shut trying to block out what was happening around her.

The bus had erupted into chaos; a vehicle of madness transporting the damned to hell.

CHAPTER FOURTEEN
STUCK

Finally, the screaming stopped and an uneasy silence fell over the travelers. Even Ben's sobbing fell quiet, his face hidden in Josh's chest, his body still hitching with silent tears. Laura's pretty features had morphed into a hideous mask of contempt and she stared at each of the travelers in turn, red-hot hatred burning into them. Her eyes narrowed and her lips thinned with spite.

"You are all *nothing!*" she spat. "You cannot fight. You are already dead."

"Why are you speaking like this?" Greg asked. "Why are you saying these things?"

"It's not her," said Sasha quietly. "It's not Laura."

Sasha knew her thoughts would not be accepted by the others, but she couldn't stay quiet any longer. Without realizing what he'd done, Alex had confirmed her thoughts.

'It's tricking us,' he'd said. 'It' not 'she'.

Sasha opened her mouth to speak but Josh's hand closing over hers stopped her.

"Sasha, don't," he warned.

"Why not? We need to accept what's happening here. This is crazy, but we need to accept something strange is happening. If we can figure out what's doing this, maybe we can fight it."

"Look at her, Sasha," he said, gesturing to Laura. "How can we fight her?"

All eyes rested on Sasha, waiting for the miracle answer she didn't have.

She lowered her head, defeated. "I don't know."

Laura started to laugh; laughter of the insane, laughter of a lunatic. Though her mouth was open and her face contorted, she didn't make the sound. Like a badly dubbed movie, the laughter was out-of-synch and distorted. But the sound was familiar. Horribly familiar.

"What the fuck is that?" said Seth, flustered for the first time, his mouth hung open in dismay.

"It's the creature," said Sasha, the words catching in her throat with fear. "And it's the same thing we heard on the road."

Greg's face was white with shock; torn between holding his wife closer and pushing her away. Was this even Laura in his arms or something else, something unthinkable?

"I won't let you go," he said, as though Laura, his Laura, could hear him. "It doesn't matter what happens, I won't let you go."

The laughter stopped abruptly and she opened her mouth. The voice that spoke was the same as the laughter. It came from her, yet was not her own.

"You can never stop me. I am..."

"All knowing."

Everyone turned and stared at Alex. The hatred had left Laura's face and was now painted on his features. He flashed a grin of triumph before launching his body against the window.

Glass smashed outward onto the road and Alex's body flew with it. With the bus still moving, his body hit the ground and he rolled. Splinters of glass tinkled around him like lethal confetti.

The driver slammed on the breaks and the bus screeched to a halt, throwing the backpackers forward.

Alex gave a howl of success before running off into the night.

Paula screamed. "Alex!"

Paula leaned out of the window, broken glass crunching beneath her arms and hands, cutting into her bare skin.

Dawn was closest and she reached over and took Paula by the shoulders, trying to edge her away from the window.

"I'm so sorry Paula," she said.

Paula swung round. "He's not fucking dead, you know!" she yelled in Dawn's face, her voice high-pitched and strangled. "Don't talk like he's fucking dead. He's still out there somewhere and we're going to find him."

Dawn cowered at the onslaught, unused to people shouting at her.

"What's going on?" Laura's voice sounded normal; worried, but normal. Ben broke from Josh's grasp to run to his mother. Whatever had held her in its grip had left her. Greg released his cramped fingers from their hold and gathered his family up in a more natural embrace. A bemused Laura accepted their frantic kisses and tears without understanding what they were for.

"We have to go and find him," demanded Paula. "We looked for the others so we have to try to find him too."

"We didn't find the others," said Josh. "And we're not going to find Alex. I'm sorry Paula, but Alex is gone."

"Fuck you!" she spat. "This is the father of my unborn child you're talking about. Did you forget that? It might be easy for you to give up on him, but there is no way in hell I'm going to leave him in this hellhole. I'm not going anywhere."

"We're not leaving you behind Paula," said Sasha. "I can't begin to understand what you are going through, but we need to get out of here. Something very wrong is happening and we can't just leave you here."

"Fine then," she said. "You can wait for me."

Before anyone could move, she swung herself out of the window.

"Shit!" Josh leapt up and dragged open the door. He jumped out of the bus and Sasha followed.

"Stay in the bus, Sasha."

"Why? It's just as safe out here. The bus isn't protecting anyone. I'd rather help than be useless."

Paula walked up the road, her body a mere silhouette in the darkness. She screamed Alex's name and Sasha heard the desperation in her voice.

"God, the poor girl," said Sasha, her heart breaking.

"Come on Paula," Josh called out. "Please don't do this."

Paula ignored him and continued to walk, calling her boyfriend's name. Josh broke into a jog and, hearing him coming, Paula picked up her pace.

"Leave me alone."

"You're not helping things, Paula. Alex wouldn't want you to be wandering around out here. Think of the baby—it's not safe."

"Nowhere is safe," she said quietly. Her voice trembled, but the mention of her baby made her stop. Her hand went to her stomach as if trying to shield her unborn child from the terror they had been plunged into.

She covered her face with her other hand, trying to hide her tears.

Josh and Sasha each put an arm around her, trying to offer some comfort. They stood on the edge of the road, looking out over the treacherous landscape. The ground underfoot was still soft from the torrential rain, and warm mud seeped into their sandals and squished between their toes. The clouds were low, coating the moon and the stars in their impenetrable blanket, making the darkness absolute. At their feet, a small rectangular sign was embedded in the ground. Bright red with a white skull and cross-bones, the writing in both English and Cambodian warned of land mines.

Paula's body shook and they stood in silence for a while, allowing her to grieve. Allowing her to say goodbye.

"Come on Paula," said Josh finally. "It's time to go."

She nodded and allowed herself to be supported as they walked back to the bus.

They reached the vehicle and Paula stopped. "I need to ask the driver something first," she said. "It's important."

"I don't think he speaks any English," said Sasha, doubtful.

"I know, but I want to try. Please?"

"Okay, I'll come with you."

Paula hesitated. "It's private. I'd rather just go around to his window."

Josh and Sasha exchanged a look.

I don't like this...

"You're not going to run off again are you?" asked Josh.

She gave them a sad smile. "I'm not going anywhere. I promise you."

They didn't want to let her go, but they had no choice? They couldn't pin her down in the same way Greg had held Laura. She was her own person; who were they to tell her what to do?

"Okay. You do what you need to."

Sasha and Josh climbed back on the bus and Paula walked around to the driver's side and mounted the step that helped the driver into his seat. His window was already open to let some of the muggy night air in. The driver, who was not expecting someone to challenge him, pulled away. Immediately, he became defensive, expecting an attack and blame for the disappearances. Instead of speaking, Paula reached in through the open window, across the steering wheel, and snatched the keys out of the ignition.

The bus was plunged into darkness and someone inside shrieked.

"Paula!" Sasha yelled.

With astonishing speed, Paula sprinted away from the bus. She had completely taken the driver by surprise and the confusion created by the sudden darkness was long enough to give her a head start.

Sasha and Josh jumped back out of the bus and took after her.

"Paula!" Sasha shouted again, but Paula paid no attention. With the bus now in darkness, they didn't even have the headlamps of the bus to light the road. Sasha and Josh only had their thin beams of torchlight and, within seconds, Paula disappeared into the darkness.

Another torch lit up behind them and Sasha looked back over her shoulder to see Dawn running behind them. "She took the keys!" Dawn yelled. "Catch her!"

Somewhere in the darkness, Sasha heard a faint plop. The sound tightened her stomach with nerves. *What had Paula done?*

The small group almost stumbled over the runaway. Paula kneeled on the ground, her legs covered in red mud. She hunched over, her breath leaving her body in short painful gasps.

They skittered to a halt around her.

"What have you done?" snapped Dawn.

Paula said nothing, but tears streamed down her face like rain.

"Come on Paula," said Sasha. "Just give us back the keys so we can get out of this awful place. The sooner we get to Siem Reap, the sooner we can get some help from the proper authorities. You know that's the right thing to do if you want to help Alex."

"Give us the goddamned keys, Paula," said Dawn.

Paula's sobs grew louder, more painful and gut wrenching, her whole body shaking with the force of her grief.

Sasha crouched next to her and rubbed her back. A roll of thunder made them all jump and a fat drop of water hit the back of Sasha's hand.

"Please Paula," she begged. "Let's go back to the bus. The storm is going to start up again and we don't want to get caught in it."

"I don't want this baby to grow up without a father," she sobbed. "I don't want to do this by myself."

"You'll be okay, and your baby will be okay, but we need to look after you now and we're not going to leave you out here in the rain.

Sasha turned to Josh. "Will you help me?"

He nodded and they both took her under an arm and pulled Paula to her feet.

Dawn noticed her empty hands. "Where are the keys?"

The tiny shorts and vest top Paula wore showed no signs of bulky keys hidden beneath them.

"Maybe she dropped them when she was running," said Josh, scuffing his feet across the ground around them, listening for the telltale jingle. The ground was too soft and he only succeeded in churning up mud.

"Great," said Dawn. "So now we're going to have a search party for the sodding keys."

Paula mumbled something none of them understood.

"What?" coaxed Josh. "Do you know where you dropped them?"

A snort of hysterical laughter caught them all by surprise.

"Oh God," Dawn groaned. "Why do I get the feeling I am not going to like this?"

"Where are the keys Paula?" Josh demanded.

Paula shrugged, and then gestured at the expanse of water and undergrowth stretching out in front of them.

"I threw them," she whispered.

"You what!" said Dawn, incredulous.

Paula lifted her head. "I threw them out there. No one's going anywhere without Alex."

The sound of Dawn's palm hitting Paula's cheek cracked like a gunshot across the empty expanse.

164

MARISSA FARRAR

"You stupid, fucking bitch," Dawn yelled. "What the fuck do you think you are playing at?"

Sasha grabbed Dawn, shocked she had hit Paula, scared she would do it again.

"She's pregnant Dawn," Sasha reminded her. "Whatever she's done, you can't go around hitting pregnant women."

"Whatever she's done?" she repeated, her voice screechy with hysteria. "What she's done is gotten us all killed! That's what she's done!"

"Don't overreact, Dawn," Josh said, trying to calm the situation. "The driver might have a spare set or maybe he knows how to hot wire the bus."

"I don't suppose there's any way we can look for them?" said Sasha. "We could try to fish them out with a stick."

Josh shook his head. "Where would we even start? Besides, we can't risk it. If we even touched a land mine we would be killed or maimed at best."

"Okay, let's not panic," Sasha said, forcing herself to take a deep breath. "We'll go back to the bus and tell everyone what's happened. Someone will come up with a solution."

"I'm not the only one who's going to freak at this," warned Dawn. "Everyone has been through a lot. This is going to be the last straw."

"We don't know it's that bad yet," said Josh.

"Yeah, well I don't know what the fuck she thought she was doing anyway."

"She wasn't thinking," said Sasha. She lowered her voice. "Paula's just lost the father of her unborn child for

Christ's sake. Things are going crazy. Have some compassion."

"I'm so sorry," Dawn said, her voice dripping with sarcasm. "How selfish of me to care about my own life, when I should be worrying about the person who might as well have written my death sentence."

"Stop being such a drama queen," Sasha snapped, starting to lose her patience.

"This isn't helping things," said Josh. The drops of rain started to fall faster, each individual droplet fat and heavy. "Come on, we need to get moving."

Sasha and Josh half-carried Paula back to the bus, Dawn skulking behind.

Lit torches now broke the darkness of the bus's interior. As they approached, the beams of light swung around and aimed at them like the sights of a sniper rifle. All four raised their arms to shield their eyes from the accusatory light.

A sense of *déjà vu* hit Sasha. Each time she had approached the vehicle, the people on board had been waiting for news. Each time, the news had been bad.

"Is she all right?" asked Steph, leaning out of the bus door.

"She's been better," said Sasha. "Can you aim your torch somewhere else? You're blinding us."

"Oh, God. Sorry." She focused the torch on the ground directly in front of them.

Seth stood up behind Steph, his large frame imposing. "I heard yelling," he said. "Are you going to tell us what went on out there?"

Josh shrugged. "I don't have much choice in the matter; you're all going to find out soon enough. Do you mind if we get on board first though? It's about to start pissing it down and I'm a bit sick of getting wet."

166

Steph backed up, but collided with Seth who stubbornly stood his ground. "I think you should stay outside until you tell us what's going on."

Steph jabbed an elbow in his side. "Come on big guy. Let's not make this any harder."

Seth scowled, but moved out of the way and took a seat. He sat bolt upright, arms folded across his chest—hostility personified.

Sasha helped Paula on the bus and sat down next to her, taking Alex's old seat. She put an arm around her shoulder. Paula was no longer crying. Her shoulders sagged, head down, her damp and stringy dark hair falling over her face.

Steph leaned across to Sasha. "If you want to sit with Josh, I'll sit with Paula. I kind of know what..." Her voice broke as she struggled to control her emotions. "I understand what she's going through. Maybe we can help each other."

Sasha nodded and reached out and squeezed Steph's hand, touched by her offer. "Thank you."

Sasha stood from her seat and let Steph squeeze in next to Paula. She moved down the tiny aisle and regained her seat at the front. Sasha couldn't help but feel relieved to be back in close proximity to Josh. Something about him made her feel safer and right now, she needed to feel safe. She had never been so scared in her life.

She couldn't explain or rationalize what was happening. Despite the excuses they'd all come up with, Sasha knew what she had seen; the terrible creature stalking the bus. The thing had moved alongside them with ease, despite the vehicle doing forty miles-an-hour.

She'd seen its eyes; the knowing and somehow human expression that had laughed, teased and taunted her.

As awful as the memory was, she could live with it. She could even live with people going missing from their party, drowned in the bomb-infested swamps surrounding them.

But she couldn't handle the madness.

Ever since Alex crashed through the bus window and ran off into the night, she had been expecting the madness. She'd been waiting for the first fingers of insanity to tease their way into her brain, to coax her to a place of lunacy. She suddenly became aware of everything around her. Was what she seeing real? Did her ears hear the truth?

The thought of losing her mind had always been a private fear. She found the loss of control terrifying; the idea of not knowing what she was doing, or knowing what she was doing, but being unable to stop. At least with something physically wrong, other people understood the disease. Physical illness could be treated with medicines or surgery, but madness didn't bring sympathy or understanding. It wasn't like cancer where people helped and supported you. Insanity was something people were afraid of.

In this situation, they had a reason to be.

"Come on," said Seth, impatient. "We're still sitting here in the dark and we're sure as hell not going anywhere fast, so do you want to tell us what the fuck she's done with the keys."

Josh took a deep breath to break the news, but Sasha stepped in first.

"Paula reacted badly to what happened to Alex and she threw the keys into the undergrowth."

Silence fell over the bus as what she said sank in.

Chay spoke first. "Hello, lady? You say we have no key?"

"We hoped you had a spare set."

Chay shook his head and Sasha's heart plummeted. "Other lady took only keys."

"Do you know how to hot wire the bus?" Sasha asked hopefully. Chay's confused expression made her rephrase. "You can start without key?"

Chay thought for a moment, said something to the driver, and then shook his head. "No key, no start."

"Does anyone else know?" she asked hoping Seth, the roughest of the bunch, had a misspent childhood and learned the trick somewhere along the line. When no one spoke up, the sinking in her gut turned to iron and dropped with a thud.

Seth turned on Paula. "You stupid cow," he said. "You stupid, selfish little bitch. Your precious boyfriend is dead so you decide to get the rest of us killed as well."

Paula cowered under the onslaught.

"See," said Dawn with satisfaction. "I told you I wasn't going to be the only one pissed off."

"If we can't start the bus," said Laura. "How are we going to get to Siem Reap?"

"I don't know," said Sasha. "I guess we'll just have to sit here and wait for some help to come along."

Steph leaned forward. "We haven't even seen another vehicle for hours. What are the chances one is going to come along now?"

Sasha shook her head. "I don't have all the answers. But morning can't be far away, we've been traveling for hours."

"We've got to sit here in the dark all night?" said Dawn. "We can't do that. People are going crazy and a creature is chasing us. What if everyone loses their minds? What if we start hurting each other? You all saw how violent Vicki and Laura became."

"Well, I'm not going to just wait," said Seth, defiant. "We'll be here for hours and as far as I can tell, you lot are a bunch of fucking lunatics. I'd be better off on my own."

"Don't let us stop you," said Laura.

Josh put out a hand. "No one is going off by themselves."

Seth sat back, his lip raised in a sneer. "You can't tell me what to do!"

"I'm not trying to. I'm just being realistic."

Seth turned to Chay. "How far to Siem Reap?"

"Not far by bus, maybe three, four hours more."

"And what's that in miles?"

Chay calculated. "Maybe one hundred miles, maybe more."

"That's fucking great." Seth hit the back of the driver seat in frustration, his dreadlocks falling in his face. "So we might reach Siem Reap by Tuesday?"

"We can't walk," Josh said.

Sasha was relieved Josh stood his ground. He seemed determined not to let this guy take control. He was too manic, too irate.

"All right, *mate*," Seth shot back, his lip curled in disdain. "I think we've established that. I assume you've got a better idea?"

Josh shook his head. "We must be able to get help somehow. We just haven't thought of it yet."

"You'd better get thinking, hero, before another person goes nuts."

"This isn't his fault," said Sasha. "What's happening here is screwed up, but it isn't anyone's fault."

"You could have fooled me," he said, shooting Paula a cruel glare.

"She wouldn't have been driven to such extremes if she hadn't lost her boyfriend."

"Like I give a shit. We're still stuck here, aren't we? And ultimately it's because of that stupid bitch."

"Christ, you're a nasty bit of work!" said Steph, wrapping a protective arm around Paula. "Don't you have a heart?"

"Actually I do and I'm planning on making sure it keeps working for at least the next twenty-four hours."

Steph scowled at him and Seth scowled back.

Sasha turned to Chay. "What can we do?" she asked him. "As much as I don't want to agree with Seth and Dawn, we can't sit here all night. The torch batteries only contain so much power and then we'll be in the dark."

"I don't want to sit here in the dark," said Paula in a tiny voice.

"Well you should have thought of that earlier," snapped Dawn.

"Can everyone stop sniping at each other so we can figure this out?" Sasha said. "Chay, is there anywhere else we can go? Anywhere else we can get help from?"

Chay opened his mouth to speak, but the driver spoke over the top of him, halting his words.

Sasha felt Josh's eyes on her, the question in her mind reflected in his gaze.

What does he not want Chay to tell us?

"Chay?" said Josh carefully. "Is there anything you can tell us that can help? The smallest thing might make the biggest difference, even if it doesn't seem important to you."

Chay's eyes shifted nervously to his companion and blurted, "Maybe..."

Again, the driver cut him short.

Seth leaned over the back of the driver's seat and shoved the driver. Seth was at least twice the driver's size and though he hadn't pushed him hard, the force was enough to rock him in his seat.

Like a cobra, the driver turned and sprang forward, his whole body raised and tensed, ready for attack.

The small man didn't intimidate Seth. Though everyone else on the bus sensed the venom in him, Seth was too thick-skinned.

"Why don't you just shut the fuck up?" he said to the driver. "Let the boy speak."

"The boy has nothing to say to you people," said the driver in heavily accented, but otherwise perfect, English.

Hearing English come from the driver's mouth caught Seth by surprise, but he quickly regained himself.

"I guess we don't need the boy to speak after all. It sounds to me like you are capable of telling us yourself."

The driver gave him the same look of disdain Seth had given Josh earlier. "I have nothing to say to you. We do not know why you crazy foreigners keep running off. It is not our problem."

"It will be your problem when that thing comes for you," said Seth, a long index finger jabbing the man in the chest. "Don't expect any of us to hold you back when it's your turn to go crazy."

The man stared him down, his black eyes sharp and intelligent. He swiped Seth's hand away. "This does not concern me."

Steph leaned forward, trying to command the driver's attention.

"How can this not concern you?" she said in amazement. "Whatever you think about us 'crazy foreigners' you have to realize that this is not normal. My best friend is missing, probably dead, and I know she didn't run off on her own accord."

The driver watched as she made her speech. No emotion played on his face.

"It is not our problem," he repeated.

"I'll make it your problem!" she said, anger bubbling to the surface.

"What's your name?" demanded Sasha. "And why haven't you spoken English until now?"

"My name is Makara. I have not spoken to you because I had no reason to."

"You've certainly got reason now," she said. "You may not care about people going missing and you may not think it's your problem, but I will promise you this: there are people on board who have lost people they love and we won't let this drop. We will report you to the authorities and to our embassies, and make sure they know you withheld information from us and put us in danger."

A sly smile crept onto Makara's face. "You will report me?" he said. "How will you report me, if you do not live long enough to see daylight?"

"Don't threaten me," said Sasha, equal amounts of anger and fear coursing through her veins. "There's hell of a lot more of us then there are of you."

"I am not threatening you," he said, amusement dancing in his voice. "I am merely making an observation."

Despite the warmth of the night, a cold finger traced its way down Sasha's spine and her whole body tensed and shuddered. Unconsciously, she slipped her hand into Josh's, suddenly desperate for human contact.

CHAPTER FIFTEEN
ACTIONS SPEAK LOUDER

Josh squeezed Sasha's hand tight–too tight. In the dark, heat rushed to his face, his cheeks burning. He tried to clamp down on the anger racing through him; every muscle tensed as he controlled the urge to leap over the seat in front and throttle the driver.

Screw this guy for saying these things! They'd done nothing to deserve such treatment. They were asking for help and he was treating them as though their lives meant zilch.

Josh's mouth clamped shut, his teeth grinding, the muscles in his jaw twitching. He wanted to speak, but he was scared he would lose control of himself.

"Listen, mate," said Greg. "I've got my scared child and injured wife with me here. I don't know what problem you've got with the rest of us, but please don't take it out on a woman and child. You're scaring everyone talking like that."

Makara reached out and took the torch out of Seth's hand. Seth began to protest, but a look from Josh stopped him. If Makara saw the child, maybe he would stop all this shit and help them.

The torchlight fell upon Ben; his blond hair glowed gold in the light. Lifting a small hand to shield his eyes, he pulled himself up to his full height.

"Ah, yes," said Makara. "The boy."

"What's that supposed to mean?" said Laura. She turned to Greg. "What the hell was that supposed to mean?"

"He's just trying to wind us up," said Greg, his eyes narrowing with hate. "Ignore him."

Makara laughed; a short, sharp bark. "You do not need to concern yourself with me. You have already experienced your enemy. I am little threat by comparison."

"You're talking about that fucking thing, right?" said Dawn. "The thing Sasha saw? She kept saying it wasn't an animal and no one believed her. Why should we be scared, yet you're not? Does the creature not like foreigners?"

Makara said nothing, simply stared at her, eyebrows raised.

"What about you?" she said to Chay. "You were going to say something before this guy stepped in. Do you want us all to die as well?"

Chay sat with his head down, unable to meet Dawn's eye.

A sudden roll of thunder clambered across the sky, coming in layers: a slow, low rumble followed by a crash like an explosion. Everyone on board cowered at the sound and seconds later, lightning lit the world.

"The storm is right on top of us," said Josh.

"Wonderful," said Sasha. "That's all we need." Her face paled with exhaustion and she put her head in her hands.

"Come on Chay," coaxed Josh. "If you know anything, even something small, please tell us." Chay's eyes flicked to Makara. "Don't worry about him; we'll make sure nothing happens to you."

Chay slowly looked up. In the diminutive, imperfect light, Josh recognized the fear in the boy's eyes. Though he pitied the boy, he couldn't let this drop. Whatever power Makara held over Chay, they needed to find a way to overrule it. Their lives depended on Chay cooperating.

Dawn jumped up. "We'll pay you! However much it takes, we'll pay you to help us. The money I've got in my personal account alone is more than both of you will see in a lifetime."

"Be careful Dawn," warned Josh. "This isn't the type of place you want to be flashing large amounts of cash around."

"They'll probably take our money and then kill us," said Steph. "What would be the point?"

Dawn ignored them both. "Come on, what do you say? You get me to safety and I'll empty my account for you. My family is loaded. I can get you even more if you want. Think of it as a thank you for saving my life."

Makara started to laugh, this time a full-bellied laugh from which he struggled to stop. Dawn stared at him, wide-eyed, two red spots appearing high in her cheeks.

"Fuck you," she said. "I hope you both fucking starve to death!"

"Sit down Dawn," said Josh. "You are not helping." He turned to the two Cambodians. Makara wiped tears of laughter from his eyes; Chay remained silent, still unable, or unwilling, to make eye contact.

"Can we do nothing to convince you to help us?" he said, hoping, somehow, to still get through to them.

"We can't help you," said Makara. "Something has started; wheels have been set in motion. This will not finish until it is over."

"So it will finish then?" said Sasha, jumping on the first positive thing to come out of the man's mouth.

"This will finish at day break," he said. "But none of you will live until then."

"Stop saying that!" she said. Her fingers tightened around Josh's hand and he glanced down. Their fingers were meshed, palms pressed together. The sight caught something in Josh's chest, squeezing his heart.

Sasha's grip loosened as she said, "So all of this will finish by morning?"

Makara shrugged. "The knowledge will not help you to survive. I have already told you your lives will not last much longer."

Unable to control himself any longer, Josh dropped Sasha's hand. He leaned over the back of the driver's seat and grabbed Makara by both shoulders, holding him at arm's length. The other man's black eyes settled on his, his expression remaining impassionate.

"Any knowledge may help us live. You know what is happening here, but you won't tell us. The fact that you won't tell us means we can do something to change things."

Makara said nothing and Josh knew he was right.

"Why are you not afraid?" said Sasha, thinking aloud. "Why is this happening to us? It can't just be that we are foreigners—there must be thousands of foreigners in Cambodia.

For the first time, Makara shifted uncomfortably in his seat. "Talk to us, damn it!" she said. "There's a reason we are here—a reason this is happening to us."

Chay turned to Makara and spoke in Cambodian. Anger boiled across the older man's features and he swung around and slapped the boy across the face. Chay whimpered and cringed away from his attacker.

"Hey!" said Josh. "What do you think you're doing? He's just a kid, you can't hit him!"

Makara sneered. "He is nothing to you. Worry about your own lives."

"I think that's what we're trying to do," said Sasha in disbelief. "But you're not making it easy."

Seth stood up. "I'm fucking sick of this. If no one else is going to do anything I'm sure as hell not going to sit around and let this little shit decide if we live or die."

The rain was falling steadily now, but Seth seemed not to notice or care as he pulled open the door and jumped out of the bus.

"Seth!" Sasha protested. "You can't walk."

Seth didn't set off down the road, however. He walked around to the driver's side and swung open the door. Before anyone had time to stop him, Seth grabbed Makara by the front of his t-shirt and dragged him from the bus.

Makara landed heavily in the dirt, winded by the fall. He gasped for breath, unable to move or cry out. Seth's fist balled before the driver's face and he started to scrabble backward, mud kicking up beneath his heels.

Josh, Sasha and Greg followed Seth out of the vehicle, but none were quick enough to stop Seth's fist from following through.

Makara's whole body flung to one side, his head snapping backward. Still the man did not cry out.

Seth's large body towered above him.

"Come on you fucking bastard! You know what's going on here. If you don't tell us I'll fucking kill you, I swear I will." To punctuate his point, he kicked Makara in the gut causing his breath to expel in a rush.

"Seth, stop it!" said Sasha, shocked.

"What? It can't hurt that much—I'm not even wearing proper shoes." To prove his point, he lifted a sandaled foot, and then kicked Makara again.

"This is awful. You can't just go around beating people up."

Greg stepped in. "Actually Sasha, I think Seth's got a point. I don't condone violence, but if we have to beat it out of him then I think we should."

"You can't be serious?"

"If I've got a choice between this guy and my family, my family will win every time."

"Of course! But this feels so wrong."

The big man folded his arms across his chest. "This whole thing is wrong, Sasha."

She hung her head, no fight left in her.

"Did you hear that?" Seth shouted to Makara above the storm. "I'm not the only one willing to beat the crap out of you."

"I can't watch this," said Sasha.

Seth sent her a scathing look. "Don't then."

Chay stood behind her, watching them. "Please don't hurt him." The rain plastered the boy's dark hair to his forehead and he looked smaller and younger than his years.

"It's okay," said Sasha, putting an arm around his shoulders. "Let's get back on the bus."

"No. I cannot. I cannot let you hurt him."

"What the hell do you care?" said Seth, surprised. "The bastard slapped you around. What do you care what happens to him?"

The boy faced Seth, shoulders squared, feet apart. "He is my father. It is my duty to protect him."

"He's your dad?" said Greg in disbelief. "And he treats you like that?"

Chay shrugged and looked back to the ground, embarrassed. "He is my father."

"Hang on," said Seth. "This doesn't change anything. So what if he is the kid's father? He's still going to tell us what the hell is going on here."

"You can't beat him up in front of his son," said Sasha. She turned to Greg. "Come on, you're a dad. What would you think if someone beat you up in front of Ben?"

"I'd be furious, but this is different. We need to learn what's happening here, and if this is the only way we can get him to talk, that's what we are going to do."

"Josh?" She turned to him; her large, dark eyes shining.

"I'm sorry, Sasha. I can't agree with you on this one."

She stared at him. "This whole thing makes me sick."

He stared back; suddenly angry with her and frustrated at her piety. "This isn't our fault, Sasha. We didn't choose to be in this position. What else can we do? The guy isn't talking and we're in the shit out here."

Seth joined in. "If you can't handle the pace little girl, get back on the bus. Let the men handle it."

She rounded on him. "Don't give me that macho bullshit! This isn't about being able to 'handle it'. It's about doing the right thing."

"Stop being such a fucking goodie-goodie, Sasha," Seth retaliated. "Saving everyone's lives *is* doing the right thing. These little shits—the kid included—are trying to get us killed. Or have you conveniently forgotten what happened to the others?"

Heavy raindrops hit the back of Sasha's neck and shoulders. Each drop felt like an accusing finger; jabbing, poking, prodding. Sasha eyes filled with tears.

Don't cry. Don't cry.

She didn't want to appear weak. She didn't want to be told to get back in the bus. She wanted to be strong, but she hated violence. Even arguments upset her; the idea of someone being beaten in front of her was more than she could bear.

Rain was falling hard now. Sasha turned to leave the men and seek out the shelter of the bus. Chay still stood just behind her. Wet and bedraggled, the sight of the boy was heartbreaking. Rain dripped off his dark eyelashes and he looked like he was crying.

"Come in where it's dry," she said, gently pushing him in the direction of the bus.

"No." He stood firm, stubborn.

Sasha didn't know what else to say. She wanted to tell him his father would be all right; that they wouldn't hurt him, but it would be a lie.

"Get in the bus, Sasha," Josh called out. "Have nothing to do with it if that's what you want, but we have to do this."

She gave one last look at the scene in front of her: the man cowering on the ground, the boy standing by in the rain. The three Western men surrounding the driver were all twice the size of their Asian counterparts and, in that moment, it seemed impossible to believe the smaller man had the upper hand. The men standing over him appeared to be no more than bullies.

Josh was watching her and she caught his eye. His dark curls were matted to his head and his t-shirt clung to his body like a second skin. She could make out the dark swirls of the tattoos covering his right arm as they disappeared beneath his shirt.

He looked both vulnerable and dangerous; the sight of him knotted her stomach.

Realization hit her. The thought of violence upset her, but what bothered her most was that she didn't want the violence to be committed by Josh's hand. She didn't want to see him differently, didn't want to touch his hand knowing only moments before he'd inflicted pain. Let the other two do what was necessary. She didn't care about them.

All eyes rested on her, waiting for her next move. Six people, all strangers before tonight, stood on a dirt track in the pouring rain, waiting to either cause or receive pain.

Sasha turned away from the bus and walked up to Josh. Her heart hammered inside her chest, her cheeks flared red in the darkness. She stopped only inches from him, his body heat radiating through his thin shirt, despite the rain. She slipped her hand into his; a gesture that had become almost habit.

"Please don't do this Josh. Come back onto the bus with me. Let the others do what needs to be done."

With the rain thundering in their ears, no one else was close enough to pick up on what she said.

He shook his head. "I can't Sasha, they need me here."

"No, no they don't," she insisted. "The driver and Chay aren't going anywhere."

"I need to hear what the driver tells us, if he says anything at all. What if Greg and Seth miss something important, something that might save our lives?"

"Maybe nothing else is going to happen now. Maybe we can wait it out until morning and get rescued."

"That's a lot of 'maybes', Sasha. Besides, you heard what the driver said—we'll all be dead by morning. We can't risk not doing anything."

She knew she was losing the battle and her head dropped.

"I just don't want it to be you," she whispered.

"What did you say?"

She lifted her eyes to meet his. "I don't want you to hurt him. Let the others beat him up if they have to, but not you."

"Why, Sasha?"

She didn't need to say why. He dropped her hand and put his arms around her, pulling her against him. He was soaked through, but she didn't care. She pressed her cheek against his chest and closed her eyes, trying to pretend they were somewhere else and Josh held her in different circumstances.

Josh rested his chin on top of Sasha's head, his emotions in a whirl.

Sasha was right to be concerned about the violence and the thought speared more guilt through his heart. What would she think if she knew what had happened in New Zealand? If using violence to save their lives upset her so much, what would she say if she found out he'd left the country because he slapped his last girlfriend?

With the memory came deep shame and regret. He had never done anything like that before and he refused to allow it to happen again. Had Sasha seen violence in him? Was aggression a part of him he had never known existed?

184

He didn't know how this had happened. Twenty-four hours earlier, he had been sitting in a bar watching a girl who caught his eye. Now, completely by coincidence, she was in his arms begging him not to beat up a man who had information that could save their lives. This wasn't the time to be worrying about his love life, but he didn't want to fall for this girl. She deserved better.

He also couldn't help but question Sasha's own motives. Did she honestly like him or was she simply on the rebound, angry at her fiancé and using Josh to try to get back at him? Something else worried Josh, even though he didn't want to admit it to himself. The thought of falling for this woman terrified him. What if the worst happened and she didn't survive? The notion made him tighten his grip around her. He couldn't bear the thought of losing her.

So do what you have to do, he thought. *If you don't want to lose her, do whatever it takes to make sure she's safe.*

"Oi! Love birds," shouted Seth. "We're standing in the fucking rain here!"

Josh released her and they parted, suddenly self-conscious.

"Everything will be all right, Sasha," he said, hoping in his heart he was telling her the truth.

Reluctantly, Sasha turned away from him and walked back to the bus. She pulled herself onto the vehicle and collapsed in her seat. Part of her wanted to hide from the events outside. She wanted to plug herself into her iPod and pull Dawn's sleep mask over her eyes, but she knew she couldn't.

"What's going on, Sasha?" asked Steph. "Why didn't they stop Seth beating up the driver?"

"Josh and Greg don't think they should. They think if the driver knows something, but won't tell us, they should beat it out of him."

"They could kill him for all I care," Paula said, her voice hard, her face stony.

"You don't mean that," said Laura. "You're just upset."

Paula turned on her, her face a mask of pain and anger. "Don't even speak to me."

The venom in her voice shocked Laura into silence and instinctively she put a protective arm around her son.

"It's okay Paula, this isn't Laura's fault," said Steph.

"It is *not* okay! It was supposed to have been her." Paula was unable to hide her bitterness. "She should have been the one who..." Her voice broke and she gripped the back of the seat, her knuckles white, as if trying to force the words out.

"Who died," she managed.

"No one was supposed to die, Paula," said Steph. "You can't blame her."

"She's got her husband, she's got her child, and I've got no one. So don't tell me who I can and can't blame."

The tension in the bus was as thick as smoke, cloying and clogging.

"Please, let's not fight," said Dawn. "This whole situation is bad enough without us fighting between ourselves."

Paula said nothing, but anger and pain radiated from her.

"And anyway," said Steph. "You're wrong. You do have someone. You've still got that tiny baby growing inside of you, and you're the only one who can give it a chance at life."

Paula's face softened and tears began to fall.

Steph put an arm around her and gave her a hug. "It's okay to be upset, but you need to stay calm. You don't want to hurt Alex's baby."

Paula nodded her agreement and sniffed, wiping the tears from her cheeks. .

Sasha put her head in her heads. Unless the men got the driver to talk, Paula's baby might not have any chance at all.

CHAPTER SIXTEEN
REVELATIONS

Seth kicked the driver again and the man curled up, his hands wrapped around his head to protect it.

"No! Please stop!" Chay shouted, struggling to fight Greg, who was holding him back.

"Not. Until. Someone. Starts. To. Talk," said Seth, each word punctuated by another kick.

Makara started to cough; a wet, gut-wrenching sound. It sounded as though something deep inside had come loose.

For the briefest instant, Seth pulled away.

Immediately, Makara stopped coughing and unfurled. He caught his breath long enough to shout something to his son. Despite the language difference, it was not difficult to understand that he had ordered him to keep quiet.

Chay stopped struggling and shouted something back to his father. His shoulders sagged, all fight gone out of him.

"This isn't working, Seth," said Greg. "You need to step things up a notch."

Makara tried to get to his feet, but another kick in the guts from Seth knocked him back down.

"You're not going anywhere buddy, not until you tell us what you know."

"Go to hell!" spat Makara, and received another kick in the guts for his advice.

"If you don't start talking, you'll be the one in hell."

"You don't frighten me! You are pathetic."

His words incensed Seth. "I'm pathetic? You're the one crawling in the dirt, and you're calling me pathetic?"

"You will cry like a baby when it takes hold of you."

"When *what* gets hold of me, you piece of shit?"

Seth grabbed Makara by the front of his shirt, dragging his body up. He punched Makara in the face. The force of the punch jolted Makara's head back, but Seth's hold kept him close.

Whack, whack.

Seth hit him again and again, the sound echoing across the empty land. A sickening crunch signaled Makara's nose breaking and still Seth did not stop.

"Christ, Seth! Stop it! You're going to kill him!" Josh struggled to catch Seth's swinging fist, trying to stop the beating. Makara's head lolled sideways. His eyes rolled back in his head, blood pouring from his nose.

"Fuck you!" Seth shouted at Makara. "How do you fucking like that, huh? Who's crying now, you piece of shit?"

"No! Please..."cried Chay. "I will tell you what I know. Please, don't kill him."

Seth dropped Makara, who slumped to the ground. He turned on Josh, catching him by surprise, and shoved him backward.

"Are you starting on me too? Is that what you want, lover-boy? I'll beat the shit out of you too, you fucking loser."

Though Seth was a couple of inches taller than Josh, he was by no means the heavier; yet the fear and adrenaline propelling Seth forward was enough to force Josh back.

Josh's right ankle buckled. Pain speared up his leg and he stumbled backward, Seth still bearing down on him. The crazed fear in Seth's eyes made Josh question if something had gotten to him to already.

Greg must have seen Josh stumble for he released Chay. The boy ran to his father's side and Greg ran to Seth. Greg, who outweighed Seth by forty pounds, grabbed the scrawny man, pinning his arms to his side, halting the attack on Josh.

Suddenly able to find his balance, Josh sprang back at Seth, shoving him in the chest in a mimic of Seth's own actions.

"What the fuck do you think you're doing? Have you lost your mind?"

Unwittingly, Greg held Seth like a punching bag. He hesitated between letting Seth go and allowing a fight to break out, or to hanging on and hoping Josh came to his senses.

"Quit it, Josh!" Greg yelled. "You're not helping things."

Josh realized what he was doing and stopped. It was too easy to get caught up in the bubble of fear and violence surrounding them.

"Are you going to behave yourself?" Greg asked Seth. The man, trembling from the adrenaline and panting like a dog, didn't answer.

"Are you going to behave yourself?" Greg asked again, giving him a small shake.

Seth nodded.

Greg loosened his grip and Seth broke free, whirling around to face them.

"We're not your enemy, Seth," said Greg. "Get a grip of yourself."

Seth glared at them both. "I was just doing what we planned. It's not my fault if you two don't have the stomach to handle a bit of blood."

"He can't tell us anything if he's dead, Seth. He's unconscious already. If we didn't still have the boy, I'd be beating you up myself right now."

Seth puffed himself up. "I'd like to see you try," he said, full of false bravado. "Try anything like that again," said Josh. "And I'll grant your wish for you."

Seth glared at Josh, but stayed quiet.

Satisfied another fight wasn't about to erupt, Greg walked over to where the driver was slumped on the ground, his son crouching next to him. Tears poured down the boy's face; the frightened eyes of a child looking up at the big man. He crouched down next to the boy, his expression a twisted mask of guilt and pity.

Makara started to regain consciousness. His eyes flicked open and he groaned through the blood coating the lower half of his face—a wet and gurgled sound. His hand flickered by his face; some part of him knowing not to touch the bloodied mess that used to be his nose. Though the rain still fell, it didn't match the rate at which the blood poured from his face.

"Shit, Seth," said Greg. "You've made a real mess of him."

"Well, you were the one who told me I needed to step it up a notch, didn't you?"

"I didn't say half-kill him!" said Greg, glaring at him.

"You got what you wanted, didn't you? The boy said he would tell us what's going on."

Greg paused, then took a deep breath, his broad shoulders slumping. "I'm sorry Chay, but I've got my own child to worry about.

You have to tell us the truth now. If you tell us, we will help your father. If you won't..." Greg looked pointedly at Seth.

Chay sniffed and swiped a hand across his face. "Okay. I will tell you. But first you must help him."

Greg glanced at Josh.

"Sounds fair," said Josh. "Let's get him back in the bus."

"If you go back on your word we'll have no hesitation in hurting him again," warned Greg. "And if we get any feeling that you are bullshitting us..."

"No, no," he said hurriedly. "I will tell you."

"Okay." Greg jerked his head at Josh. "Give me a hand, would you?"

Greg stood at Makara's head, Josh at his feet.

Makara cowered, assuming another attack was imminent. His eyes flicked between the two men and, though fear haunted them, Josh also recognized a kind of cold defiance. Something in them that said, 'do as you will, but know you will get what you deserve'.

The size of the driver made it easy for Greg and Josh to lift him. Chay hovered anxiously. Seth grabbed the boy by the scruff of his t-shirt, pulling him away.

"Leave him be, Seth," said Josh. "He's going to do as we asked, so leave him alone."

"I wanted to make sure he wasn't getting in the way."

"Just get the door."

Seth held open the driver's door. Josh and Greg maneuvered the driver so he lay across both the driver and passenger seat. Sasha and Dawn leaned over the backs of the seat to see what was happening.

"Jesus Christ!" said Dawn. "What the hell did you do to him?"

"Only what was necessary," said Seth, quick defend his position.

"He looks like he's been in a car crash," said Sasha. "Surely you didn't have to do all that?"

"Don't you bloody start!" said Seth. "The boy is going to talk, so you should be thanking me, not getting on my case."

"Is he really?" said Dawn, unable to hide the relief in her voice. "He's going to tell us how we can get through this?"

"I think that might be a bit optimistic," said Greg. "But at least he's going to tell us what has happened to the others."

"I'm not sure I want to know," said Dawn, shivering slightly at the thought.

"Anything might help at this stage. We have to listen to what he's going to say."

"How do we know that he's not just going to lie to us?" said Steph. "He could make up any old rubbish and we wouldn't know any different."

"We've already warned him about the consequences of him lying. I don't think that's something we need to concern ourselves with."

In the moderate dry and comfort of the bus, Makara gave in to unconsciousness once again. The blood flow from his nose had started to congeal, making his injuries appear even worse than they were. From where Josh stood, the bottom half of his face looked like it had caved in. Greg tilted Makara's head to one side, making sure he wouldn't choke on either blood or vomit.

"He'll be okay," he said to Chay. "I think you should get in the back with us so you can tell us what you know."

Chay gave his father one last anxious glance before resigning himself to his fate. His father would be furious with him when he woke; so furious Chay would suffer beatings for a week, but he had no choice. These Westerners would kill his father if he did not tell them what he knew. His father would have his own people to deal with when this was over, people who would be livid, but such a thing was out of Chay's hands.

"Come on Chay," said the big Australian, they called Greg. "Get on the bus."

Chay climbed on board and slid into an empty seat at the front of the bus. He felt torn between wanting to sit close to his father and staying as far away from the guy with dreadlocks as possible. He did not trust himself to be anywhere near the man who had so violently beaten his father. As far as Chay was concerned, Seth was already dead.

All eyes were on him and he took a deep breath, preparing himself. This would not be easy; his words would be met with scorn and disbelief. These travelers had no idea about his world and culture. They would not understand the history of his country, the power that descended from generation to generation.

However, he had a story he need to tell.

"You will not believe what I tell you, but I make you promise, on the life of my father, that I tell you truth. I will tell you what I know. I ask only that you do not threaten me or my father." He looked around the group, trying to read each of their faces in the small amount of light from the torches. The thunder and lightning had stopped again for the moment, but rain continued to thrum steadily on the metal roof of the bus.

"Just get on with it," said Seth.

Chay's whole body tensed with anger at the sound of Seth's voice. He clenched both fists, resisting the urge to leap at the bigger man and tear his eyes out. He felt for the other travelers and did not wish for them to die. For Seth, however, he wished nothing but the most painful of deaths.

Chay started this journey not truly believing his father when he predicted the night's events. Though he'd heard the stories since childhood, he'd thought them to be nothing more than myth. Even after the first two went missing, he still tried to convince himself the disappearances were simply a coincidence. The stories his father told him were just that—stories. When he finally accepted what was happening, he'd begged his father to stop it; tried to make him realize to sacrifice these people was wrong, but his father had other ideas.

These people were here for a reason, and the men who put them here would not take kindly to hearing the travelers had lived.

It would not be easy for these people to believe him. He had struggled to believe what was happening himself and he'd been brought up with this knowledge. However, the travelers had one thing that, until tonight, he had not.

Proof.

They had seen what *it* was capable of. Some of them had even seen the being with their own eyes. Aside from that, none of them really had a choice; if they did not believe him, what were they left with?

"I will tell you story as it was told to me," he said to them. "Please, no interruptions."

"What is this, fucking story time now?" said Seth. "Should we all be..."

"Shut up, Seth," said the man who seemed to be their leader, Josh, cutting him off. "Just listen for once in your life. This is what we've been fighting about for the past hour and you never know, you might actually learn something."

"It's okay," Dawn, the pretty blonde, reassured him. "You carry on."

Chay looked once more around the group's expectant faces and took a deep breath.

"Cambodia was not always poor country," he said. "Ten thousand years ago the Khmer empire ruled and Cambodia was a powerful and wealthy place. Angkor was a sacred temple city built by gods, for this is what the people believed their kings to be. Yet a dark cloud hung over city. This cloud came in form of their king, Jahard—a war-like man; his temper and stubbornness known before any other trait.

"Jahard took a wife, Arana, a trader and traveler from another Kingdom. She did not want to marry the king, yet could not leave for fear of Jahard taking his revenge on her family. Arana soon became heavy with child, but she could not be happy about the child. Instead, she fell into depression, sleeping most days, visiting her family and homeland in her dreams."

"What the hell has this got to do with us?" Seth interrupted.

Sasha shot him a daggered glare. "Shut up, Seth!"

Chay tried to judge the rest of the group, but other than the obvious hostility of the man with dreadlocks, the rest were impossible to read.

"She gave birth to a boy," he continued. "A son for Jahard, but things only became worse. Arana saw the child as another Jahard and she could not love him. She felt only violated; defiled by the man who gave her child, betrayed by own body for creating the boy and debased by the child who suckled her like a parasite."

"Are we supposed to be starting up some sort of women's support group?" Seth interrupted again.

This time he was ignored.

"Arana could take it no longer. One night, her maid woke to find Arana stood on balcony of room, the boy in her arms. Arana climbed onto balustrade that divided balcony from one hundred-foot drop below. Before maid could stop her, Arana jumped.

"When king found out he became most angry. Instead of being sad for his son, Jahard turned his hatred on people he believed responsible. Jahard order his men to round up all travelers, traders and nomads in country and have them brought to Angkor Wat, his greatest temple.

There he watched as they were sacrificed. He watched the blood run down the great staircase, listened to screams of pain, rejoiced in their deaths, but most of all he wanted their children. Before he had the men and women killed, he sacrifice their children before them.

"He sacrificed their children so the gods would give him his son."

CHAPTER SEVENTEEN
CURSED

"You have got to be fucking kidding me!" said Seth. "What did you think we wanted, a goddamned fairy story?"

"No! No." said Chay, holding his hands up in defense. "I said you will not believe, but I tell you truth. I promise you."

In the torchlight, Seth's eyebrows raised, his lip curled. "You expect us to believe we are being attacked by some... by some... "

By some... what? thought Sasha. *Exactly what had the boy explained?*

"We're being attacked by what, Chay?" she asked. "That was one hell of a story, but we're all still as clueless about what's happening to us as when you started."

Chay looked at her as if she was stupid. "Jahard," he said. "Jahard is what is happening."

"The king?" she said, confused. "How can a king who has been dead for thousands of years be following us?" A memory flashed across her brain, a memory of a dark, sleek body and four loping legs.

"And that wasn't a king I saw," she said. "There's no way that thing was human."

Chay nodded eagerly.

"It was king once," he said. "The gods punish him. It is said gods never want Jahard to rest. Every one hundred years, for one night, he rises to take revenge on travelers and look for a son."

Chay's eyes flicked to where Ben slept.

Laura gasped and pulled the boy closer to her body.

"Nice fucking gods!" said Seth. "Not that I even believe in God, but they're not only punishing this king. As far as I can tell, we're the ones being punished."

Chay shrugged. "I cannot explain what gods do."

"If you ask me, this is all bullshit," said Dawn. "I've never heard such a load of mumbo-jumbo in my life. An animal is out there and everyone is getting carried away with a local kid's fairy tale."

Sasha turned to her. "That thing is *not* an animal, Dawn! Don't forget what happened to the others..."

"Drugs then," she interrupted. "Anything makes more sense than the pile of crap the kid has come up with."

"Dawn, you were the one saying it *wasn't* an animal or drugs. You can't change your mind because you don't like the alternative."

"So, you believe him? You think this is some cursed king chasing us around, driving us crazy and making us run off into the night."

Sasha ran a hand through her hair. "I don't know what I believe, but I think we've got to keep open minds. If we just dismiss the story, we might be signing our own death warrants."

"Sasha is right," said Josh. "The idea is insane, but then so is what's been happening tonight. We've already ruled out all logical explanations, so what does that leave us with?"

"So what do we do?" asked Steph. "Say we do believe him, what are we supposed to do about it?"

"And why us?" said Dawn. "Why did we get the short stick? There must be thousands of backpackers in Cambodia, so why are we being hunted down by a fucked-up dead king?"

"No travelers day," said Josh, half to himself.

Sasha turned to him. "What?"

"No travelers day, remember? We were both told we couldn't travel today. You thought this was a kind of bank holiday."

"I don't understand."

"Think about it," said Josh, impatience sharpening his tone. "If other travelers were all told they couldn't travel today, we're the only ones on the road. That's why this is happening to us!"

Paula spoke for the first time in what seemed like hours.

"They told Alex and me there were no buses," she said shakily. "But Alex got angry and shouted at the guy selling the tickets. We wanted to stick to our flights because of the baby and we were on a tight schedule. Alex didn't want to waste another two days in Bangkok." She stopped and wiped the back of her hand across her face. "The guy came back to us a couple of hours later and told us we could go."

Josh nodded. "The same thing happened to me."

"I practically begged them to sell me the ticket," said Sasha. "I paid a goddamn fortune to be on this damn bus."

"I didn't want to stay in Bangkok." Dawn stared at her hands.

"Why not?" Sasha asked, urging her on. "What's wrong with Bangkok?"

Dawn shrugged. "Dirty, noisy, smelly. The place is just like London. Just like the place I've flown thousands of miles to escape."

"So you asked to be able to travel today?"

She smirked, the old Dawn back. "Demanded more like. They shouldn't advertise if they're not going to stick to a timetable."

"I assume the same story goes for you and Vicki?" she asked Steph.

Steph nodded miserably. "We were on our way home after a year away—an around the world ticket. We had one flight left to use up and only a couple of weeks to do it. We thought we would travel overland, see as much of Cambodia as we could, head across the border and into Vietnam, and then fly back from Laos. We wanted to fit in as many countries as possible and time was running short. God," she sighed. "I'd give anything to be able to go back and change that decision."

Sasha turned her attention to Greg and Laura who sat in the back, huddled together.

"How about you guys?"

Greg and Laura exchanged a glance but didn't meet Sasha's eyes and didn't respond.

"Guys?"

Finally, Greg spoke. "Nobody said anything to us about not traveling. We booked the trip as easily as any other bus journey." He looked at his wife. "They did treat

202

us differently though; kept staring at us, like they felt sorry for us or something."

"They knew, didn't they?" blurted Laura, hysteria in her voice. "They wanted Ben for something so they put us on this bus!"

"Is that true?" demanded Greg of Chay. "Did they know this was going to happen?"

Chay shook his head. "They are told only that they must put you on bus."

"But they must have known something bad was going to happen..."

"More to the point," Josh interrupted. "*Who* told them to put us on the bus?"

Chay glanced back toward his father—a huge mistake. Seth and Greg were both on him in an instant.

"It was him, wasn't it?" said Greg. "All of this is his fault."

Seth shoved Chay in the chest. "If he thought the last beating was bad, wait till he experiences this one."

"No!" said Chay, his dark eyes filled with fear. "My father, he only works for the men. He drives bus, he not plan anything."

"He knew what was happening," said Greg, a snarl in his voice. "And that makes him as bad as whoever he works for."

"You'd better tell us who the fuck he works for and why we've ended up here, or you're going to end up the same as poor old papa." Seth punctuated his sentence by hitting the boy across the back of the head.

Chay cowered, expecting more blows to fall. When none came, he lifted his head and looked around at the group nervously.

"You might as well tell us," said Dawn. "We're no closer to making it out of this alive."

Chay seemed to consider this for a moment. He sighed in defeat.

"You are payment," he said. "Thai, how do you say... mafia? The Thai mafia pay with you to Cambodia mafia. They owe because Cambodians allow the Thai to build their casinos on Cambodian soil. They cannot gamble in their own country. The people who allow this to happen, they are bad people and they ask for their debts be paid to keep their gods happy."

"You have got to be kidding!" said Dawn. "*We* are the payment for rent on casinos? We're not theirs to fucking pay with."

Chay shrugged again.

"They must keep their gods happy—their crops and livelihoods depend upon it." He paused for a moment. "Our lives are not like yours. Our gods are real and they determine our fortune."

"So screw everyone else?" Laura said. "Is that how you think? Sacrifice other people's children and yours will survive?"

"This world has always been about sacrifice. If a bird is raising too many chicks, she will sacrifice the weakest so the strong will survive."

"I don't give a shit about what bloody birds do! We're human. We are supposed to respect other humans and take care of the weak. If we can't do that, we are nothing more than animals." Laura's outburst woke her son and he looked up at her face. He caught the fear there as easily as a cold.

"Mummy?" he said, pulling on the front of her vest top. "Mummy, what's the matter?"

"It's okay, baby," she said, pulling him closer to her body as though she could press him back into her womb; back into a place no one else could touch him. "The bus has broken down, but they'll fix it soon."

Ben cuddled up to her and put his thumb in his mouth, an unconscious gesture for comfort.

"I don't know about anyone else," said Josh. "But I still don't get it. Why did they pick us as their 'sacrifice'? How the hell are we suppose to keep their so-called 'gods' happy?"

"Ten thousand years to the day, Jahard murdered the travelers and their children," said Chay. "Jahard has finished his punishment. When his sentence is over, the gods will give him the ability to return to the land of the living. He can only do this through the life of a traveler; of a child, a boy. But his connection to the living is weak, he has not inhabited a living body for thousands of years, and the mind of a child is the strongest of all. To reach his goal he must first start small; to feed on weaker minds and become stronger.

"Ten minds to feed upon, to grow strong upon, until daybreak when he is able to take the child's body as his own."

Laura moaned pitifully and rocked her child as if he was a baby.

"But there are eleven of us," said Sasha. "Or at least there was when this started."

"Goose wasn't supposed to be on the bus," said Josh. "It was a last minute thing. The girl at my guest house must not have known."

"So one of us might survive?" said Dawn, clearly hoping the one would be her.

Chay's eyes flicked from them. "Or he will simply do whatever he wishes and then take the boy as his own."

"No crazy, dead king is taking my son!" said Greg. "You can say whatever you like, but I'll do everything I can to stop this from happening. I will make sure that..."

A bump against the side of the bus halted him mid-sentence.

"Oh God," said Dawn grabbing Seth's arm. "What the hell was that?"

Every one of them sat frozen; listening, watching, waiting.

The bump came again, but this time from the other side of the bus. The force rocked the vehicle and both Paula and Laura screamed. Josh and Sasha jumped up to the window and Josh shined his torch out onto the road.

It was empty.

"The thing is out there, isn't it?" said Dawn, on the verge of panic. "It's going to come in here and kill us all!"

"Shut up Dawn," said Josh. "You're not helping."

"Someone do something," Laura begged. "Please don't let it take my boy, he's only a baby."

Greg stood up. "I'm sure as hell not going to sit here while some creature tries to destroy my family. If the monster is out there, I'll catch it and break its bloody neck."

"Don't be ridiculous, Greg," said Sasha. "You've seen what it's capable of. You need to be here with your family. They need you."

Laura caught his arm and looked up at him with big, wet eyes. Ben, who still had no idea what was going on, did the same.

"I have to go," he told them. "I can't just sit in here, hiding like a coward, when it might start playing with our minds again."

206

A high-pitched screeching ripped through the bus. The sound was that of incredibly sharp claws being dragged down the side of the bus. The noise tore through them like glass. The girls clamped their hands over their ears and Ben started to cry.

"It's going to open us up like a tin of sardines!" cried Steph.

"I'm going out there," said Greg, defiant.

Josh stood. "I'm coming with you."

"What the hell are you going to do?" said Sasha, some of the panic Laura was experiencing creeping over her. "You've got no weapons, nothing to protect yourself with! You can't just beat it up like you did the driver."

"Who says we can't?" said Seth, rising to his feet.

"Fine, you go out there," Sasha said, starting to lose her temper. "Go and get yourselves killed. See if we give a shit."

"This bus isn't going to protect us, Sasha," said Josh. "I know you're scared, we all are, but hiding in this tin can till daylight is not going to save us. If whatever is out there wants to take one of us, then it will. We can't stop it."

Greg interrupted. "Yes we can. We stopped it with Laura didn't we?"

Paula spun around, ferocity glinting in her eyes. "Yeah, saved your wife and got the father of my baby killed."

"She's right," said Josh. "We didn't stop it; it just transferred to someone else."

"Oh God," Dawn sobbed. "Is this really happening? We're actually going to die."

"No one else is going to die," said Greg, moving towards the front of the bus. "I take it you guys are with me?"

Sasha was powerless to stop them.

The three men stepped out of the vehicle and onto the road. As soon as their feet hit the ground, each one spun around, using their torches like searchlights, peering into the darkness.

Josh expected a huge, dark creature to launch at them with teeth and claws, and murder on its mind.

Apart from the sound of the rain, the distant grumble of thunder and the heavy breathing of three frightened men, he heard nothing.

"Where are you, you piece of shit?" Greg yelled into the darkness. "Come on. Show yourself!"

Again only silence met them as they braced themselves, waiting for hell to break loose.

Frightened faces pressed against the windowpanes. All eyes searched the night, collective breath baited, poised to shout out a warning.

Josh nudged Greg. "Let's move to the other side."

Seth grabbed Josh by the shoulder and said in a whisper, "Shouldn't someone check *under* the bus?"

Mimicking his actions during his search for Goose, Josh got on his hands and knees. Flashbacks of being a child and hunting under his bed for the bogeyman taunted him. He couldn't help but expect a huge, clawed hand to appear and drag him, screaming, under the chassis.

Pushing the thought away, Josh took a deep breath and peered beneath the bus.

It was empty.

He let the breath out in a whoosh and got to his feet, his legs weak and shaky. He wasn't ashamed to admit he was terrified.

"Okay," he said. "Let's do this."

With Josh leading, they moved slowly around the bus. Josh had to resist the urge to mimic cops on television shows and use his torch like a gun; pausing before springing around the corner. The image struck an inappropriate chord and he snorted back laughter, feeling at once manic and crazed.

A shove from behind pushed him forward and, rather than the smooth entry he imagined, Josh ended up stumbling.

Nothing lurked on the other side of the bus. Whatever had bumped them was gone. He spun back around to face whoever had pushed him. He could easily have guessed the culprit. Seth gave him his crooked sneer, but before Josh retaliated, Seth's ice-blue eyes flicked to the side of the bus and widened in shock.

Following his gaze, Josh shined his torch down the side of the bus. Despite the rust and dents in the bodywork, he easily made out the five claw marks running as deep cuts down the length of the bus. The strength needed to make such marks would have been extreme.

Whatever the creature was, it had gone, but there was no denying it had been here.

"Damn!" said Greg. He punched the side of the bus in frustration, making the people inside scream in surprise. "Now what are we supposed to do? Just sit around and wait for it to come back?"

"I'm sure as hell not going to," said Seth. "I'm going to stick to my earlier plan and try to walk out of here. I'd rather be doing something than sitting in that shit-heap waiting to be attacked."

Josh looked from one man to another. He didn't share Greg's desire to face the creature, nor Seth's desire to start trekking, but he did agree with them on the 'not sitting and waiting to be attacked' side of things. If their torches ran out, they would be sitting in the dark waiting for something to happen. There was no greater invitation for something terrible than doing nothing.

"Maybe the boy has an idea for what we can do?" Josh suggested. "He obviously knows a lot more than we do."

"I don't know," said Greg. "He might not even be telling the truth about this whole thing and even if he is, why the hell would he try and help us? His balls will be on the line if we get to some kind of civilization and report him and his father as being responsible for getting the others killed."

"So we lie to him," Seth suggested. "If he can feed us a load of bullshit, why can't we do the same to him?"

"And say what?" said Josh. "What the hell could we say to make him help us?"

Seth smiled; a sly, lop-sided grin revealing his one fang-like tooth. "What we said to make him talk in the first place of course."

Josh realized what he implied and his heart sank. "You can't keep beating on the father. The guy won't last through much more."

"So we start on the boy. It won't take much before he starts howling."

Greg stepped in. "No. I won't have you beating up a kid. It's not right."

"You think you can stop me?" Seth said, squaring his shoulders; his usual 'don't fuck with me' attitude returning to his voice.

Greg rounded on him. "I could squash you flat, you scrawny little..."

"Stop it, you two," said Josh, moving between them. "We don't need to be fighting each other right now. That's not going to solve anything."

The two men glared at each other, but they both backed off.

"Let's try to think about things logically," he said. "We've been standing out here for the last ten minutes or so and nothing has happened. I've got a feeling this thing could come and take us if it wanted to, so there must be a reason it hasn't. Things were happening to us when we were in the so-called safety of the bus, so there's no reason things will be any worse in the open."

"At least the bus is dry!"

The voice came from behind and Josh turned to find Sasha standing on the road.

Josh smiled at her. "I would have thought you were used to getting soaked by now."

She smiled back. "And I thought I was running away to the sun."

Seth coughed theatrically and Josh pulled himself from Sasha's brown-eyed gaze.

"Anyway," said Sasha. "I hope you guys aren't making any decisions without us."

"No decisions," said Josh. "Just throwing a few ideas around."

"Yeah, I heard, and I have to say I agree with you. I don't think we're going to achieve anything by sitting around, waiting for that thing to pick us off one by one."

"Well, you would agree with your *boyfriend*," muttered Greg. "You don't have to worry about an injured wife and a child."

Josh frowned. "Greg's got a point. Laura would have to be carried. Same with Ben."

"Maybe we could split up?" suggested Greg. "Half of us could stay here and the other half could go and get help."

"No," said Josh. "That's not going to happen, we have to stay together. If we split up, we'll be weakened. Safety in numbers."

Seth gave a snort that was somewhere between amusement and disbelief. "Why am I starting to feel like a bloody gazelle being stalked by a lion or something?"

Greg looked at him in contempt. "Because that's exactly what we've become."

Sasha felt the atmosphere flare between the two men and tried to divert an argument before it started. She wasn't Seth's biggest fan, but Greg really seemed to hate the guy.

"At least the rain seems to be easing up. If we do decide to risk heading off on foot, we're not going to get a soaking."

"Yeah, well I think getting wet is the least of our worries," said Greg, still giving Seth the evil eye.

Sasha sighed and turned away from the men. If anyone could help them now, it would be the boy. She walked up to the bus and rapped her knuckles on the window next to where Chay sat. The sharp noise made the boy look up, his dark eyes wide with surprise. She beckoned him with a finger, signaling for him to come outside. He looked around at his father, clearly thinking of his last trip outside of the bus.

Sasha walked around to the open door. "We won't hurt you, I promise you. All we want to do is talk."

Steph popped her head up from behind Chay. "Do you think it's safe out there? What about the thing chasing us?"

"It's no safer in there than it is out here. I think recent events have proven that. The rain has all but stopped, so at least we're not going to get wet."

Chay stared at her, his eyes full of fear and distrust. She hated that she caused such emotions in a child.

"It'll be okay," she said gently. "As long as you do what you can to help us, everything will be all right."

Sasha saw him glance back, once again, at his father. "He'll be all right too," she said. "You have my word." She wished, hope against hope, she would be able to keep her promise.

Reluctantly, Chay climbed off the bus. Dawn, Steph and Paula followed; each one wary. It was something about human nature; whatever the proof to the contrary, the human race always felt safer under shelter.

Whatever their fears, none could resist the pleasure of stretching cramped calf, thigh and back muscles.

"So what do we need to do?" Sasha asked Chay.

He didn't respond, just gave his head a small shake.

"To beat this thing, what do we have to do?"

"I do not know," he said, his head continuing to shake, his small forehead creased with worry. "I only tell you story we are told as children. I thought it to be no more than a story until tonight. How do I know how to beat it?"

"You must know something!" Sasha persisted. "Even if you don't realize you do, something in these childhood stories might give us some idea, some *hint*, about what we can do. This is our lives we're talking about!"

213

She broke off as a lump built in her throat and her eyes burned with hot tears. She swallowed hard, angry with herself for allowing her emotions to break through once more.

Chapter Eighteen
On Foot

Chay watched the dark-haired, pretty woman struggle with tears, and guilt clutched at his heart. He felt torn between fear from the repercussions he would suffer at the hands of his father and the men he worked for, and guilt at the fear and misery of these strangers.

Part of him wanted to help; wanted to click his fingers, magic them back to the border and warn them all not to get on the bus, but that was impossible. He was scared of what would happen to him and his father if these people did survive. If the authorities didn't catch up with his father, the men he worked for would.

He wasn't only worried about tonight, but what happened after. Things were getting worse and the men here weren't going to let him get through the night unscathed. They had already hurt his father and fear pushed people beyond what they would normally do.

His choices were limited. If he helped these people and they survived, his life would be in danger because of what he had done. If he didn't help, they would probably kill him and his father anyway.

Anger toward his father blazed through him. How dare he put them in this situation. His father was often angry and violent toward him, but he was still his father. He was supposed to look after him, protect him from danger; not put him right in the middle of it.

Why was he trying to protect his father when his father had done nothing to protect *him?* If they survived this thing, the men his father worked for would go after his father, but Chay would be all right. They probably weren't even aware Makara had a son.

At least then the backpackers might stand a chance at survival.

Even if he chose to help them, what was he supposed to do? He had been truthful about not knowing any more than he'd already told them.

Chay looked around at the angry and frightened faces surrounding him. The angry faces bothered him most, particularly Seth and the father of the boy. Chay had seen how he treated the child—with love and affection and tenderness—things he'd always craved from his own father. Greg wouldn't allow his son to be taken without a fight. If they couldn't fight this thing, they would fight the people who put them here.

He needed to think of something.

"We're not going to stand here forever, kid," said Greg. "You know more than you're letting on and if you don't tell us soon..."

Chay understood the threat and shot Sasha a look of reproach. This time, his mournful eyes fell upon a hardened heart and, despite her earlier promise, she turned her face away.

Inspiration hit.

"You are travelers right?" Chay said to scornful expressions.

"That's obvious," said Seth. "Try telling us something we don't know."

"No, no. You must think. The king is here because he needs travelers. His wife was a traveler, his son the child of a traveler, the people he murdered—all travelers. So what if you are no longer travelers?"

Each of them stared at him in disbelief. They were trapped in the middle of nowhere, in a country unrecognizable from their own with transport they couldn't start.

Chay recognized the doubt in their eyes and continued in a hurry. "What if you get to village? Make them take you in? Other foreigners are in the country, but he wants you because you are traveling!"

They stood in silence for a moment, allowing what Chay had said to sink in.

Sasha looked at Josh's face, trying to read his thoughts. He caught her eye and, for once, he did not smile.

"Is it possible?" he said. "Could it be so simple?"

Chay grabbed his arm. "Is not simple," he said with alarm in his eyes. "Next village several miles away. Villager know who you are, be scared. You will be very bad luck to them; make crops fail, children die."

Seth butted in. "A village isn't far from here and you've only just told us? They might have a phone and we could call for help."

"I don't think that's likely," said Josh. "I expect this village is nothing more than a few run down shacks in the same spot. I doubt they have electricity, never mind a phone."

Seth's shoulders sagged. "Great. So we've got to beg some locals, who think we're going to make them starve and murder their children, to take us in and hope this fucking thing leaves us alone?"

Josh cocked an eyebrow. "We've got to get to the village first."

"Exactly how are we supposed to do that?" said Dawn.

Chay grinned at her; an expression completely out of place given the circumstances. "We must walk."

She turned up her nose. "Walk? How far?"

"A few miles—maybe more."

"And what am I supposed to do with my bag? I've probably got a couple of grand worth of stuff. I'm not deserting it for some scabby looters to help themselves to."

"Shut up Dawn," snapped Greg. "We've got more important things to worry about than your stupid clothes. What about Laura? Her leg is still bad; there's no way she can walk any distance."

"So we're going to do this?" asked Sasha. "We're going to walk to the village?" Something stirred uneasily in her stomach. They didn't even know if there *was* a village. This might all be a setup, a way of exposing them to even more danger. She didn't like the idea of setting off in the dark, knowing that thing was out there watching their every move, skulking along beside them and waiting for the perfect moment to take its next victim. The problem was if they didn't go, what else could they do? Their options weren't exactly abundant. It was either sit and wait, or try to do something to save themselves.

"We have to at least try," she said. "We have no other choice."

"Well, we're not going," said Greg. "Laura can't walk any distance, never mind miles."

"Then we'll carry her," Josh said. "We'll fix up a sling between us and take it in turns. Same with Ben."

Greg's face crumpled in doubt.

"This will work." Josh reassured him. "There are three men, four if you include Chay. Two can carry her between them and then we can swap, and we'll all help with Ben."

"What if it doesn't work? What if we get to the village and they want nothing to do with us? What if this thing just picks us off one by one while we're struggling to get there?"

"What's the alternative, Greg? If you've come up with any better ideas, be sure to let us know as I'm sure we'd all love to..."

Laughter, like that of a madman—harsh, coarse and guttural—drifted from across the plains. The sound grated through Sasha's soul, taking a little piece of her forever.

The group froze like deer sensing a predator. Dawn gave a tiny moan of despair.

"What do we do?" said Sasha, her voice a feeble whisper.

"It's teasing us," said Josh. "Playing with us."

"Should we get back on the bus? Wait it out?"

Greg suddenly made up his mind. "Let's get the hell out of here."

His sudden change of heart spurred Josh into action. He jumped up on the side of the bus and unstrapped the tarpaulin covering their bags. Quickly, he found his own rucksack and dragged it off the roof and onto the ground.

"Go and get Laura and Ben," he told Greg before turning to the others. "Everyone needs to grab the basics. The less you can carry the better."

Another laugh came to them, but this time a cold snarl accompanied the sound.

Dawn ran to the side of the road.

"Just *fuck off*!" she screamed in the direction the laughter was coming from. "Fuck off and leave us alone, you fucking bastard!"

She let out a scream and stumbled backward.

"Stay on the road for God's sake, Dawn!" shouted Josh.

"It hissed in my ear," she said, tears running down her face. "I heard it! I felt its breath against my face." Her hand trembled beside her cheek as if its breath had dirtied her and she was too scared to touch her own skin. "Oh, God. It's going to come for me next, I know it is."

Sasha ran to Dawn and put an arm around her shoulder. She trembled violently and her body odor hit Sasha's nostrils—sharp and rank—the scent of fear.

"Come on, Dawn. Move away from the side of the road. You need to get your stuff together so we can get out of here."

Dawn nodded mutely, her usual brass persona swallowed by terror. She didn't argue and climbed back onto the bus to rummage through her things and gather what was important to her.

Sasha went over to where Josh was pulling things out of his rucksack.

"Why is whatever you want always at the bottom of your pack?" he said, glancing up at her.

She smiled at him and shrugged. "I think they call it Sod's Law."

"This whole fucking thing feels like Sod's Law."

Josh pulled a length of rope and material from his bag.

"A hammock?" said Sasha, confused. "What are we going to need that for?"

"To carry Laura in. We can use it as a sling between two of us and she can sit in the middle."

His thoughtfulness touched Sasha and she had to resist the urge to crouch down, wrap her arms around him and bury her face in his neck. The desperate need for physical contact hit her like a thirst, but now wasn't the time and she forced herself away from the moment.

Sasha turned away and stared out into the night, almost willing the thing to come to her, as it had Dawn. The soothing chirp of cicadas and the high-pitched whine of a mosquito filled her ears. With a heavy heart, she turned and walked to the bus to get her things. Back on board, she picked up her small backpack and rifled through the contents, making sure she had everything: passport, wallet, useless mobile phone. Her fingers came across a photograph and she pulled it out to see herself and a man staring back at her.

The man she stood next to looked like a stranger.

Nick no longer seemed real to her and she hurriedly pushed the photo to the bottom of her bag, strangely embarrassed by its presence.

"Is everyone ready?" Josh's voice came from the doorway and she jumped, heat rushing to her cheeks. Chay leaned over from where he was perched on the front seat. "What about my father? He's not waking." As if to demonstrate his point, he pulled the older man up by the shoulders and allowed him to fall back onto the seat.

"Then we leave him," said Josh. "We have enough to carry without having to worry about shits like him."

"I must stay with him," said Chay.

"No chance. You're coming with us and you've no choice in the matter. You're the only one who knows where this village is and the only one who can persuade them to take us in. Right now, you're the most valuable thing we've got."

Chay glanced back at his father, his lips thin with worry.

"His injuries aren't enough for him to die," said Josh.

Chay's troubled dark eyes fixed back on Josh. "Okay, I will take you."

"Too bloody right you will," said Seth, catching the end of the conversation. "If you didn't, I would beat you every step of the way!"

"Nice, Seth," Sasha said. She was tired with his constantly aggressive attitude and he was starting to sound like a broken record.

"I'm the only one around here with the balls to do something instead of just standing around talking, so don't look down your snooty nose at me."

Sasha hackles rose, but she gritted her teeth and forced herself not to react. He wanted to get a reaction out of her. He was probably enjoying this whole thing.

Greg half-carried Laura out of the bus and Ben followed, wide-eyed.

"I don't know about this, Greg," Laura said. "That thing is out here."

"The bus won't offer us any protection. We'll stand a better chance if we try to get to safety than if we just sit here and wait."

222

"Maybe someone will come along and help us," she protested.

He cradled her in his arms. "That's not going to happen. You need to trust me, okay. I'll do everything I can to get us out of this."

She sighed and rested her face in the crook of his neck. "I know you will. I'm just scared and tired. I want this to be over."

"Mummy?" came a little voice from beside them. "Are you okay, Mummy? Why can't we stay in the bus? I don't like it out here."

"Everything will be fine," she said, reaching down to stroke his fine blond hair. "We're going for a walk now because the bus is broken and we don't want to stay out here all night, okay?" Ben nodded. "And don't worry about being too tired because everyone is going to help you, give you piggybacks and stuff! That will be fun, huh?"

The strain in her voice was clear and Ben's forehead wrinkled at the sound.

"Are we ready?" asked Greg.

"As we'll ever be." She gave him a weak smile and he carefully put her down, though kept one arm wrapped around her waist for support. She tried to put some weight on her leg and sucked air between her teeth. Greg shot her a look of concern and she smiled again, though the expression seemed forced.

"I'll be fine."

One by one, everyone climbed out of the bus and stood on the roadside, expectant. Sasha listened for the hideous laughter that had taunted them only minutes before. Tension hung in the air like electricity. Greg and Josh had swung the hammock between them and Laura was perched in the center. Ben was happy to walk for the moment, but Sasha, Dawn and Steph all agreed to take it in turns helping him when needed. Chay strode out in front, while Paula and Seth brought up the rear.

They walked only one hundred yards before a shout from Seth halted them. Everyone turned back, fearing the worst.

"It's Paula," he said. "She's gone back to the bus."

"What!" said Sasha. "What the hell did you let her do that for?"

Seth shrugged. "Not my problem is it? She said something about not being able to leave her bloke, Alex, or whatever his name was."

"And you've only just said something? Christ! You are unbelievable!" Sasha shoved past him, purposely pushing a little harder than necessary.

Laughter, cruel and mocking, came from the bus and Sasha broke into a run.

"Sasha. Wait!" yelled Josh, running after her. He caught her with ease and pulled her to a stop.

A blood-curdling scream cut through the night.

"Paula!"

A crash sounded from the bus and the whole thing rocked up on its side and smashed back down again. Like a ship in violent waters, the bus bucked from side to side. What was left of their belongings was strewn around like driftwood. The sound of the metal chassis crunching against the earth echoed in Sasha's ears and the force of the vibrations pulsed through the ground. Paula's screams came fractured and broken, and each movement of the bus cut her voice off with its impact. The forceful thrashing of the bus grew stronger and stronger, faster and faster. The bus should have split apart; the pressure exerted on its rigid frame too much to take.

The violence stopped as suddenly as it began. The stillness was almost as loud as the crashing of the bus had been.

Sasha started at a run toward the vehicle.

A piercing scream, final and horrific, cut through the night, and something wet and dark splattered across the windscreen.

"Oh God, no," cried Sasha. She started to run again, but Josh reached out and grabbed her. She struggled against him, but he held her tight.

"You can't help her, Sasha," he said gently. "She's gone."

Sasha pulled away from him and walked with determination back to the group. Shaking with fury and grief, she walked straight up to Seth and slapped him hard across the face. His head jolted with the blow, leaving her hand stinging.

"You fucking bastard," she said, her voice low in anger. "I hope it gets you next and I hope it tears you to shreds."

They stared at each other, eyes locked in fury and hate. Seth's blue eyes glinted in the torchlight and Sasha could have sworn she was staring into the eyes of an unblinking snake.

"Serves the silly bitch right," he said. "If she hadn't chucked the keys away in the first place we'd be half way to Siem Reap by now."

Sasha choked on his audacity. "You are unbelievable. Don't you care about anyone but yourself?"

"Right now it's every man for himself."

"We'll be sure to remember that when it's your turn."

Seth gave her a narrow-eyed smile that was more of a snarl. He turned away and started walking down the road, away from the carnage.

"You guys can stand around having a group hugging session if you want," he called back over his shoulder. "But I'm getting the hell out of here."

Dawn and Steph both broke into a jog to catch up with Seth. Greg looked back at Josh to see if he was coming to help him with Laura.

Sasha glanced back at the bus. They couldn't go back now. They had to keep going and simply hope what Chay told them was the truth and they'd be able to make it to the village without anyone being hurt.

She turned to catch up with the rest of the group, but stopped when she noticed Chay still stood, staring at the bus.

Realization hit her.

"Oh, Chay. I'm so sorry." The boy stood frozen with his back to her. She called to the others. "Wait a minute, everyone. Chay's father was on the bus."

The group stopped and looked back at her.

"We're not going back for him," said Greg. "He got us in this mess. If he's dead, it's his own goddamned fault."

"Greg is right," said Josh. "We wouldn't go back for Paula, so we're definitely not going back for Makara."

With his head down, Chay turned his back on the tin can that had become his father's grave and resumed his position at the head of the group.

CHAPTER NINETEEN
ENDURANCE

An hour had passed since they started walking and the group was exhausted, both mentally and physically. It hadn't taken long for Ben to tire, so the girls had taken turns carrying him between them. Though a small child, his weight soon became too much to bear and they tried to get him to walk intermittently to give their aching arms a rest.

Greg and Josh continued to carry Laura and, though small-framed like her son, the strain of her weight made their muscles cramp and their bones cry out in protest. Laura begged to be put down and allowed to walk, but any pressure on her leg made her cry out in pain. They could only move her position to allow some relief; Laura using one man like a crutch whilst he half-carried her and allowed the other to rest.

Chay was small, but strong, and helped when needed; but Seth strode on ahead, neither offering to help, nor having it asked of him. He'd made his position clear and no one had the energy to waste arguing with him. Even though the pace of the group sometimes became excruciatingly slow, Seth never allowed himself to get too far ahead to lose sight or sound of the rest of them.

So far, whatever was chasing them had left them alone, but that didn't do anything for Sasha's nerves. At the slightest sound, she froze in position, waiting for the attack, only to find the person next to her had coughed or someone groaned in pain.

They had been walking in near silence, none of them knowing how to express what was happening in words, when a small sob came from Dawn.

"I've got people back home," she said, her voice tight and high. "People I fought with before I arrived here. The last thing I said to them was that I hoped they'd rot in hell." She gave a tiny, sad laugh. "I guess it's ironic because that seems to be where I've ended up."

Sasha could tell Dawn wanted to talk. Her words felt like a final confession.

"Do you think we can leave something behind? Leave some kind of message to tell the people back home that we love them and we want them to be happy?"

"Don't talk like we're not going to get out of this," said Sasha. "You'll freak me out."

"We have to be realistic, don't we? I'm sure everyone has people who will wonder what happened. People they need to say things to. People who will blame themselves..."

"What happened, Dawn?" Sasha said gently. "Why are you here?"

She gave a small sniff. "I wasn't supposed to be here by myself. I was supposed to be traveling with my boyfriend—sorry, *ex*-boyfriend now. We were all packed the night before we were due to leave and I went out with some of the girls from work. My best friend Amie cancelled at the last minute, claiming she'd fallen ill. Perhaps I should have known something was wrong, but hell, I was a naive idiot.

"I arrived home after my night out, not too late or drunk because we had to be up early the next morning to get our flight, and I walk into the lounge to see Amie sitting on our couch with her head in her hands and Pete pacing the living room. I didn't even click when I saw them together, instead I thought, *oh God, something's happened to Mum or something* and they both wanted to be here to tell me themselves. I think I even *said* that, which is even more humiliating. Good old trusting me, too dumb to think anyone would ever screw me over. Then Pete told me to sit down and Amie wouldn't meet my eye and I started getting that horrible, cold, sinking sensation you get right before your world is ripped out from under you."

Sasha turned her head as she walked, offering a smile of sympathy to show she understood.

"So I sat down and listened while Pete calmly told me he wouldn't be able to go traveling because he and Amie had been seeing each other and she had just found out she was pregnant, and yes, it was his, and yes, they were in love and wanted to make a go of it. They said they wanted to tell me together because they respected me and they didn't want this to ruin our friendship! What a fucking joke." She paused and shook her head, her blonde hair falling in her face. "I told them I hoped they rotted in hell, went in the bedroom, picked up my backpack and passport, walked out of the door and got a taxi to Heathrow. So here I am, straight out of one hell and into another."

"That's awful, Dawn," Sasha said, feeling for her. "You poor thing."

Dawn shrugged. "Thing is, now all of this has happened, their affair doesn't seem as important. Do you know what I mean? I hate them for what they did, but I don't want them to spend the rest of their lives blaming themselves for my death. Part of me still thinks 'that'll teach you, you bastards', but I don't really mean it. Up until a few days ago, I loved them both deeply and I would hate to think they would have this hanging over them for the rest of their lives. They would always think my disappearance happened because of them, that I was too distraught and I did it to myself somehow."

The two women continued to walk side by side, a companionable bond created by Dawn's revelation—her insight into herself. Sasha realized Dawn wasn't as hard as she appeared.

"We're going to get out of this, Dawn. Please try to believe that."

"I want to, I do. But no matter how much I tell myself, I just can't bring myself to believe it. Do you know what else? I'm somehow relieved Pete isn't here. At least I don't need to be scared for the lives of the people I love as well as my own."

They both looked to the small family limping before them. Dawn's eyes flicked to Josh helping them. When Dawn turned back, Sasha recognized pity in her eyes. Mistakenly, she thought the sight of the family had evoked the emotion.

Dawn lowered her voice so the men couldn't hear them. "You really like him, huh?"

Sasha glanced away, guilty, and held up her left hand. "I'm already taken."

Dawn shrugged. "I shouldn't say this considering what happened to me, but only a crazy person wouldn't notice there's something between the two of you. One thing I've learned is life's too short to be with the wrong person."

The women walked on and Sasha stole glances at Josh. His whole focus was on the people around him, people he'd not even met before today. She might be being stupid, but she couldn't help but feel they had a connection. Of course, she might be reading something into nothing. What if he was simply being as attentive towards her as he was to everyone else?

Their feet squelched in the mud and they plodded onward, the night wrapped around them like fog.

"I don't want to pry," said Dawn. "But what are you doing here by yourself if you're engaged?"

"Long story. I'm supposed to be meeting him here, in Cambodia, but..." she trailed off, shaking her head.

"But what?" Dawn prompted.

"I'm not sure the relationship is right anymore. I haven't seen the guy for a year. He isn't exactly desperate to get home and I don't even know if he'll be waiting for me when I turn up. I've been fantasizing about a big, romantic reunion, but even if all this hadn't happened I'd still struggle to see that happening. He wants a different life now and I don't think I feature."

Dawn gave her a rueful smile. "Bloody men. Can't live with them..." She thought for a minute. "So you're engaged, but you don't think you have a future with him, so what's stopping you with Josh?"

Discussing their love lives considering their situation was ridiculous, yet somehow, the conversation made them feel better. Made them feel *normal*.

"This isn't the time or the place." Sasha said. "I mean, we can hardly go out for dinner or a drink."

"Maybe not, but you're the one telling me we'll get out of this alive, so perhaps you should start listening to some of your own advice. You could ask him out when you get back home."

Sasha cheeks flushed at the idea. A long time had passed since she'd asked anyone out and the idea was mortifying.

"I couldn't. I still need to sort things out one way or another with Nick. I couldn't have someone waiting in the sidelines. Besides, I don't even know if he feels the same way."

"Course he does. He couldn't sit beside you quickly enough."

"He only wanted to get away from Goose." Saying the name of the man who had died only hours earlier felt strange.

"You tell yourself that if you want, but I think deep down you know differently."

Sasha's stomach clenched and adrenaline made her muscles tense. She wasn't a believer in love at first sight, but something about Josh attracted her and it wasn't just the dark curls and serious green eyes. He had an aura about him, a sense of strength and kindness. He'd naturally become the leader of the group, the one everyone turned to, and she couldn't help but admire him.

But she still needed to consider Nick; the man she'd thought she'd spend the rest of her life with. Did he not have these qualities? She struggled to believe she'd fall in love with someone who didn't encompass such traits. She thought back to their life together and everything seemed so superficial and fake. They'd been the perfect couple; successful jobs, great home, but what lay beneath?

How had so much changed in a matter of hours? She'd been on her own for a year now and never even considered being with someone else. Yet here she was, only miles from Nick, and she was seriously thinking about another man. The situation must be affecting her emotions; the intense certainty she was bordering the threshold between life and death. Or perhaps somewhere, deep down, she knew she shouldn't have come here in the first place?

She shoved her hands in the pockets of Josh's jacket and buried her face in its depths. His subtle scent—the lingering musk of his deodorant—filled her senses.

If Nick wanted to be with her, he would have come back home as promised and not decided to go to Bali instead. Why hadn't his choice in itself told her enough? She couldn't help wonder; if she had met Josh in different circumstances would she be feeling the same way?

Sasha allowed herself to take another look at Josh. He carried Ben. Something about the strength of the man, combined with the tenderness he showed the child, made her heart lurch.

"Hey, guys!"

The shout from Seth interrupted her thoughts.

"I think we've got a problem."

He'd stopped about seventy yards ahead and was staring at something in front of him.

"Oh God," said Dawn. "What now?"

Everyone stopped where they were, with the exception of Chay, who ran on to catch up to Seth. With the sudden stillness and everyone quiet, a noise became noticeable.

"Does anyone else hear that?" asked Steph, her head cocked to the side. "It sounds like more thunder."

"It's not thunder," said Josh. "It's water."

233

Chay reached Seth, then turned back and beckoned the rest of the group to join them.

The noise grew louder as they approached. Ahead of them, cutting across the dirt road, was a fast-running river. The river wasn't wide, only about ten feet, but the heavy rain had deepened and swollen the waterway, churning up the red earth so the river seemed to bubble blood in the torchlight.

Chay shined a torch along the edges of the bank to reveal a couple of splintered, fractured planks of wood sticking out only inches across the water.

"Bridge is down," he said.

"Thanks for that," said Seth. "Next time we need someone to point out the obvious you'll be the first person we turn to."

"Oh great!" said Steph. "This is all we need. How do we get across? Can we go around somehow?"

Thick undergrowth and marshy land spread out on either side of the road. Even if they didn't have the threat of land mines, they would have struggled to get through to find a better place to cross.

"What are we supposed to do?" said Sasha. "It's not like we can build a bridge or anything."

"We'll have to swim," said Josh. "We don't have any other choice."

"I don't know if I can," said Laura. Her voice was weak and she was shaking with the effort of simply keeping her balance on the hammock. Despite the best efforts of the men, she'd had to support herself some of the way and the journey had sapped her energy. The paleness had returned to her face and her skin appeared clammy.

"She needs a doctor," said Greg.

"That's going to be a bit difficult right now," said Josh, irritation sharpening his tone. "We need to be practical and think of a way to get her across."

"What about the hammock?" said Sasha. "Couldn't we use that to carry her across?"

Josh shook his head. "I can't see how. Each of us crossing is going to be dangerous enough without having to worry about carrying someone else. The hammock would catch in the water and pull everyone downstream."

He bent down and plunged his arm deep into the water. The pull dragged his arm downstream and he almost lost his balance.

"There's no way we can swim. The flow is too strong."

"What about using the rope from the hammock?" Steph suggested. "If we could get it to the other side, we could use the rope to pull each other across."

Josh looked at her as if he might kiss her and Sasha experienced an absurd stab of jealousy.

"Brilliant! That's exactly what we can do. If one of us tries to get across first, the rest left on this side can hold the end of the rope so they aren't swept away. Then we'll just take turns getting across. The strongest of us will have to go first and last, so the rope will be held on both sides of the bank."

"What about Laura?" said Greg "She's not going to find the crossing easy. Someone is still going to have to carry her."

"I'm becoming a bit of a liability," said Laura, trying to smile to show she was joking when they knew she wasn't.

"Don't be daft," Greg scolded her. He turned to Josh. "Her getting a soaking isn't going to help things either." He lowered his voice so only Josh and Sasha were close enough to hear. "She doesn't look good, mate. She must be suffering from an infection or something. I'm worried about her."

"How can we carry her across and keep her dry? To do it on your own, you'd need both hands to keep her out of the water but then you wouldn't be able to hang onto the rope."

"What about someone holding onto Greg?" said Steph, stepping in closer. "They could use one hand for the rope and hold onto Greg with the other."

"I don't know." Josh said. "That would take some strength."

Dawn shook her head. "Wouldn't it be easier to tie the rope to Greg, let him get across that way?"

Josh angled his body slightly to her. "It wouldn't work. He'll need the tension in the rope to keep his balance, especially if he's also going to be supporting Laura."

"It might not be as difficult as we think," Sasha said. "The first person might get across to find the crossing isn't so bad."

"I don't think wishful thinking is going to get us anywhere right now," Josh said. His words left Sasha stung. She turned away, scuffing her feet in the dirt like a child, feeling stupid and angry.

"So how are we going to do this?" asked Greg. "I take it Josh is going first."

"Thanks for volunteering me, mate," Josh said with a wry grin.

Greg tried to smile back, but it was forced. "No worries."

"I'll go next," said Sasha, forcing herself out of her sulk. "I'll take Ben across."

"Are you sure?" said Greg. "He can swim, but not in this water. Are you sure you can manage?"

"One of us is going to have to take him and I'm stronger than I look." She squatted down in front of Ben. "You can hang onto me so your Daddy can help Mummy across, okay?"

The little boy nodded, but his gaze flicked over her shoulder at the rushing water behind.

"We'll be fine," she reassured him. "You hang onto me as hard as you can and I'll get us across." She turned to Josh. "So who's going to help Greg get Laura across if you're going to go first?"

They all turned to the tall, solitary figure standing silently in the background.

"It has to be you, Seth," said Josh. "You're the only one big enough to take their weight."

Seth raised his eyebrows. "You may have figured this out by now, but I'm not really into this whole altruistic thing."

"No shit." Josh's shoulders squared. "Well, how about you put your charming personality aside for a minute and help us out. If you don't, you're going to be walking the rest of the way by yourself because we're not going to leave them behind."

"I thought that might be the case." Seth gave a heavy, over-dramatic sigh. "Okay. Fine. But don't expect me to make a habit of it."

"Good. Thank you. Chay, you can come last."

"Is that a good idea?" said Dawn. "If he gets washed away, we'll be screwed. No one else knows where we're going."

"I'll go last," said Steph. She gave a little smile. "I'm tougher than Dawn."

Dawn made no moves to argue with her.

"Okay," said Josh. "So I'll go first, followed by Sasha and Ben; Laura, Greg and Seth; Dawn; then Chay, and finally Steph. Is everyone all right with that?"

Seth gave a small grumble of complaint, but everyone else nodded.

Josh picked up one end of the hammock and twisted the rope tight around his wrist. By twisting the rest of the hammock, over and over again, it formed a tight, thick coil of material: solid and strong. Greg picked up the other end and copied Josh's actions, twisting his end of the rope around his wrist and pulling it tight.

"You ready?" he asked Josh.

Josh nodded. "Can someone keep a torch just ahead of me so I can see where I'm going?"

"Sure," said Sasha, and then added, "Good luck."

"Thanks." Their eyes met—a spark passing between them—and Josh turned to the racing water.

CHAPTER TWENTY
DEEP WATER

Josh crouched at the edge of the bank, preparing himself for what he expected to be a struggle. His hands sank into the marshy bank, mud seeping between his fingers, and his feet slid down the bank and into the water. Immediately, the power of the water threatened to drag his feet from beneath him. Slowly, he lowered himself in and was relieved when the water only came to just above his waist. The earth beneath his feet disappeared downstream as erosion displaced the ground he stood on. He gripped the rope as tight as he could. The rope-hammock was his lifeline and if either he or Greg dropped it, he could easily be swept away. At least none of the others would struggle as much as he would. Once he'd crossed to the other side of the river, the tension in the rope would make it easier for them to get across.

Josh made sure he had his balance and took another step. Immediately, he plunged chest deep and the surprise made him lose his balance. He flailed and slipped. His head ducked under, echoing water rushing past his ears, and he gulped a mouthful of warm, silted water. He burst back through the surface and coughed, grit and dirt catching in the back of his throat, choking him. For what was only seconds, but felt like so much longer, his feet found nothing but water, then solid ground met his soles and with relief he regained his footing.

"Are you okay?" Sasha called from the bank, and he flashed her a thumbs-up. Already, he was a quarter of the way across, but if the water got any deeper he might not make it. The water had reached the middle of his chest and he bent his body against the flow to prevent being pushed over again. He took tiny steps, scuffing his feet through the detritus. This way he felt more grounded—less unstable— and he pushed forward, knowing the opposite bank was only an arm's length away.

Josh reached out and his fingers scraped soil and foliage. With a final push, he wrapped his hand around the thick roots of a plant and used it to pull himself against the bank. The water was shallower here and he allowed himself a moment to catch his breath before he heaved himself up onto dry land. A cheer broke out and Josh punched the air with both hands as though he'd won a marathon.

Quickly, he turned his attention back to the river. Sasha was next across and she had the added burden of Ben. Josh crouched down, so the rope-hammock skimmed above the water, and Greg copied his actions. Josh leaned back on his heels and pulled on the rope, hoping he was strong enough to resist the weight of both Sasha and Ben. He prayed he wouldn't just slide through the mud and be pulled back into the water. He would dive in after Sasha and Ben if he had to, but he would much rather get them both across safely.

"Ready?" he called across to both Sasha and Greg.

"Ready," they echoed back.

Ben wrapped his arms around Sasha's neck and straddled her waist, his warm face pressed into her neck. Sasha took hold of the rope just ahead of where Greg held it. She edged toward the bank, her thighs trembling as she lowered herself to a squat. Her heart hammered in her chest and she took short, sharp breaths.

"Wait!" called out Laura and Sasha paused in position. Grimacing in pain, Laura limped to her son, pulled the top half of his body away from Sasha's, and grasped him in a ferocious hug.

"Be good for Sasha," she said. "Hold on tight and don't wriggle, okay?"

"Okay."

"I love you."

"Love you too, Mummy."

Laura let go.

Sasha wrapped one arm around Ben's torso and used the other to hold onto the rope. Her heart lurched in her throat and she forced herself to take a deep breath, trying to steady her nerves. Though she'd volunteered to be the one to take Ben, the responsibility consumed her. If something happened...

No. She couldn't even think about it. Concentrate on getting across and freak out when they were all safe.

The speed of the water hit her like a torpedo and she braced herself. Ben's grip around her tightened. Stones and dirt, carried along in the flow of the water, hit her bare skin and she hoped they wasn't hurting Ben.

"Take little steps," Josh called to her. "You're less likely to lose your balance."

She did as he said and her toes felt the drop Josh had fallen down. She edged her feet forward, hanging onto the rope for dear life. As she moved down the drop and the water grew deeper, she hoped against hope the water level wouldn't come above her head. She would struggle to swim with Ben on her back.

The water edged higher. It churned and bubbled around her as if it wanted to take her; like a living, breathing force, consciously trying to pull her under. Sasha's heart tripped in an erratic, frantic beat and she breathed through her nose in tiny gasps. She was too scared to open her mouth; scared the water would get in and she would start to choke, that she wouldn't be able to breathe.

Josh must have noticed something was wrong. "Sasha?" he called out to her. "Sasha? Are you okay?"

She didn't answer, but stood frozen in one spot, her eyes wide with Ben clutched to her.

"What's happening?" yelled Greg. "What's she doing? Should someone go in and get her?"

Josh shouted back at him. "No, that's not going to work. I won't be able to hold the weight if someone else is on the rope. My feet are already slipping." Josh's attention turned back to Sasha.

"Sasha, listen to me. You're doing fine, okay? You need to keep moving and you'll be out in a second. I won't let anything happen, I promise you. Come on, I know you can hear me. The river isn't going to get any deeper."

Josh's promise got through to her. She blinked and gave her head a slight shake. She needed to move.

Standing here in the middle of a river wasn't going to get any safer. The only safe place was on the other side.

With Josh.

She started to move again, tiny steps that brought her closer and closer to the opposite bank. As soon as she was within arm's reach, Josh bent forward and dragged her and the child out of the water. She clung to him, trying to fight tears of relief, Ben squashed between their wet bodies.

"Shhh. It's okay," he soothed her. "You're safe now."

"I'm so sorry. I don't know what happened—I just froze."

A little voice piped up between them and they parted, remembering the child sandwiched between them.

"Oh! I'm sorry Ben," said Sasha. "Are you okay? I'm sorry if I scared you."

"I'm wet," he said, holding up his arms to show that he was telling the truth.

"I know you are, honey. We're all wet, but it's warm out here so you'll soon dry off."

"Mummy says if I'm wet I'll get a cold," he insisted.

"Well, maybe your mummy will have some dry clothes in her bag. But you'll have to wait till your daddy brings her across, okay?"

Ben nodded, his gaze flicking over Sasha's shoulder to where Greg, Laura and Seth all waited their turn to get across.

"Sasha, I'm going to need your help," said Josh. "I hope you're feeling strong because you're going to have to hang onto me, make sure the weight of those three doesn't drag us into the water."

"I'll be fine," she said. "And I promise I won't freak out on you again."

He grinned at her. "I trust you."

"Is Ben all right?" Greg shouted at them.

"He's fine," Sasha shouted back. "Wet, but safe."

Greg was relieved. There was nothing worse than trusting someone else with the most important people in your life. Unfortunately, now he had to do it all over again. This time he needed to put both their lives into Seth's hands: someone he could probably throw farther than he trusted. He had a bad feeling about the whole thing, but there was no other way. Seth was their only choice.

"You'd better not screw this up, buddy," Greg said to Seth, under his breath.

"Don't give me that shit," said Seth. "I'm doing this because I have to, not because I want to."

"I mean it. You might not give a shit about anyone else, but we're depending on you. This thing isn't a joke. Our lives literally depend on you."

Seth held up both hands. "All right. Enough of the speeches. Let's just get this over with."

Greg turned away from him, his heart sinking, but he forced himself to smile at Laura. He didn't want her to see the worry in his eyes. She had enough to deal with.

"Okay hon. I'm going to cradle you so I can lift you above the water when it starts to get deeper. Seth is going to hold me around the waist with one arm and hold on to the rope with the other so we don't get swept away. I know this is scary, but you need to trust me when I lift you up. Don't struggle, because losing my balance is the last thing I want to do."

Laura smiled back at him. "You sound like me telling Ben not to struggle."

"I do, don't I? Sorry. I just want us to be safe."

"I know, honey. But you're strong. I trust that you won't drop me."

Greg wasn't worried about him dropping her; it was Seth he was worried about.

"We'll be fine," she said in a sterner voice. "Let's get this over and done with so we can get off this goddamned road."

Greg bent and lifted Laura in his arms. He was thankful for the differences in their body shape in a way he'd never been before. His height and strength would make it easier to lift her small frame above the water than if they'd been closer in size. He could wade into the shallower water by himself, but in the deeper parts, he would need Seth's strength to hold them steadfast.

With Laura in his arms, he crouched and scooted down the bank and into the water. Even in the shallows, the water pulled on his limbs, threatening to take him with the flow. Greg took a deep breath, preparing himself. He'd seen what happened to Josh and so took the next few steps carefully, feeling with his feet for the drop he knew was coming.

The moment he stepped down the incline, Greg realized he wouldn't be able to go much further without Seth's help. The force of the water threatened to push him off balance and he dare not lift a foot until Seth reached them. Laura's arms were wrapped around his neck, her head buried in his shoulder as if hiding. He pulled her body as close to his as possible. The water already bubbled around her feet. If it got much deeper, he would struggle to keep her above. He heard Seth's large frame plunge into the water behind him.

"This is fucking ridiculous!" Seth said as the water pummeled against him. "I'm supposed to be on holiday."

Seth took hold of the rope, grateful to have something to hang onto. Greg and Laura were frozen nearly halfway across, Greg almost chest high in the water. The torchlights were all trained on the couple, leaving Seth in near-darkness. The water rushed and churned like black oil, swallowing him up to the waist. Something bumped against his calf, something cold with the texture of rotting flesh. It seemed deliberate, trying to wrap itself around his legs, like gelatinous fingers grabbing at him, trying to pull him down into the dark.

"For Christ's sake, Seth. Get a move on!"

Greg's voice snatched him back to reality and he continued to push forward, trying to forget that something hid beneath the surface. He clung to the rope with both hands, pulling himself through the water.

In less than a minute, he reached Greg and Laura. Greg's arms shook with the effort of holding Laura above the water and Seth saw he was weakening. Holding Laura might have been easy, but doing it whilst fighting the fierce push of the river drained him.

"Damn it, Seth!" the big man swore. "I need some help here. Don't just stand there staring at us."

Still holding onto the rope-hammock with one hand, Seth reached out and wrapped his other arm around Greg's waist. Immediately, he felt Greg's relief as the bigger man leaned some of his weight into Seth; both men now providing a more solid barrier against the ton of water trying to push them downstream.

"We need to move, Seth," Greg shouted above the roar of the river.

"I'm ready," said Seth. "Let's go."

As Seth stepped forward, something moved in the water beside him. Something with a thick, snake-like body and limbs tipped in pointed claws pushed its way like a crocodile beneath the water. Scales flashed on the surface for a fraction of a second before it disappeared into the dark.

"Oh fuck!"

Something bumped against his waist and he screamed in surprise.

"What? What's wrong?" yelled Greg.

"There..." Seth's voice broke. "There's something in the water."

"Don't fucking start, Seth! We need to get out of here."

The bank was only feet away, but Seth stood paralyzed with fear, his eyes fixed on the water around him, watching for the thing beneath. Around his body, the rushing water suddenly became still and the dark fluid began to shimmer like oil on a wet road. Seth stood with one arm raised above the water, his lower body motionless, as though frozen in a block of ice.

Claws cut like knives across the back of his ankle, slicing his Achilles tendon, and Seth screamed. White-hot pain seared up his leg and sheer panic blinded him. Seth plunged forward, shoving past Greg, knocking him off balance.

CHAPTER TWENTY–ONE
LOSS

Instantly, water engulfed Greg and he became submerged under the fast-flowing river. Water rushed into his lungs, thick and suffocating. The darkness was absolute and a muffled roar filled his ears. Caught in the river's grip, his body tumbled. Laura's arms slipped from his neck and the water dragged her away. He grappled; desperate to find her, but the ferocity of the water had torn her from his grasp.

His fingertips touched her skin for a fraction of a second and then she was gone.

Greg burst through the surface. He could barely breathe, the taste of silt and dirt clogging his mouth. His throat burned as he choked up the thick, dirty water. None of these things mattered; he only wanted to find Laura.

He tried to turn in every direction, fighting against the current, desperately trying to spot her in the darkness, praying she had somehow made it to the bank. In the depths of his heart, he knew there was only one direction she could have gone. He heard Seth, still screaming in pain, pulling himself out of the water and onto the other bank. Greg prepared himself to let go of the rope and allow the water to take him to his wife.

Taking as deep a breath as his burning lungs would allow, he let go of the rope and pushed himself after Laura.

A hand grabbed his ankle in an iron grip. Greg kicked back at whoever held him. He fought against the person stopping him from finding his wife, but their grip was too strong. Greg had weakened from the time he'd already spent in the water. His energy was dissipating and he wasn't going anywhere.

"You can't go after her, Greg," came Josh's voice. "You'll both drown."

Greg continued to struggle, desperation in his heart, images of Laura fighting for her life filling his head. She was being washed farther away with every passing second.

"You've got a son and he needs you."

The truth of Josh's words hit home and all the fight went out of him. He couldn't risk Ben losing both parents; not on a night like this. Laura wouldn't have wanted that.

As he stopped his struggles and allowed Josh to drag him to dry land, his heart tore in two. Never before had he experienced this type of pain. The thought that his wife, the mother of his child, his best friend, was gone, cut through his soul. How could he go on now? How could he spend the rest of his days knowing he had lost her?

The ball of pain seemed to grow in his chest, welling up inside his throat. It was a bright, burning lump that choked him; engulfing every synapse in his body. The pain was more intense than anything physical could ever be. It was the pain of lost hope, lost dreams, and a lost future. The pain of a lost life. Laura would never see her son grow up, would not be there to pick him up when he fell, to wipe his tears when he cried. She would never watch him marry or experience the joy of her grandchildren.

As Josh helped him out of the water, he saw Ben and pain hit him afresh. Greg didn't have to explain what had happened; the look in his son's eyes said he already knew.

The boy rushed at him, throwing his small arms around his waist and Greg bent and scooped him up in his arms. They clung together, united in their grief, and Greg's own tears came as his son's small body shook in his arms.

"I'm so sorry," he whispered to his son. "I'm so sorry I couldn't save her."

Seth lay on the ground, clutching at his leg and screaming, "My ankle! Something cut my fucking ankle!"

Deep inside Greg, rage began to build, swallowing his grief.

"I'm fucking hurt here! Someone do something."

Greg did something.

With care, he disengaged his son's arms from his neck and gently put him down. Then he turned and launched himself at Seth.

Leaping on him, Greg straddled the smaller man's chest, pinning his arms down with his knees.

"What the..."

Seth didn't get a chance to say anything else. A large, balled fist smashed him in the mouth, knocking the words out of him.

"You fucking bastard!" Greg punctuated his sentence with another punch. "You stupid, fucking bastard." Another punch landed. "I knew we couldn't trust you, you selfish piece of shit!"

Seth's head lolled backward, blood pouring from his mouth and nose.

Josh leapt onto Greg's back and Greg felt the other man trying to pull him off but, suddenly, he felt like he had the strength of two men.

Without considering his actions, Greg stopped punching Seth and wrapped his hands around his throat.

"Oh my God," Sasha cried from somewhere above.

She rushed over and grabbed Greg's hands, trying to pull them from Seth's neck. Seth's eyes bulged and he looked wildly at Sasha: a desperate plea for help.

"Stop it, Greg," she pleaded. "This isn't his fault. Something attacked him."

Greg ignored her, his fingers tightening, single-minded in his mission to destroy the man he thought responsible for his wife's death.

"Please Greg, don't do this," she begged him. "Not in front of your son. Don't let him have the memory of this on top of everything else."

Something about her words got through to him. He still had a child who needed him. What would Ben do with his mother gone and his father locked up in a Cambodian prison? Slowly Greg's fingers loosened from Seth's throat and he released his grip. Dazed, he climbed off Seth and turned to Ben, who watched him with a mixture of love and fear.

Sasha almost collapsed with relief. While the others going missing was horrific, watching someone murdered in front of her was simply too much to bear.

Seth gasped for breath, a harsh, whistling sound, his struggle heightened by the blood clogging his airways. Bright red bubbles burst from his mouth and nose, splattering his skin. His hands clawed at his throat, as though he could still feel Greg's hands and was fighting him off.

Greg sat on the ground a few feet away, his back to Seth. His knees pulled up to his chest, arms wrapped around his legs, head down. Though silent, his whole body shook with sobs. Ben went to him, his small face a tight mask of confusion, and wrapped his arms around his distraught father.

Seth was a mess. His Achilles tendon had been severed, his nose broken and the fanged tooth that had made his smile seem so strange was missing. Red abrasions branded his throat and he still fought for breath.

Sasha knelt over him, feeling useless and scared. They weren't going to make it. Whatever happened, this thing would get them one way or another. If it didn't kill them directly, it would make them turn on each other.

She realized Seth was trying to say something and she leaned in closer. Blood matted his dreadlocks, like short lengths of intestines hanging down his face. He seemed deflated and suddenly younger. The harsh, aggressive man banished; replaced with a frightened, damaged boy.

"I'm sorry," he said, his voice a harsh whisper. "I didn't think. I'm so sorry."

"Hush," she said, placing a hand on his shoulder. "It's not your fault."

Seth shook his head, tears welling in his eyes.

"I killed her," he said, a tear running down the side of his face and falling to the earth. "I didn't help them."

A tight ball constrict Sasha's throat and she fought back tears. How had this happened to them? They were all regular people supposed to be having the trip of their lives, and instead they'd been plunged into hell.

Josh crouched beside them.

He rubbed Sasha's back. "I need your help, Sasha. We still need to get the others across."

Sasha lifted her head and realized she had completely forgotten about Dawn, Steph and Chay. She turned to look at them, but they were mere shapes in the torchlight. Despite the lack of light, she could tell by their hunched figures they were scared.

"Is it safe?" she said. "After what happened?"

"Nowhere is safe right now," he replied. "But we need to keep moving and we can't leave them there."

Sasha realized they had no other choice. "At least let Dawn and Steph come across together. They can try to help each other if something happens. They won't be alone."

"So Chay comes last?"

"I know we can't risk losing him, but he's a hell of a lot better off than the girls. At least he's not going to get attacked half-way across."

Josh nodded. "You're right. Chay will be fine."

He yelled over the new plan and then picked up his end of the rope. Chay picked up the other end and, clinging to one another, Dawn and Steph made their way into the water. They hung onto the rope like the lifeline it was, scanning the surface of the water, watching for the thing that had hurt Seth, but nothing materialized. Slowly, they edged their way through the river, fighting the determination of the water to take them the same way it had taken Laura.

Together, they crossed to the other side. Josh and Sasha bent to haul them, wet and frightened, out of the water.

"You two okay?" Josh asked them.

They nodded in unison.

"Chay," he called across the river. "Tie the end around your waist and hold on with both hands."

The boy did as he was told and they pulled him through the water and up onto the bank.

Thank God we made it across, thought Sasha. But she caught sight of Greg and remembered, with a sinking feeling, they hadn't.

"Hey, guys!" exclaimed Dawn. The excitement in her voice grabbed everyone's attention. She pointed into the distance. "Look over there."

Everyone's eyes followed the line of Dawn's finger to the horizon. At first, no one understood what she meant and Sasha felt a stab of fear that Dawn was starting to see things like the others. Then she saw what Dawn was talking about and her breath caught in her chest.

Where previously there had only been darkness, a line now marked the earth from the sky.

Daybreak.

"Oh my God!" said Sasha. "It's getting light."

"If the sun's coming up, then this is over? Right?" said Steph. "Chay said the king has only one night to take revenge on the travelers and to find his son. If that night is over, we must be saved."

"It can't be that easy," Josh said, shaking his head. "The king isn't going to go to all this trouble only to let us go because he's run out of time."

"Why not?" Dawn interrupted. "Why the hell can't something go our way for once?"

"Yeah," agreed Steph. "Maybe he wasn't expecting us to challenge him."

From his huddled position on the ground, Greg laughed; a sound that was both forced and unnatural. He got to his feet, surveying the people left.

"How the hell do you think we challenged him?" he said to them. "Five people are dead—my *wife* is dead. We've no more challenged him than a mouse challenges a cat when the cat allows the mouse to run for entertainment." He paused, steadying his voice. "This thing isn't over yet."

As if in response to Greg's statement, the cruel laughter that was becoming horrifyingly familiar floated across to them. The laughter didn't seem to come from any one direction. Instead it came from the very ground they stood on, the water flowing past them, the air they breathed. The creature was part of the place they inhabited.

They could not escape.

Sasha realized something had changed in the laughter. The pitch and tone had lightened, the sound somehow sweeter, yet still with all the horror and menace of before. The direction also, had changed. It was close to them, so close the laughter could have come from one of their own mouths.

All eyes slowly moved to the small blond child standing amongst them.

The hideous laughter came from Ben's mouth like a terrible voiceover.

Dawn and Steph screamed and backed away from the child. Sasha's fingers wrapped around Josh's, squeezing hard.

"Ben?" said Greg, his voice full of fear. "Stop that Ben, it's not funny. You're scaring Daddy."

The laughter continued, evil laughter coming from the throat of an innocent child. Greg fell to his knees in front of his son and grasped him by his narrow shoulders.

"I mean it, Ben. You stop that right now or you will be in so much trouble."

Still the laughter came as Greg shook Ben roughly. "Damn you. Stop that right now. I won't put..."

Ben raised his head to look at his father and Greg jolted back, as though he'd been slapped. Ben's eyes, once as blue as cornflowers, were now as black as night.

"It has started," Chay said quietly.

Greg rounded on him. "What the hell are you talking about? What has started? What the fuck is the matter with my boy?"

"Jahard is taking his son."

"Ben is not his son! He is *my* son and I won't let him take him."

"He has already taken the minds of the adults, fed on each in turn. He has grown stronger with each mind he destroys, and now he is strong enough to start to take the child."

Greg's posture changed as the acceptance of Chay's words finally sank in. His shoulders fell and his chest seemed to cave in on itself.

"Is he going to kill him?" Greg asked, his voice not much more than a whisper.

Chay shook his head. "He will not kill the boy. He will continue his life *in* the boy."

Greg did not take his eyes off Ben. "I still don't know what you're talking about."

"Jahard will become the boy. He will be the child, but will have the mind, thoughts and power of a ten-thousand year old king."

"No, that can't be," Greg said in disbelief. "That's impossible."

"Daddy?"

256

Greg turned his attention to his son. The voice was now Ben's own, but darkness still filled his eyes. Ben seemed to see right through him, beyond him, like a blind man.

"Ben? Is that you?"

"Of course it's me, Daddy." The eyes were still dark and unseeing in the small, innocent face. "What do you mean? You're scaring me."

"Oh my God." Greg clasped his own face in his hands. "I can't handle this. I can't do this on my own."

Josh put a hand on Greg's shoulder. "We'll do whatever we can to help you. We won't let this happen without a fight."

"This can't be happening," he said, still in shock. "It's a dream or something; a terrible nightmare. I can't believe my wife is dead and my son is becoming..." His voice broke and he barked out a hysterical sob.

Josh squeezed his shoulder, a gesture of comfort that seemed pathetic given the circumstances.

Ben's strange black eyes still showed no emotion, but the rest of his face crumpled in hurt and confusion. A chill ran down Greg's spine. Hearing that laughter coming from his own son was enough to turn blood to ice, but now his eyes, the thing that opened onto a person's soul, had changed. The child no longer seemed to be Ben.

He no longer even seemed to be a child.

As these thoughts went through his head, Sasha crouched next to Ben and put her arms around him and pulled him close.

"For God's sake, Sasha!" said Josh. "Be careful!"

Sasha stared at him. "Don't be ridiculous, he's only a little boy."

"Yeah, but..." Josh started to protest.

"He's a boy who has just lost his mother and whose father is in no fit state to take care of him right now, so show some compassion."

Her words jarred Greg to the soul.

Ben cried into Sasha's chest and, now that he no longer faced them, he appeared to be like any other distraught five-year old. Yet Greg couldn't bring himself to go near the child as he stared at Sasha and his son. He felt torn between wanting to take Sasha's place and running away screaming.

He is still my son, Greg tried to tell himself. *He needs me now more than ever.*

But he couldn't throw off the feeling of malevolence from the boy's eyes. The idea that something else lurked behind them, speaking with his son's voice, living within his son's mind, was too much for him to take. He could not bring himself to go near him.

"Greg," said Sasha, her tone firm. "Whatever is going to happen hasn't happened to him yet. This is still Ben. He's still your son, whatever he looks like on the outside. He's just a little boy who is scared, and crying, and asking for his mummy. Since she isn't here, you need to grow some balls and take care of your child."

Greg glanced nervously at the boy.

"Imagine what Laura would say if she knew you were abandoning your son. It would break her heart."

At the mention of his wife, disgust and shame at his weakness filled him. His own fears were allowing him to fail at the only thing he had left in his life—being a father.

Greg dropped to his knees and pulled his son close. Just before Ben buried his head in his father's arms, Greg saw his eyes had changed back to blue.

Relief washed through him like a tonic and he held his son in a fierce hug, knowing he was squeezing too tightly, but unable to let go. If this creature wanted Ben, it would have to take him first. He wouldn't allow himself to be weak again.

The sense of relief did not last long. From behind them, a woman screamed and another joined in chorus.

Sasha spun around to see Dawn and Steph standing facing each other. Steph clutched her face and Dawn pointed at her, her mouth open wide in shock.

"What's wrong?" asked Sasha.

Dawn continued to point, her hand shaking. "She's bleeding."

Sasha ran up to Steph and pulled the other woman's hand away from her face. Blood smeared the bottom half of her face and Steph looked down at her bright red fingers.

"It's okay," said Josh. "It's just a nose bleed." Steph didn't seem to hear him; she just stared at her blood-drenched hand, her eyes full of fear.

Josh took hold of her hand, commanding her attention.

"It's okay Steph, it's just a nose bleed," he repeated. "Is it something you suffer from?"

Steph opened her mouth to answer, but instead of words, a strange gurgling noise erupted from her throat. A bubble of blood ballooned from her mouth and burst like a blister.

"Oh my God." Sasha covered her own mouth with her hand.

"What's happening to her?" said Dawn, panic clear in her voice.

A thin whine came from Steph and a rivulet of blood trickled from the side of her mouth and down across her chin. Her eyes darted from side to side, searching each of their faces for an answer, but finding none. Steph pulled her hand from Josh's grasp and wiped across her chin. She stared at the blood with fresh fear in her eyes.

"This isn't normal," said Josh. "This hasn't happened to her before."

"Of course this isn't normal!" Dawn shrieked, near to hysteria. "None of this is fucking normal!"

A roll of thunder rumbled across the sky and cracked right above them.

Dawn screamed and Sasha cowered, as though afraid the sky would cave in.

"We need to keep moving," said Josh. He turned to Chay. "How much further to the village? Do you think we can make it?"

A nervous twitch tweaked at the corner of Chay's right eye but he looked in the direction they were headed. "I do not think is far now. Maybe one more hour, maybe less."

"Will we reach the village before daylight?"

Chay's gaze flicked to Steph, still bleeding from the nose and mouth, and then down at Seth who was barely conscious.

"I do not know."

Greg must have read Chay's thoughts and jumped in. "If anyone can't keep up, I say we leave them."

"How can you say that?" said Sasha. "Especially after we all helped to carry your wife and son this far."

Greg stared at Seth in hatred. "He didn't help."

Greg had a point, but Sasha couldn't bring herself to abandon someone in the middle of nowhere. They'd already left enough people behind, even though it felt like they had little choice at the time. The idea of walking away while someone begged for help was unthinkable.

Steph now crouched on the ground, blood dripping between her fingers. She looked up at Sasha and opened her mouth as if trying to speak. Her eyes were beseeching, but her effort was rewarded only by a flow of flesh blood. Steph turned her attention to the ground and her bloodied finger began carving lines in the dirt.

"Josh, quick!" Sasha said. "Give me your torch, Steph is trying to tell us something."

Steph drew the words with careful precision. When she finished, she hung her head and waited for the others to read:

THE MONSTER IN MY HEAD MAKES ME BLEED

Dawn screamed again and turned away from the words, falling to her knees.

She covered her eyes with her hands and repeated, "No, no, no ..."

Steph raised her head and Sasha saw her eyes were wet and dark. She blinked and Sasha realized the tears running down her face were blood.

"Christ!" said Josh. "Is that thing doing this to her? How is that possible?"

"He is strong now," said Chay. "Now it is not only the mind he is able to control."

"So he can do anything to us?" said Sasha. "Anything he likes?"

"He must take the weakest first, but then yes. He can do anything he wishes."

CHAPTER TWENTY-TWO
WHEN THE PAST IS PRESENT

The group continued their walk along the dark road, but the helplessness of their situation hung like thick smoke in the air. Their struggle grew with every step. Josh and Chay dragged a half-conscious Seth along in the hammock and Sasha guided an almost blind and quickly weakening Steph.

Greg carried Ben, walking with fierce determination out in front. Dawn— hysterical and crying—was no good to anyone. Between tears, she muttered prayers and begged for her life from a creature she'd never seen.

Sasha had her arm around Steph's waist, but, because of the words Steph had written in the dirt, Sasha expected her to go crazy like the others. She kept reminding herself of the speech she'd given Greg about the same person still being on the inside, no matter what they looked like. Though the sky gradually grew lighter, it was still dark enough to hide the horror of Steph's face and for this, Sasha was grateful. The girl grew weaker by the minute; her will to live ebbing along with the blood. She couldn't imagine what was going on in Steph's head, how frightened she must be. Steph could no longer speak or see. Her contact with the outside world was slowly being shut off.

I've walked this road before.

The strange thought leaped into Sasha's head as if somebody had spoken the words in her ear.

She frowned at her own memory, but struggled to shake off the feeling that she'd been here before.

The sensation grew stronger, almost as though she were being transported back in time. An impression of carrying something came to mind and she almost sensed the weight of baskets pressing down on her head and shoulders, and the texture of the reeds she used to weave them molded against her skin.

Sasha shook her head, trying to dispel the notion. The stress and exhaustion must be taking its toll. Yet another memory rose in her head and she suddenly found herself back in a market place, a place she knew and loved. The charred scent of roasting meat assaulted her nostrils and people shouted out their wares in a foreign language she somehow understood.

Sasha stopped dead, the memory receding like a dream.

"Something's not right," she whispered. A jolt of panic spiked through her body.

Josh must have noticed Sasha had stopped and called back to her, "Are you okay?"

Sasha nodded. She must just be tired and her overactive imagination was going haywire. She tightened her grip around Steph's waist and began to move, but

Steph slumped forward. Sasha managed to catch her before she fell on her face.

"I need some help here," Sasha shouted to the others.

Josh and Chay ran back and helped her to gently lower Steph to the ground. Josh placed two fingers against the inside of Steph's wrist.

"Her pulse is faint and erratic," he told the others.

Sasha glanced down. Dark smears of blood marked the inside of Steph's thighs. She was hemorrhaging from every orifice.

"Oh, God," said Dawn. "She's going to die, isn't she? We're all going to die."

Josh didn't argue with her. "I don't think she'll last much longer."

"Should we stop for a while?" Sasha asked.

Josh glanced at the sky. "I don't think we've got a while. I think we might have to leave her."

"We can't just leave her here," Sasha said in dismay. "She'll die alone."

"We can't carry her as well, Sasha. She isn't going to make it."

"She'll die alone," she repeated and a tear ran down the side of her face. The idea of leaving Steph in the middle of the road, barely conscious, blind and unable even to scream was unforgivable. Sasha didn't know how aware Steph was of what was happening to her, but if she was even remotely conscious, yet unable to reach out...

She would be like the victim of a too early burial, with her own body as the coffin. She would be completely defenseless against the creature that used to be a king. Even if the thing had already done what it needed to claim her life, what other unspeakable horrors might the ancient king put her through if they abandoned her?

Steph's breath rattled up through the thick blood in her lungs and snatched the tiny amount of oxygen needed to keep her body alive. Sasha had no way of knowing if she could hear or understand the decisions being made around her. Sasha took hold of her hand and squeezed, hoping for a squeeze in return, something to show she was still with them enough to make it.

Steph's fingers remained limp.

Josh got to his feet. "I know this is hard, simply leaving her, but we need to think about what's most important: getting the people who are still alive to safety."

No one answered him. No one wanted to be the one who called time on Steph's life.

Dawn sat on the ground a little way off, crying into her hands. Josh bent and gently pulled her to her feet. She clung to him as if he was the last person alive. Greg, Ben and Chay had already started to move up the road and Josh began to walk after them.

Sasha stayed crouched next to Steph, her back to the others, blocking their view. What she was about to do broke her heart. She struggled to get her head around her intentions, but the other option was even worse. She couldn't let Steph suffer any more than she already had.

Sasha bent and stroked Steph's short, pink hair back from her face. Somewhere deep inside, she felt stronger than she had in years. The strong part of her took over, knowing she was acting out of selflessness; her actions stemmed from something she would have done before...

Again, the strange idea—a distant memory of another life—filled her, but she pushed it away, concentrating on what was important.

Sasha placed her hand over Steph's mouth, pinching her nostrils closed with her thumb and forefinger.

Sasha braced herself and held her breath. She prepared herself for a struggle, for Steph to fight back, but Steph might already have been dead. Tears of horror and grief poured down Sasha's cheeks and she turned her face away, squeezing her eyes shut, trying to block out what was happening.

Within a minute, Steph's chest fell still.

"Sasha?" Josh's voice traveled along the road.

Sasha released her hold on Steph's face and turned to them.

"It's okay," she said, her voice choked. "She's gone now."

Sasha turned back to Steph. "Rest in peace."

She stood, wiping Steph's blood from her hand onto her shorts, and walked toward the others.

Josh looked at her, concerned. "Are you all right? You seem strange."

"Could anyone experience this and not be different?"

"As long as you're all right."

Another memory, a vision, flashed in her head like pictures on a movie screen. Three women, each with dark hair and eyes, stood beside a river, washing clothes. They seemed to sense her presence and lifted their faces to Sasha. They welcomed her with wide smiles and waves. Affection toward these women swept over her. She knew everything about them, and they about her, and she accepted this without question.

"Sasha?"

The touch of Josh's hand on her arm brought her back to reality, but her name seemed somehow strange and foreign. Even Josh's face had faded to unfamiliarity and in her mind another man, a man with smooth, brown skin and deep, black eyes, replaced him.

"Something is happening to me, Josh," she said, a stab of fear puncturing her heart. "I don't feel right."

Josh looked into her eyes, studying her. "Are you sick?"

"No," she gave a small, frightened laugh. "In fact, I feel stronger than I have all night. I can't explain it. I'm seeing things..."

"Like hallucinations?" he interrupted.

"No. Seeing things in my head, remembering things I've never experienced." Her heart pounded and her words caught in her throat. "I feel... I feel like I am forgetting who I am."

Josh stared at her as if she was crazy, concern in his eyes.

Dawn interrupted them. "Ben's changing again."

All attention turned to the child.

Greg stood beside him, distressed. "His eyes are back to black."

Everyone stared at the child, watching him expectantly. They were waiting for the laughter to start again, or for the boy to say, or do, something strange. They didn't have to wait long.

"They will both be mine..."

The voice grated and rasped as it contorted vocal chords into its own.

Only the voice did not come from Ben; but Dawn.

She stood frozen in one spot, every muscle in her body rigid with tension, straining from the effort of having him inside her. She stared at Ben with a strange affection. Though Dawn's eyes had not completely changed like

Ben's, they still weren't her own. Something hid behind her pupils, a shadow that passed across them like a cloud across the moon.

Sasha didn't just see a shadow but something in those eyes she recognized. A frozen spear of fear lodged in her heart. He was there. She would never forget the eyes of the man who had stolen her life.

Jahard.

Even the thought of his name made her flesh crawl. She desperately wanted to turn and run, but every muscle in her body seemed to have been cut, leaving her impotent and helpless.

Dawn's eyes moved from the boy to Sasha. As soon as Dawn's gaze landed on her, something shifted inside Sasha's body, inside her mind. The images of smiling, welcoming faces were swallowed by other, darker memories; a baby screamed, crying for her, and the thought filled her with repulsion. She remembered a night of intense and excruciating pain; when she'd thought her body was being torn apart and she only wanted the gentle touch of her mother to ease her suffering. She remembered rough hands on her skin, lips hard against her mouth, the coarse hair of his beard against her face. She remembered the horror of his fingers pushing up inside her, the shame of her body reacting, even as her mind screamed out in revulsion. She remembered him forcing himself inside her, his large body smothering her, his breath panting against her ear, liquor on his breath and the roar of satisfaction as he came.

Deep inside, such despair and loneliness overwhelmed her; she thought she might go mad. It was a loneliness that ran like a deep ravine within her soul, fracturing her into pieces. She wanted to cry out, to plead for help, to tell everyone she was screaming inside, but she couldn't connect with her mouth. She remained frozen under the stare of the man she had thought she escaped forever.

Dawn lifted her hand and placed her palm against Sasha's cheek.

"Ah, my Arana," she said in that terrible, rasping voice. "I know you are in there."

"No!" Josh leaped forward and knocked Dawn's hand away from Sasha's face. For a moment both of the girls were themselves, but it did not last for long.

Dawn opened her mouth and the laughter came again—cruel and mocking.

"The rest of you will die. Ten minds to make mine whole," she said. "But the woman and the boy belong to me."

"I don't know who the hell you think you are," said Greg, trembling with fear and fury, "But you're not going anywhere near my son."

Dawn laughed. "You know who I am. And soon the whole world will know. Your son will be the most powerful man in the country, with strengths and knowledge no other will surpass."

"He's just a child! You can't expect him to fend for himself. Who will look after him?"

"The child will know nothing about it—his soul will be no match for mine. It is I, who will be him. His body is merely a vessel, a way for my becoming part of this world again. Even if his body is still alive, his soul will be dead." The creature that had once been Dawn turned back to Sasha. "Do not despair. His body will be well looked after. I have brought back the woman who stole my son from me so she can complete the job she started."

Dawn grasped Sasha's face, her thumb and her forefinger digging painfully into her cheeks. "And this time she will have no way of escaping. Her soul will belong to me. She will be my mother, my wife, my slave. I will put her through a living hell until she repays what she has done."

Dawn let go of Sasha and looked around the group. "But for now," she said, "I must take three lives before the sun rises and I am reborn."

Then Dawn screamed—a scream that pierced their souls. Above them, a crash of thunder joined her cry.

Her eyes stretched wide and her mouth rounded in an 'O' of shock. Her bare arms raised out in front of her and she stared as though she expected them to attack her.

Starting at her shoulders and running down to her fingertips, a ripple of something dark undulated beneath her skin, like caterpillars trapped between muscle and membrane. They moved slowly but with deliberation.

Dawn screamed.

The things reached the back of Dawn's hands and each one split into five, the smaller versions moving down the back of her fingers, the skin rippling.

The group watched in horror as the things started to force their way out of the ends of her fingers. The skin beneath her nails stretched as though someone forced pegs from inside of her. With an audible 'pop,' the things pierced Dawn's skin and black claws emerged, like young reptiles clawing their way out of their eggs, facing their new world.

"Help me," she pleaded in a thin whine.

Josh started forward, though by the expression on his face, he seemed unsure of what he planned to do.

Dawn's head whipped around, her eyes focused in hatred. "You will not touch her!" she snarled in a voice not her own.

Lightning forked through the sky.

Dawn lifted her head and howled.

The skin of her chest and legs bulged and wavered, hiding a secret desperate to get out. Her breath left her body in short, frantic pants and she held her clawed hands above the undulating skin; part of her desperate to use her new appendages to rip out whatever was plaguing her. Another side of her held back, seeming to understand she would not be able to stop what she started and would tear herself to shreds. She screamed again as pain ripped through her, growing with the swollen flesh, and then dissipating as whatever lived beneath her skin sank back in and moved to another area of her body, only to rise again.

The thing fought its way out of Dawn's body, taking her humanity with it. Some part of her mind had shifted, unable to comprehend what was happening to her. Her pain and the terror swiftly destroyed any moments of insight and she finally raised her hands and tore at herself. The claws pierced her skin, pulling, stretching and ripping, exposing the flesh.

She shrieked in agony and frustration. From each cut, darkness flowed from her body, ebbing around her. At first, it only enveloped her chest, but quickly swelled, submerging her arms and legs. Like a person drowning, Dawn tried to raise her head above the black fluid, but it climbed, sending tendrils of its self crawling up her face.

Her mouth opened wide in another scream, but the darkness flowed between her lips, choking the sound in her throat. Wisps, like thick acrid smoke, wound up each nostril, blocking her last breath. Like an inkblot, the black seeped across each of her eyeballs, drowning the white and the last hints of sanity.

"Jesus Christ!" Josh said to no one in particular. Of all the terrible things he had seen so far that night, this was truly the worst.

A black balloon of tar surrounded Dawn.

The mass rippled around her like a spider weaving a cocoon of silk around its prey. Dawn's face froze in horror and she made no sound as she continued to rip at herself. More and more of the black entity engulfed her, until Josh struggled to make out the person beneath the heaving, shifting mass.

Greg hid Ben's face against his legs and instinctively Josh reached out to Sasha. He touched her hand, but she pulled away. There was no hint of recognition in her eyes. She looked at him as though he were a stranger.

Josh stared at her in hurt and confusion. She stared back but there was something haunted about her eyes; like those of a drug addict or someone who'd been abused as a child—dark and pained. The Sasha he knew, even when hurt or scared, still had a light about her. The woman staring back at him now was not just terrified or angry, she was broken.

Josh managed to tear his gaze away, a small part of him frightened if he looked into those eyes for too long, they would draw him down into the wretched world she inhabited.

He turned his attention back to Dawn. With relief, he saw the black fog had disappeared. Dawn slumped on her side on the ground, her long blonde hair covering her face—a tangled mass of blood and dirt. Gaping wounds tipped each finger, and the shorts and tank top she wore were in tatters. Crisscrossed over her body, like the marks of a grill on a well-cooked steak, were cuts deep enough to severe skin, muscle and flesh. If it wasn't for the amount of blood flooding each wound, he would have been able to see the white glint of bone peeping at him. The metallic scent of blood filled the humid air, but beneath that lay the stench of feces and death.

"I can't handle this!" Josh said to Sasha, forgetting she was no longer the woman he knew. He remembered and his gut wrenched with loss; his confidant was gone.

He looked around at those left, his heart sinking further. Seth was barely conscious. His eyelids flickered and he moaned in pain, but seemed unable to talk or walk. Josh wondered if he even was aware if what was happening around him.

He couldn't help but think Seth not knowing was partly a blessing; Josh didn't think he would last for much longer.

Greg stared at Josh in fear.

"He's going to take my son," he said, his voice tiny and fragile for a man of his size. "The bastard took my wife and now he's going to take my son."

He'll take you first, Josh thought, but didn't say. *But I'm probably next.*

He didn't want to die like this, stuck out in the middle of goddamn nowhere, the bodies of two other travelers—people he had come to know and like—lying in the dirt only meters from each other. He didn't want this poor man to die knowing his son's body was to be used by some murderous king from centuries ago and he was frightened for Sasha's soul; unsure of what would happen to her once Jahard had his way.

Then he realized he had forgotten someone; Chay.

Josh scanned around for the boy, knowing he couldn't have gone far. If it had still been the middle of the night, Josh would have missed him, but in the growing light, he was easy to spot. Chay sat on the side of the road about thirty feet away, his back to the diminishing group and his head in his hands.

I won't let this happen!

With sudden, fierce determination, Josh sprinted over to the boy and dragged him to his feet. Chay must have only weighed fifty kilos and Josh lifted him with ease. Chay's body went limp and Josh tossed him into the center of the road. Emotions bubbled inside of him: anger for the deaths, fear for his own life, hatred at the people responsible and he believed he would kill the boy. He would kill the boy with his own bare hands; rip him to shreds for doing this to innocent people.

But there was no fight in the child, only sadness.

Chay lay in the fetal position, trembling. Tears streamed from his eyes and his lower lip quivered. He looked up at Josh with big, wet eyes. No malice resided in their depths.

"I did not know," Chay said, his voice hitching. "I am so sorry, but I did not know." He turned his face to the ground. "Kill me if you wish. I deserve to die."

Thunder growled above and Josh crouched next to the boy. He put a hand on his shoulder and Chay jerked away, certain the touch would be a blow.

Josh didn't intend on hurting him; his anger toward the boy had gone. Chay was only a child dragged into something he didn't understand. The boy's father had been the one at fault. Chay had lost someone too. However much of a scumbag he'd been, Makara had still been the boy's flesh and blood.

Instead, Josh directed his anger toward the 'man' doing this to them; the man who lived ten thousand years ago, but was now getting a second chance to complete his lineage.

A sudden thought occurred to Josh.

"Why would they do this?" he asked, partly to himself and partly to Chay. "Why would the gods allow Jahard to kill thousands of people and then give him a second chance? It doesn't make sense."

Chay lifted his head, his eyebrows arched in surprise. "They did not curse Jahard because he killed the travelers. They cursed him because he drove Arana to kill herself. To kill is part of human nature, part of animal nature. Those species that have lived through centuries all kill to survive. But to kill yourself, to murder your child, is an abomination against the gods. Jahard has been in hell for ten thousand years and that was the punishment for driving Arana to kill herself. He is allowed a second chance because she took his child with her."

Chapter Twenty-Three
Someone Else

Sasha sensed someone inside her, sharing her mind. The other woman tried to push her out, as though only a finite amount of space existed inside her head. The terrible things the woman had experienced engulfed Sasha's own feelings, thoughts and memories; taking the place of her own:

A distant memory of her as little more than a baby and being somewhere hot, the sun beating down on top of her head, warming her back. The clear, slightly too-blue water of an outdoor swimming pool, the cool liquid surrounding her like fluid in the womb, her body supported by the safe and gentle hands of her grandmother; hands that, in her more recent memories, were covered in skin as delicate and fragile as silk.

Gone.

Her fifth birthday and her mother's smiling face as she presented a cake in the shape of a butterfly, the wings covered in brightly colored icing; the reds and yellows swirling together like a sunset on an autumn day. How

276

absurdly pleased she'd been to blow out the candles and make her wish with everybody watching; such pride in her clever mother and thinking she'd gotten the best birthday cake ever.

Gone.

Eleven years old, Christmas time and her dad was sick with appendicitis. She'd spent Christmas day sitting anxiously in the hospital, her nostrils assaulted with sickness and bleach. She sat watching people rush past, tension taut in the air, while everyone tried to force Christmas cheer in a place that epitomized everything but.

Gone.

The memory of Josh's arms, his dark, unruly hair, green eyes and the horror of their journey...

With fierce determination, she hung onto this memory. She needed to remember everything that had happened.

If she didn't, she would never survive.

One by one, the mind of another claimed her memories. On one level, Sasha was still aware of her surroundings. She knew something terrible was happening, but not on a level within reach. She might have been a coma victim, with her mind still alert, aware of people speaking around her, but unable to move or talk back. Someone else controlled her body and Sasha sensed her presence. The other woman's thoughts and feelings seemed to be her own.

They were anguish.

The torment she'd suffered for thousands of years, emotions that had never dissipated. She felt the violation of what she'd experienced, guilt for deserting her own family, for murdering her own child and failure at giving up on herself.

Yet, Sasha sensed something else deep inside all of the pain and loneliness and madness. Like a tiny nugget of gold in the churned mud at the bottom of a river, it was lost in the depths, waiting to be rediscovered. It was the woman who'd visited her as she walked the road; the strong woman with the wide smile and the family who loved and depended on her. Somewhere deep beneath everything, she still existed. If Sasha made contact with that part of the woman, she might be able to break the strange bonds holding her prisoner deep inside her own body.

She was still Sasha, but now diminished, her past ripped away. She only existed in that moment, yet she wanted to live. A future was out there for her and she would grab it with both hands and never take life for granted again. She would make the most of every day and not allow herself to put her life on hold. Why these thoughts seemed so important, she didn't know, but they gave her an energy and determination she desperately needed in order to keep hold of who she was.

The thoughts gave her hope.

'*I know you are there,*' Sasha said, speaking to the woman who now seemed to be controlling her body. '*Can you hear me? Do you know I'm here?*"

Sasha focused every part of her consciousness on trying to sense whether the woman had heard her.

There was no change in the spirit encasing her, nothing to make Sasha believe she'd been heard. The other woman's thoughts and emotions bound her like a cloth around a mummified body, smothering Sasha from the outside world. They prevented her from reaching out to the people, or person... *there was really only one person she needed...* who could help her.

Like a form of meditation, Sasha tried to hold her own thoughts still and concentrate on the other woman. She tried to pinpoint something she could use to connect to her, so she could find a way out of this.

The other woman seemed to live in a churning mass of emotion and Sasha couldn't distinguish a single, clear thought. It was all just fragments of memory, each running into the other, layering one on top of another; single words, repeated over and over again:

The baby the baby the baby the baby... parasite... sucking... its hurts so much... why did they not... the baby the baby... come...

Beneath all of the guilt and pain, one underlying emotion controlled the rest.

'You're scared of him aren't you?' Sasha called out. *'You're scared of this King...'*

Sasha thought for a moment, desperately trying to grab the name from her rapidly receding memory.

'Jahard!' she declared.

The moment his name filled her head, the woman's soul squeezed in on her own, crushing her in a vice-like trap. Panic wrapped its steel bands around her. Like air in a balloon pulled deep underwater, she felt as though she were compressed inside of herself and didn't know if she would explode or simply vanish.

Determined not to allow panic to take over and wash away what was left of her, Sasha fought, trying to break free. The amount of pressure reached a plateau and then its grip gradually released.

As her heart rate slowed and the adrenaline began to dissipate, Sasha found the experience didn't leave her frightened of what the woman could do to her, but instead triumphant. She had reached her and however deep Sasha was buried, she had communicated. Sasha became more and more certain she knew the other woman's identity.

'Arana?' Sasha called out the name pensively; suddenly scared she might be wrong. She felt a strange quiver around her, a sign of recognition, and she tried again.

'Arana? If that is you, please don't be afraid. I can't hurt you.'

The dark madness moved like a cloak, trying to smother the person beneath, but despite this, Sasha heard someone.

"What's happening to me?' The tiny voice sounded far away, as if from the end of a tunnel. 'I'm frightened.'

High-pitched, hitching sobs, like a child crying, filtered through to Sasha. The cries broke Sasha's heart. Whatever this woman had become was because of the same terrifying creature that had been tormenting them since nightfall. Her memories were patchy, but she remembered hateful blood-red eyes staring at her and the pain of the people left behind. If she survived this, Sasha didn't think these things would ever leave her.

'Don't be frightened,' Sasha called to her. 'I want to help you.'

'I'm so tired.' The voice was soft, like the whisper of wind through the branches of a tree.

'I know you are, but I need you to stay awake for awhile, then you can rest'.

'No, I don't want to,' the voice came back stubborn, sulky. 'I'm scared.'

Sasha couldn't shake the feeling she was talking to the child the woman had once been; that somehow what Jahard had done to her had reverted her back to childhood and taken away everything that made her a strong woman. The tiny piece of the woman who survived the torment Jahard put her through and the horror of killing her own baby was the child she'd been before she even knew men like Jahard existed. A time of innocence. Arana had lost all of her defenses and crawled back to a time where she no longer had to take responsibility for her life.

This was not the person to take on Jahard, but Sasha still believed the strong, grown woman existed in here somewhere. Yet time was running out.

How the hell would she find her again?

"So, it's because Arana killed herself that all of this is happening," said Josh in disbelief. "Not because Jahard killed all of those people?"

"It is still because of Jahard," Chay insisted. "If he had not driven Arana to take her own life, the gods would not have cursed him."

"Jesus," Josh grasped his hair in a fist. "Whoever these gods are, they don't have much sense of justice."

Chay shrugged. "No one say the gods are fair."

Josh glanced at the sky. It was no longer black, but instead deep cobalt blue. Though a dark bank of cloud still hung over them, it seemed to be growing lighter by the minute.

Josh waited with his heart in his throat, his whole body poised, certain he would be next. This creature was running out of time. If he still needed to take the lives of those left in order to take Ben's body as his own, he didn't have long. Seth balanced on the brink of life and death—the creature´s job apparently already done. Josh suspected Greg would be the hardest for Jahard to take, the love for his son making him more of a challenge than Josh would ever be.

Josh could barely bring himself to look at Sasha. She appeared to be almost catatonic, standing with her mouth slack, her arms hanging by her side. Her dark eyes were scared and haunted, but did not seem to see him. She gazed into the distance as if peering into a place that no longer existed. Josh had tried shaking her, but he'd gained no response and it pained him to do anything more violent to try to bring her back.

Despair slowly weaved its cold fingers around his heart and, for the first time that night, tears threatened. He wiped at one eye and turned his head from Chay. That he was even concerned about crying in front of the boy was ridiculous. What did it matter now? What did any of it matter?

But people still lived.

Greg grabbed him by the arm, hard enough to hurt.

"We need to do something, for fuck's sake!

Josh turned and they locked eyes. Joshes emotions reflected directly in the eyes of the bigger man and he was immediately ashamed at his own self pity. He couldn't imagine what it must be like to not only be terrified for your own life, but also lose your wife and watch something change your son.

"It's hurting him," Greg said, his eyes pleading.

The boy lay on the ground, small and defenseless. His fine, blond hair was still wet and matted to his head. His face screwed up in pain, his small mouth tight and thin. His fists clenched and unclenched. Somewhere, he had lost one of his blue flip-flops and his naked foot twitched and kicked out, as a dog kicks in his sleep.

Both men crouched in the dirt beside him and Greg stroked his son's matted hair. The boy's eyes opened to reveal only darkness. The twitching stopped. He lay still and looked up at his father.

"I want Mummy," he said, a fat tear rolling down his cheek. "Where's my mummy?"

Though the eyes did not appear human, to ignore pleas of a frightened child was impossible.

Then, like a wild animal, Ben snarled. His lips drew back, revealing small, white teeth and he snapped at his father's hand, just missing Greg's fingers. Greg yelled in shock and pulled away, confusion and distrust distorting his features.

Ben laughed; the laughter of the mad.

Thunder cracked directly overhead and, almost immediately, lightning cut the sky in two. The first drops of rain hit the top of Josh's head hard, like fingers drumming the top of his skull. A downpour threatened, but the weather was the least of their worries.

Ben was crying again, his small fists balled up over his eyes, sobbing in that uninhibited way only small children do. Once more, Josh found himself wishing for Sasha's presence. Despite the people around him, Josh had never felt so alone in his life.

"Josh?"

Greg's voice came out as little more than a whisper, but something underlay his tone that filled Josh with fear.

"It's happening," he said, his face white and eyes wide in terror. "Something is moving inside my head, I can feel it."

He raised his hands to his head, his fingers pressing as if expecting to feel something pushing back out at him.

"It's like he's touching my brain... Oh God, it hurts!" Greg roared in pain, anger and frustration.

His face contorted in agony; his fingers pressed against his temples. His knuckles whitened with strain and his hands shook. Like a puppet whose strings had been cut, the big man fell to his knees.

He looked up at Josh, his eyes imploring. "I can't let him see this," he said. "I can't let Ben watch him do this to me." He reached out in desperation, gripping Josh's forearm, his fingers digging into Josh's skin, and begged:

"Please... Don't let him take my son."

She floated inside herself like a fetus inside a womb. Like the unborn, she heard noises from the outside: a jumble of words, the crying of a child, the muffled roar of thunder. But she couldn't process them or understand what they meant. Her past had completely disappeared. Her memories now belonged to a different time, a different world; one where people did not rely on machines to transport them, supermarkets to buy food, and computers and cell phones to communicate with other people. Life was about producing enough food to feed your family and working to put a roof over their heads. It was a hard time, but a happy time.

Sasha realized these memories, but she knew Arana did not. Arana held them too deep inside, as though scared to remember who she was. The person Arana had become was the person Jahard created—the woman who had taken her life and the life of her newborn child.

Had Arana been like this before she died, or had death driven her insane? Sasha didn't know, but the only memory Arana allowed her to keep was the memory of what happened tonight. Had Arana done so consciously—stuffing Sasha so deep inside of herself in order to hide Sasha's existence from Jahard? Maybe, unconsciously, Arana *wanted* Sasha's help. She knew she couldn't defeat him alone, so she kept Sasha deep inside of herself to give her the strength to stand up to him.

Arana's memories felt real to Sasha—as though they were her own—so maybe she could also control them? Maybe she could take Arana back to her past, before Jahard destroyed her, to a time when she was herself? Whatever control Jahard held over her *must* be broken. If Arana stood up to him—used the hate she harbored toward him, without being scared of him—then perhaps they stood a chance.

Arana's personality had been broken into three: the child she'd once been, the shell of a person Jahard created, and the woman she had once been... and needed to be again.

An idea began to form in Sasha's mind. Could she go into Arana's past and bring the strong Arana back with her? The idea seemed crazy, but surely no crazier than everything else that happened tonight.

The thick, black fog of the broken Arana still hovered around her. The child Arana cried softly in the darkness.

By going into Arana's past, she would need to churn up old emotions. To do so without scaring the child Arana further would be difficult.

Sasha had no idea if her plan would work and she didn't want to lose the only contact she had with another human being. But, she had to try. There were no other options.

She closed her eyes and took a deep breath. She plunged into Arana's past, pushing herself deeper and deeper. Terrible memories swamped her, but this time it was different. Though she witnessed the memories as if they were her own, with complete clarity and understanding, she now understood the memories were not hers, but Arana's.

Sasha saw a woman standing on a balcony. Stars dotted the dark sky and the cold puckered her skin. Clutched to the woman's chest was a tiny baby, her baby; crying with a hunger that would never be satisfied.

She wanted to reach out to her, wanted to stop her, but she wanted the impossible. The events she watched had already happened; she didn't have the power to change them. She sensed the anguish and confusion Arana was going through. Arana had no control over her actions. She couldn't see any other choice. In her eyes, Jahard was evil. She didn't want the child to grow up to be another version of him.

Though watching from a distance, Sasha felt everything Arana did. Like a dream she once had where she witnessed herself as a separate person, watching her own actions, Arana was her, but not her. Though happening to someone else, all the thoughts and emotions were as clear as her own.

She needed to push further into Arana's past.

With a mental thrust, she moved back in her mind. Each of Arana's memories moved *through* her, so she relived each of them, if only for a moment.

Plunged into the excruciating pain and fear of childbirth, she understood how shell-shocked Arana had been once it was over; the feeling a piece of her had been torn away. She experienced the horror of rape, not just once, but over and over; each time by a man who had made her a prisoner. Shame and guilt that she'd not fought against him swept over her, the humiliation of having a man do anything he wanted to her. Sasha learned Arana allowed Jahard to take her in order to protect her family. Jahard had threatened the lives of the people she loved. He'd used them to make Arana his slave.

Still she needed to get past this. She had to reach the person Arana was before all of this happened to her.

'Please, help me,' Sasha begged. 'I need to find you.'

She continued to move back. The soles of her feet ached from walking hundreds of miles, her arms and shoulders always had a burden to carry. Yet the aches and pains were good; a feeling of satisfaction and contentment.

Suddenly, a strange, sucking sensation pulled against her limbs and her ears popped.

She was in a village.

Sasha looked around in amazement. Fresh, clean air filled her nostrils, purer than she had ever smelled before. Bread cooking only served to sweeten the air. A warm sunlight blessed her skin and above her stretched a brilliant blue sky. Soft dirt crushed underfoot and cattle grazed nearby, their bony spines jutting from under their skin.

In front of Sasha a dozen small, round huts built from sticks, woven reeds and mud were arranged around a larger building, possibly a communal dwelling. Moss grew up the walls of the huts, so there seemed to be little distinction between the homes and the ground they'd been built on.

Calm surrounded the place, as though the people who inhabited the village lived in peace with their surroundings.

Sasha was not alone. Two boys and a girl, all with coffee-colored skin and shiny dark hair, played outside of the bigger hut. They practiced a game with a stick and a ball made of the same kind of reeds that bound the walls of the houses. Their laughter and squeals were happy sounds, and Sasha's sudden appearance hadn't appeared to interrupt their fun.

Scrawny chickens scratched in the dirt around them and as one got too close, the boy poked at the bird with the stick. The action reminded Sasha of Ben doing exactly the same thing earlier at the restaurant. The chicken squawked and flapped with meager wings, sending dust and dirt flying.

Sasha stood among them like a ghost. Although the ground was firm beneath her feet and the sun hot on her skin; the children showed no sign of acknowledging her presence.

'Arana?' Sasha called out with her mind; instinctively knowing her voice would not be heard in this world.

Movement from one of the huts caught Sasha's attention. From the doorway climbed a woman with long, dark hair. Her height caused her to bend to get through the gap. As she did so, her hair fell over her face. Sasha's heart caught in her throat, but then, as the woman straightened, her heart sank.

The woman was not Arana. Though the same color, this woman's eyes were rounder, her mouth thinner, her cheekbones not as high. Despite these differences, there was no questioning the resemblance.

Sasha stared at Arana's sister.

Sasha took a step toward her and hesitated. Would the other woman be able to see her? What would she say to her if she did?

The woman turned and spoke to the children. They stopped their game to listen. The boy said something in response and the indignant expression on his face told Sasha more than the words she could not hear. The woman put her hands on her hips, flung her head back and roared in laughter. Sasha couldn't help the smile that automatically came to her lips; the woman's laughter was infectious.

Arana's sister caught sight of Sasha out of the corner of her eye and turned toward her; no unease in her face, only curiosity.

She smiled, revealing straight white teeth, and nodded to the hut she had just emerged from, beckoning Sasha. Sasha looked around in case the woman nodded at someone stood behind her, but she was alone.

Arana's sister turned and walked back inside the hut. Sasha had no choice but to follow.

Sasha stepped inside the cool, dark depths of the hut. Unable to make out the people inside, she blinked a couple of times, waiting for her eyes to adjust to the gloom.

Three women, each of them similar in appearance, sat cross-legged on the ground. The ground underfoot had been covered in a thick moss and a coarse cloth. The woman from outside patted the cloth, motioning for Sasha to sit.

'Where is Arana?' Sasha asked, still standing. 'I need to see Arana.'

The woman smiled. 'You will. Arana will be here soon. She needs to see you too.'

Her voice was like chocolate; smooth, rich and luxuriant.

'*You're her sisters, aren't you?*' Sasha asked, already knowing the answer.

'*I am Sophea,*' the woman said. She touched the arm of the woman to her left. '*This is Mau.*' Repeating her action, she touched the woman to her right, '*And this is Vanna.*'

Sasha smiled at them, but felt awkward, as if she'd walked in on a private party. '*My name is Sasha.*'

'*We know who you are.*' Sophea said. It was a phrase that could have sounded threatening, but in her tone, was welcoming.

Sasha squatted on the ground and lowered herself further to sit cross-legged like the others. The four of them now sat in a circle with Sophea and Sasha opposite each other, and Mau and Vanna on either side.

'*She needs our help,*' Sophea said. '*She needs your help too.*'

'*I know. That's why I'm here,*' Sasha said, at the same time wondering where the hell 'here' actually was. '*Arana's in trouble and so am I.*'

Sasha remembered the things she had experienced—the pain, the humiliation, the anger. A shiver wracked her body.

'*I just don't understand how any of this is possible?*' Sasha said. '*I'm back in a woman's past, and I don't understand how any of this can be real? How can I be sitting here with you? Are you ghosts or something?*'

Sophea smiled, but this time sadness filled in her eyes. '*Maybe we're not real, but maybe you're not either. The truth is we are here now, we are experiencing this now. If that is not real, then what is? As for us being ghosts—what are ghosts? Surely, every person, if held in someone else's heart, will live forever. They have left a piece of themselves, something their loved one can call on when*' *things are hard. With family, this is even more so. We are part of Arana both spiritually and physically and now she has become part of you.'*

'She's not just become part of me,' Sasha interrupted, anger heating her voice. *'She* is *me!'*

'No. She doesn't want what is happening. She wants to be left in peace, but that man—that thing—he wants only to hurt and control her. He is doing so even after her death. She knows you can help her; this is the reason you are here now, the reason she has allowed you to come to us.'

'And you?' Sasha said. *'Why are you here?'*

The three sisters exchanged glances as Sophea reached out and took Mau and Vanna's hands.

'We could not help her when he took her,' Sophea said, her smooth voice suddenly choked. *'We did not know where she had gone. She was the one who loved to travel. We three stayed in the village, looking after the children and growing crops. She would leave for many weeks at a time, selling and trading things she had made, bringing us back luxuries for our home, grains for new crops. She would learn things from different tribes: new ways to irrigate our crops, ways to dye our clothing, medicines to heal our sick. We did not know where she went on these journeys and we did not know when he took her.*

'The news of the king of Cambodia taking a new wife was told to us, but he was not our king and it seemed of little relevance. Nobody thought to link her disappearance with the king's new wife. Why would we? In our eyes, we are simple people. The chance of the king wanting to marry someone like us was so unlikely, we never considered it.

'*Besides, there are many dangers for travelers,*' Sophea continued. '*Especially for women. We thought an accident had occurred—perhaps someone tried to steal from her and used violence. You have to understand; we were a family with no brothers and our father died many years ago. Arana was always the strongest and she took on the role of a brother.*

'*Weeks passed and she did not come home. We made sacrifices, praying for her safe return, but by then months had passed and still no word came of her.*'

Sophea's dark eyes filled with tears. Sasha resisted the urge to reach out and touch her.

'*It wasn't your fault.*' Sasha said, trying to offer some comfort. '*None of this was your fault.*'

'*We failed her. We let him destroy her. Now we have the chance to help her beat him.*'

'*But how?*' Sasha asked.

'*Arana knows something that will save them—the others who are left— but she needs to break through the state Jahard has left her in. She needs to communicate with the people on the outside, to tell them what they need to do to stop Jahard taking what he wants.*'

People's faces and fragments of memories appeared in Sasha's mind: Ben's innocent blue eyes, Josh's easy smile, and the people Jahard had already taken: Steph with her short pink hair, matted with water and dirt, the tightening of her body as she died. Her friend, Vicki, running off into the darkness to a fate they'd not witnessed. Laura, so kind and loving towards her family, who would never get the chance to watch her son grow up. Paula, Alex, and their unborn child. Dawn and the hurt it would cause her friends and family back home, knowing they'd left on unkind words. Even Goose, who surely had people who loved him.

A painful ball constricted her throat and the backs of her eyes burned hot with tears.

'I'll do whatever it takes,' she said quietly. *'Just tell me what to do.'*

Mau and Vanna reached out and each took one of Sasha's hands in their own. Both of their hands were rougher than Sasha's—years of physical work having taken their toll—but they were warm and safe.

'We are forming the circle of sisterhood, with you in Arana's place. She will use your strength, passion and essence as her own. She will channel herself through you to break through the madness Jahard has created and stop him.'

What about me? Sasha wanted to ask, but felt too selfish and petty to say it.

She didn't need to.

'We don't know what will happen to you,' said Sophea. *'I am sorry.'*

'How will I know what to do?' Sasha asked with her heart in her throat. She was more frightened then she'd ever been in her life.

'Just give yourself up to her. Stop fighting her and become part of her instead. Arana already knows what to do.'

The thought that this could all be a trick, that Jahard might be trying to get what he wanted by making her surrender, went through her mind. Then she realized she had no other options. This was her last chance.

Instinctively, she closed her eyes. In her heart, she focused on the people left: Ben, Greg and Josh. Could she give up her own life to save the lives of people who'd been strangers before tonight? Could she live with herself if she allowed Jahard to take Ben's life as his own? If she didn't do this, what would become of her anyway?

So many questions spun through her head, but essentially her choice came down to one simple thing: did she believe in herself enough to have the strength to survive this?

A tingling bolt of pain, like a thousand bee stings, shot up each arm. Sasha gasped and tried to pull away, but Vanna and Mau's firm grip kept the circle strong.

'Don't fight it,' said Sophea, staring at her intently. 'In your heart, you have already accepted this is the right thing to do.'

Sasha stared down at her hands. Palm to palm, fingers entwined, she was bound to each of the sisters. In front of her eyes, sparks of blue light fired from their skin. Each of their hands looked like an electricity ball, like the ones Sasha had seen in a science lab at school. Each tiny spark joined with another until the blue light played and danced between her fingers. It leapt up her arms and across her chest, to join with the woman sitting next to her. Fear mixed with amazement and wonder. Gradually, the sharp stabs of pain subsided into mere pinpricks. A ball of blue light bathed each woman and Sasha's fear disappeared. Something inside Sasha's mind jolted.

And everything went dark.

CHAPTER TWENTY-FOUR
SACRIFICE

Around him the storm grew stronger. Raindrops pummeled Josh as if deliberately trying to hurt him. Thunder rolled and crashed above his head. The rapidly lightening sky had become a stage for the light show the storm created.

Josh sat on the ground with Ben's head in his lap. He was trying to keep the child from drowning in the rain which collected in puddles on the road. Chay sat beside them, his head in his hands. He looked as miserable as Josh felt.

"Just leave us," Josh said to the boy. "You'll be safe without us."

Chay shook his head. "This is my fault. I won't abandon you. And I do not have anywhere else to go.

Sasha still stood motionless, with little sign of knowing where or even who she was. Josh had tried to get her to sit down with him, but she wouldn't take a step and no amount of coaxing had made any difference. He considered using the hammock Seth lay on to cover her, but she didn't seem to notice the rain pounding against her and Seth had groaned in pain when Josh tried to move him.

Greg paced back and forth along the side of the road, his hands clutching each side of his head. He muttered words Josh struggled to hear. Josh caught the occasional word, but Greg either spoke a language Josh didn't know or was speaking gibberish. Every so often, he stopped and lifted his head at the sky and screamed.

Josh watched with understandable wariness, unsure of what would happen next. He didn't doubt that he too would die in some horrific, inexplicable way. Now he was playing a waiting game: waiting for Greg to die, waiting for death, waiting for the sun to come up. The storm was doing a good job of hiding the rising sun, but daylight was inevitable.

Josh had given up.

From the corner of his eye, he saw Sasha jerk, as if she'd fallen asleep, then jolted herself awake. Her head turned and Josh realized she was looking around.

"Sasha?" Josh called her name, but got no response.

Carefully, he lifted Ben's head from his lap and motioned for Chay to take the child. Josh got to his feet and walked over to where Sasha was standing.

"Sasha?" he said again.

Her head turned in his direction. Josh reached out a hand to touch her, but she recoiled and he dropped his arm. He moved carefully toward her, in the way a man may walk toward a nervous animal, but he realized, though she showed no signs of recognizing him, she also did not fear him.

"Sasha? What's happened to you? Are you all right?"

She opened her mouth. "Saaa... sssh... ahhh." she said, as if trying to form her lips around the sounds for the first time.

With sudden certainty, Josh knew the person he was speaking to was no longer Sasha.

"Who are you?" he said, his voice coming out in a harsh whisper.

She spoke like someone who had been deaf for most of their life, but had been suddenly blessed with the ability to hear again and was now learning to speak.

"You... must... stop... him," she said, slow and deliberate. She stared him directly in the eye, her dark pupils fathomless. Dizziness and nausea overwhelmed him and he stumbled slightly. He gave his head a shake and forced himself to look back into her face. His gaze flicked across hers, not wanted to focus back on those brown depths, the sensation like falling.

"But how?" he said in dismay. "I don't know how!"

A crash of thunder drowned out her reply and she repeated herself, almost shouting in her strange voice over the sound of the storm.

"Someone... must... die."

"But people have already died!"

Her words came slow and forced. She looked at him in desperation. "You do not understand. Someone must *choose* to die. They must die because Jahard has driven them to it. They must start the curse again."

The knowledge slapped Josh across the face. Of course, he'd missed the obvious—the answer had been staring him in the face since Chay told him! Then his heart sank. He was the only one left who was *able* to do it.

He needed to kill himself, and he needed to do it soon.

But how?

Josh opened his mouth to ask the woman now inhabiting Sasha's body, but the light went out of her eyes and her limbs fell limp. She'd reverted to the same catatonic state as before, all of her energy apparently used up in her effort to tell him what he needed.

This was impossible. He had no weapons: no guns, knives or drugs even. He looked across the marshy lands spanning either side of the road. Could he drown himself, would he be able to do that? Could hold his head under the water long enough to die?

Josh barked out a laugh at the thought and the hysterical sound scared him.

Then he remembered what lay in the ground beneath the water and the reason they'd been unable to leave the road in the first place.

"Land mines," he said aloud.

Could it work? Would he even be able to find one? He might end up blowing off one leg and end up writhing in agony while Jahard came to finish the job. The thought terrified him—the thought of death terrified him. He didn't want to die. He wanted to stay and fight, but he remembered Greg pacing like a madman and the shell of a person Sasha had become.

He would be fighting. By doing this, at least the others stood a chance. It was his only option.

Josh turned to walk to the side of the road and then changed his mind. He turned back to Sasha and kissed her on the cheek, his lips pressing against the cool softness of her skin.

"I hope you'll be okay," he whispered to her. "I think I would have liked to have gotten to know you."

Josh turned back the way toward the road. He steadied himself, mentally and physically, and began to walk to the water. He moved with determination, promising himself this would be over with as quickly as possible.

He reached the side of the road and his right foot stepped off, but something slammed into him, knocking him off his feet and back onto the road.

Josh landed heavily on his back and the huge thing that had hit him landed on top, winding him. He gasped, unable to fight whatever was pinning him down, unable to suck in another breath. Time moved more slowly than he'd ever experienced before. Each second that passed with no oxygen felt like a minute. His lungs burned and his brain seemed to shout at him, 'Breathe. Breathe!'

The thought he was drowning came to mind and he was almost relieved that he wouldn't have to do it himself. But he remembered what the woman had said, 'someone must choose to die' and realized someone else doing the job for him wouldn't renew the curse.

The weight pressing down on him shifted slightly and Josh sucked in a huge gasp of desperately needed air. The relief was so immense he almost forgot the immediate problem of the man who had knocked him down in the first place. As the man partially lifted his weight up, Josh thought him about to get off, but instead he grabbed Josh's arms and pinned them above his head. Though Josh hated being held down, the movement lifted the pressure on his chest and allowed Josh to catch sight of his attacker.

Greg.

The rain poured down half-blinding him. Josh thrashed about, trying to get some leverage, but Greg was bigger and stronger. Due to the rain, Josh now lay in a pool of mud and he sank into the ground, Greg's weight forcing him down. For all his efforts, he produced little more than a wriggle like a worm stranded in a puddle.

"Don't do this, Greg," Josh pleaded. "I know you're still in there somewhere."

Greg looked down on him, the whites of his eyes blood red. Josh was certain he saw something close to hunger in those eyes. Greg snarled and bared his teeth just as his son had done earlier. A thin line of spittle hung from his mouth, narrowly missing Josh's face.

Josh had the hideous sense that, like something from the cheap horror flicks he'd loved to watch as a teenager, Greg would turn into a werewolf. In his mind's eye, he saw the claws that had pierced the ends of Dawn's fingers.

Anything was possible.

But it was not claws he needed to be concerned about, but teeth. Greg snarled again revealing incisors that had grown long and pointed, so they protruded from beneath Greg's top lip.

Panic set in—clutching his heart, blinding him in terror. Josh bucked in the dirt, trying to fling his head up to butt his attacker. He only managed to kick the lower half of Greg's legs. Josh screamed for help, knowing the only people close enough to hear him were mere children. Greg's head lowered, teeth as sharp as razor blades, to rip out his throat.

In the chaos and panic, a small figure darted out of the fading dark and jumped on Greg's back. Chay clung to him, riding the big man like a bronco. It allowed Josh the briefest respite while Greg let go of one of Josh's arms and reached back, plucking the boy from his body with ease and tossing him onto the road.

The release wasn't enough to escape, and even as Josh tried to crawl out from under Greg's mass, the man-creature whipped back around, flashing white canines.

With one hand free, Josh grabbed hold of Greg's throat, trying to hold him away. His force was nothing against the possessed, transformed being and Greg lunged down, aiming, once again, for Josh's throat

A deafening explosion smashed against Josh's ears, accompanied by the sound of tearing earth and flesh. The ground shook as though in the midst of an earthquake. Water exploded around them and pieces of vegetation and dirt splattered down on top of them. Thunder crashed so loudly Josh would hear its echo for days to come. Lightning tore from the sky and hit the road not far from where he lay.

Screams filled the air all around; as if the ground, the sky, the very world they stood on, shrieked in rage and fury. The air vibrated with its power. They were the screams of the thousands of people who had been murdered: men, women and children, all crying out for their lost lives. They screamed with rage at the person who had taken them, for their pain and suffering, each layering on top of the other.

As suddenly as it started, the cries of anguish stopped. The rain grew lighter and thunder grumbled in the distance like a sulky child.

Greg stared down at Josh in surprise and let go of his wrists, shocked he'd found himself holding them. He looked around in confusion.

Ben sat up, rubbing his eyes as if he'd just woken from a long sleep. Seeing his son, Greg climbed off Josh and ran to the boy.

Chay pulled himself to sitting, rubbing the side of his head, injured in the throw. The boy was hurt, but otherwise safe.

Josh rolled over to his side in relief, catching his breath and steadying his nerves. He'd believed himself to be a dead man.

A hand on his shoulder made him spin back around, half expecting it to be the vampire-Greg-creature again. Sasha stared back at him.

"Is it over?" she asked in a hopeful whisper.

"Sasha?"

She gave a small smile and he grabbed her. Josh wrapped his arms around her and crushed her hard against him. Tears filled his eyes and he pressed his lips tightly together to stop himself from sobbing.

"Is it over?" she asked again, her breath hot against his neck.

"I don't know," he said, still overwhelmed at having her back. "I'm not sure what happened?"

"Well that makes two of us." She bit her lip. "Did she speak to you? Did Arana speak to you? Did she tell you how to end it?"

"Was that who I was speaking to—Arana?"

Sasha nodded.

"She told me someone had to die by their own hand to resurrect the curse." He shook his head. "Jahard must have realized what I was planning because he used Greg to stop and almost kill me, so I didn't get the chance to do it."

"So what the hell happened? Because it's over, isn't it? Everything feels different."

She was right. Everything did feel different; lighter, less oppressive.

The sun peeped over the horizon as the last traces of darkness disappeared from the sky. Josh saw something else as well.

He grabbed Sasha's arm and pointed to the empty hammock where he'd last seen Seth. A trail of blood and a deep track gouged in the mud showed where Seth had dragged himself off the road.

Seth had saved their lives.

GOING HOME

It was lunchtime in Siem Reap and the hot sun beat down on their heads, browning their bare arms and legs. Sasha and Josh sat on plastic chairs outside of a local restaurant, each of them nursing a beer. A pool of water collected around the bases of their glasses, the sun threatening to warm the beverage if they didn't drink quickly enough.

They had given their statements to the authorities that morning. They didn't know how much the police believed in ancient curses, so they'd stuck to the story of a vicious wild animal and an explosion on the bus. Even that story had seemed far-fetched, but the real one would have only gotten them locked up in an insane asylum. The local police took their passport numbers and home addresses, together with promises that the survivors would be available for questioning should they be needed. The foreign embassies had also been notified, but as the stories of each of the four survivors matched, and the authorities had no reason to suspect foul play, the whole incident would be put down to a tragic accident and unfortunate circumstances.

As soon as they reached the town, Chay disappeared. None of the travelers thought they needed to mention him. They'd only cause him trouble. After spending time at the police station, Sasha and Josh left Greg and Ben with many hugs and tears. Promises were made to stay in touch but they all knew the small family would need to put the horrific memories of what had happened behind them in order to grieve for Laura properly. Sasha and Josh made up part of those memories.

"I can hardly believe we made it," said Josh.

"For a while, I didn't think we were going to. Being here feels surreal." Sasha shook her head, her gaze cast down to the table. "We're lucky, aren't we? All those other people..."

Josh reached across the table and squeezed her hand. "We're lucky we lived, but we couldn't have done anything more for the others. I don't want you to go home feeling guilty for surviving."

"I know. I'll try not to, but it won't be easy. I don't think I'll ever be able to forget what happened."

Josh thought for a moment. "Do you blame her?" he asked.

Sasha looked up in surprise. "Blame who?"

"Arana? Do you blame her for killing herself, for killing her child? If she hadn't done that none of this would have happened."

She shook her head. "I know what she did was terrible, unforgivable even, but when she was a part of me I experienced everything he did to her..."

Sasha broke off, her skin crawling as she remembered the awful things Arana had been through.

Josh must have seen Sasha pale for he changed the subject.

"So what about your fiancé?" he asked. "Are you still going to try and meet him?"

Sasha glanced down at the finger on her left hand. Only a thin band of white skin marked where the ring had been. She held up her hand to show Josh.

"I guess I must have lost my ring somewhere along the way, in the river perhaps." She shrugged and lowered her hand. "I don't even care, and no, I'm not going to meet him. I'm going to book a flight back home and I can't wait to get there." She paused for a moment, thinking. "One thing I've learned from this is that life really is too short. I've been hanging around for the last year, waiting for Nick to come home to me, waiting for him to live his life so I can get on with mine. It's pathetic and I've got no intention of doing the same thing again."

A smile hinted at Josh's lips. "So if I promise not to keep you hanging around, would it be too presumptuous to ask if we can meet up back in London?"

Sasha tried to look annoyed. "I suppose as long as you promise..."

The frown cracked and she broke into a smile. They caught each other's eye, and looked back down at their drinks in sudden shyness.

Josh seemed to remember something and his face darkened.

"Before we take this any further, I need to tell you something about me. I need to tell you the reason I left New Zealand in the first place."

Sasha looked up at him. "Do I really need to know?" she said. "I think everything that has happened in the last twenty-four hours is enough to change anyone. I mean, look at Seth. If you had told me at the start of the trip that he would end up sacrificing himself to save us, I never would've believed you. Do you think whatever it is will affect us?"

Josh thought and then shook his head. "No, never. I've seen enough anger, pain and violence to last a lifetime."

Sasha reached across the table and squeezed his hand. "That's good enough for me."

They sat in reflective silence for a moment.

"You know, I still can't believe what Seth did for us," said Josh. "We'd all given him such a hard time and he went and sacrificed himself for us."

"I think he did it for Laura," Sasha said. "He felt so guilty about her. He thought her dying was his fault. I guess it was his way of making things up to Greg and Ben."

Josh shook his head in amazement. "I still can't believe it. It shows how strong the human spirit can be. I thought the guy was barely alive, never mind awake enough to hear everything that was said. He must have been alert enough to understand and pull himself through the mud and off the road."

Despite the hot day, another shiver jolted up Sasha's spine. The thought that they had been so close to bombs the whole time was almost as scary as Jahard.

"People can have amazing reserves when they're put in extreme situations," she said.

The waitress, a young girl with shiny black hair and coal black eyes, approached the table and immediately they stopped their conversation. What had happened to them was something they would only ever talk about with each other; it wasn't for anyone else's ears. Neither of them would be able to retell the story of that night to another soul without being met with looks of disbelief. Even if someone else did believe them, they would never truly be able to understand what they had gone through. Their experiences would follow them for the rest of their lives and the ghosts of the people who had died would haunt their dreams, but they knew they had each other.

Whatever might happen between them in the future, the dark road they'd traveled would bind them forever.

MARISSA FARRAR

By Marissa Farrar

The 'Serenity' Series

**ALONE
BURIED
CAPTURED**

THE DARK ROAD

Coming Soon...

UNDERLIFE

About the Author

Marissa Farrar is a multi-published horror and paranormal author. She was born in Devon, England, loves to travel and has lived in both Australia and Spain. She now resides in Devon with her husband, two children, a crazy Spanish rescue dog and four hens. She has a degree in Zoology, but her true love has always been writing.

Her dark take on a vampire romance, Alone, was first published in 2009 and has now being re-launched, together with the next books in what is now the 'Serenity' series.

Her short stories have been accepted for a number of anthologies including, Their Dark Masters, Red Skies Press, Masters of Horror: Damned If You Don't, Triskaideka Books; and 2013: The Aftermath, Pill Hill Press.

If you want to know more about Marissa, then please visit her website at www.marissa-farrar.blogspot.com or her facebook page at www.facebook.com/marissa.farrar.author.